CHECK ME OUT

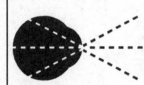

This Large Print Book carries the
Seal of Approval of N.A.V.H.

PROPER ROMANCE

Check Me Out

Becca Wilhite

THORNDIKE PRESS
A part of Gale, a Cengage Company

Farmington Hills, Mich • San Francisco • New York • Waterville, Maine
Meriden, Conn • Mason, Ohio • Chicago

Copyright © 2018 by Becca Wilhite.
Thorndike Press, a part of Gale, a Cengage Company.

LIBRARY OF CONGRESS CIP DATA ON FILE.
CATALOGUING IN PUBLICATION FOR THIS BOOK
IS AVAILABLE FROM THE LIBRARY OF CONGRESS

ISBN-13: 978-1-4328-6260-2 (hardcover)

Published in 2019 by arrangement with Deseret Book Company/Shadow
Mountain

Printed in the United States of America
1 2 3 4 5 6 7 23 22 21 20 19

For Scott
Just right for me, inside and out

CHAPTER 1

You know that quote people attribute to Confucius? The one that says, "Choose a job you love, and you will never have to work a day in your life"? I know that quote. I've had paper copies of it stuck to various household mirrors. I believe in it. I love it. For three years of college, it was the lock screen of my phone. I'm a fan of Confucius, but I'm a disciple of that quote — whether he said it or not.

Here's the thing Confucius didn't mention: Even if you love your job and going to it doesn't feel like work, you still have to get out of bed on time, brush your hair, and put on pants that weren't created for yoga. You know — pants with button fasteners.

I checked my phone. It was four minutes before ten, and I was less than one minute away from the library door. In a skirt. Success.

I put my phone back in my pocket as I

passed the giant, crooked oak at the edge of the library block. The tree must have been centuries old. It had, throughout my life, starred in all my borrowed book fantasies. When I was a little kid, it was "The Giving Tree." When I was twelve, it was Hogwarts' Whomping Willow. Later, it was the tree outside the Radley place. Then Treebeard the Ent.

The tree guarded the old Greenwood house, which was — historically and architecturally speaking — pretty awesome. The brick had worn smooth after decades of weather. It soared up from the lot, looking taller than its three stories, with cool turrets and angles and weathered beams. And if the actual architecture wasn't interesting enough, consider the rumor that it had been part of the Underground Railroad. I couldn't count the times I'd wished I'd been brave enough to kneel at the foundation and peek into cellar windows. I never did, though.

If the tree starred in the fantasies, Old Man Greenwood starred in the horrors. He was famously reclusive, sketchy. And he seemed to have never in his life used a garbage can. My beautiful tree, perfect for a romantic-swing situation, was surrounded by a rusting car frame and assorted dumpy garbage. Walking past the Greenwood property, I felt sorry that the library had to sit next to it, like the yard was the dirty little kid in elementary school whose nose is always running and who never bathes.

Poor library. Couldn't help its neighbors. I took a deep breath of autumn morning air as I turned up the sidewalk. When I climbed the stone steps and unlocked the library's wooden door, the scents all shifted. Inside, the air smelled like a grandma's house with a pleasant undertone of dusty books and that puppy-smell that comes from little kids running around.

The light was different, too. More golden, with lines of morning sunbeams cutting through dust in front of every east window. The original Victorian bones of the building made for tall, skinny rooms with windows everywhere. Here on the main floor, several walls had been removed to make an entryway big enough to run the library. The circulation desk — a sprawling, mammoth, wooden monstrosity cobbled together from several sources — was the beating heart of the place. Librarian Julie's perch, at the center of the desk, faced the door and allowed her to smile at every patron who walked in.

The narrow staircase, leading up to the

children's section, had been widened enough for two people to pass each other with only minimal elbow bumping.

The main room, spreading out in all directions from the huge desk, wandered into computer cubbies, research stacks, a room full of newspapers and magazines that nobody read, and eventually to the back of the old house where the adult nonfiction was housed. The windows back there were my favorite, stretching in mock-gothic arches to the tall ceilings. And my most favorite of those windows were the replica stained glass, donated by a library patron several generations ago. Four window panels showed local plants in four seasons: tulips and irises for spring, wisteria for summer, oak and maple leaves for autumn, and holly for winter. The windows went largely unnoticed, except by me because it was my job, as the only full-time employee under forty, to climb the tall ladders and clean them every Saturday.

I started up the circulation desk's three computers and flipped the main light switches. If I'd been five minutes earlier, I'd have had time to walk around turning on lights in all the rooms. Instead, I took the stairs to the kids' section two at a time, flipped on the overhead lights and the three lamps by the miniature reading chairs, and was back at the desk with a librarian smile on my face (and possibly panting) by 10:00.

The wooden door creaked open. Bonita Honeycutt, the sweet woman who had been a white-haired assistant librarian my entire life, walked in. "Morning," she chirped as she opened the book-drop closet and rolled the cart to the desk. "No crowds yet?"

Every day she asked. And every day I made myself smile when the answer was no.

"When I was a girl," Bonita said, a dreamy, distant lilt in her words, "we loved the library. And the swimming pool. I was dynamite in my bathing suit." She put her hands on what I could assume was once a waist.

I loved it when Bonita talked like that. Her history fascinated me, in a mild and totally non-stalker-ish way. She hadn't grown up in Franklin — I knew, because I'd asked — so I wondered about her past. Hearing her talk about when she was a girl, I wanted to ask her, when did you *stop* being a girl? Why do you consider yourself a girl only in the past? And why were you dynamite only in the past? And did you know it then?

Instead, I pushed the wheeled box away from the night book drop and up to the desk

11

to check in the books.

Within a minute, I heard some of my favorite words. "Greta, I'm glad you're here."

"Hi, Boss." I waved a paperback copy of *Anne of Green Gables,* read practically to tissue paper, in Julie Tucker's general direction as she walked in from the back door. "What can I do for you?"

I always asked, even if I was already doing it.

"After you check in last night's drop, I need these books pulled." She waved a handwritten paper at me. It looked like there were about ten titles on it. No sweat. I was always pulling books for people who, for one reason or another, couldn't get in to find their own books. "And I have some new picture books that I need someone to read. You game?" She pretended this wasn't the world's biggest perk to this job.

Putting on my serious face, I nodded. "I'm sure I can find some time to take care of that."

Julie smiled. I'd known Miss Julie Tucker as long as I could remember. She gave me my first job, the job I had all through high school. The job that decided my career. She'd kept me on during summers between semesters at the university, and she hired me as assistant librarian after I'd finished my master's degree. She had run the library forever.

I reshelved the stack of overnight returns. Moving to the periodicals room, I slid new magazines into their protective plastic covers and placed them on the reading racks. I stacked the older issues, noting that it looked like nobody'd read them at all. There weren't even creased pages. People didn't come to libraries to read news or magazines. This was not a surprise. I'd spent all my masters research writing about how libraries should — ought to, *needed* to — pull themselves into the present so they would stay relevant.

More than anything, I needed my library to stay relevant.

I pulled out my phone and opened up my librarian account on Twitter. As part of my job to keep the library relevant, I was in charge of social media. Some people were surprised to see how much library chatter happened on Twitter. It was a great resource, and I felt zero guilt for checking it at work. After scanning through a few news stories about a big city branch closing due to funding concerns, I wrote the morning tweet: "It's a perfect day to get lost in a good book. #GetLost #CheckOutTheLibrary"

An extremely old man leaned over a table beside the reading racks. Unfolded in front of him, a newspaper fluttered under the air conditioning vent. He pulled his brown cardigan tighter around his chest.

So, okay, maybe some people still came to libraries for news. I caught his eye and smiled at him.

I headed back to the circulation desk and checked the Card. This was a game I played with Kevin, our high school intern. The Card was short for "Across the Desk without Context" Card. We would write down the weirdest, dumbest, or craziest things people asked us across the desk and leave them for each other. (If it was really a good one, we bent the rules for "Over the Phone without Context.") There was this gorgeous old Underwood typewriter in the workroom — it had probably been in the library since the thirties — and we used it to type up the Cards on old card catalog cards from storage. This was not a subtle endeavor. You had to hit the round keys like you really meant it. Everyone in the vicinity could hear us when we typed.

Kevin had done two Cards on his last shift. One said, "Do you know much about

Europe? Because I have a question about Japan. (Adult male, early 20s)." The other one said, "I'm looking for a book about a guy that has a dog. Do you know that book? (Adult female, late 50s)."

I grinned. I loved my job.

I was carrying a stack of adult fiction back to the shelves just before lunch. As I came around the corner, I saw him. The most perfect looking guy I'd ever encountered in my entire twenty-four years. Standing in front of my favorite stained-glass windows, looking incredibly handsome and a tiny bit lost.

I shifted the load of books in my arms and leaned in, just a little: a completely professional lean. "Excuse me, can I help you find something?"

He turned toward me, and I got the full effect of the messy, curly dark hair, the chocolate-brown eyes, the eyebrows, the jawline. My thoughts immediately melted into *Oh my goodness, what am I supposed to be doing?*

He wore a button-up plaid shirt layered over a black T-shirt. There were words on his T-shirt, which I wanted very much to read (reading words is a weakness of mine), but I couldn't seem to drag my eyes away

15

from his face. That face. It was almost too perfect to be real. But here it was, right in front of me, balanced perfectly on a perfect neck that connected to perfect shoulders . . .

"Rilke?"

I shook my head. "Greta." Shifting the books to my left arm, I stuck out my right hand. For a shake. Because I am an idiot. Then I realized what he'd said. "And you're looking for Rilke poetry?" Thank goodness for a liberal arts bachelor's degree. At least I knew Rilke was a poet.

When he nodded and smiled, he looked precisely and directly into my eyes, and I swear I saw our future. It had great hair.

It's possible I stood and blinked for a minute or three. Then I remembered I was a grown-up. With a job. "Please follow me," I said, hoping I didn't sound as breathless as I felt. I led him around the stacks to the poetry section. "Here is Rilke in German and French, and in translation if you prefer English." All of which I read off the spines of the books quickly. And efficiently. I don't think he noticed I was cheating.

He stopped close to me. Not uncomfortably close. Near enough for me to know that I wouldn't mind if he stood closer. He wasn't terribly tall, which was good — sometimes I felt dwarfed by people who were terribly tall. Not that I was tiny or anything. I could smell something vaguely musky, like deodorant or cologne or aftershave. It blended nicely with the dusty book scent of the nonfiction section.

He put his fingers on top of the Rilke books and slid three of them off the shelf and into his hand. He somehow managed to look half at the books and half at me. It occurred to me that he probably didn't need any more help and I should get back to work.

I didn't leave.

As he flipped through a slim collection, I pulled a different book from the shelf. Since I knew exactly nothing about Rilke — aside from the fact that he was a poet and what I'd just read on the book spines — I read the back cover copy and discovered that he'd written this whole collection of sonnets in a little over a month. I tried to find a way to use that little gem to start a conversation, but even I couldn't make small talk about a guy who busted out several sonnets a day.

I put the poetry back and straightened a few straggly books. It was possible that nobody had touched some of these books in years, maybe even my entire lifetime.

When it became clear that I was lurking, I

asked, "Anything else I can help you with?"

He looked up from the book. Right through his long, thick eyelashes. He had to know that was a trick, and probably that he'd perfected it. His slow smile nailed me to the floor. "I'm new here. What's good to eat?"

Well. I knew the answer to that question. "Happy's has the best burgers and fries. Ornello's for pizza. There's this little Mexican place by the university that makes the most perfect carnitas. If you're looking for cold-weather food, there's this amazing soup-and-sandwich place not far from here. And Brooklyn Bagel, which has bagels, if you can imagine. But I've been to Brooklyn, and I ate a bagel, and it was way better than anything I've ever eaten in Ohio."

I must have stopped to take a breath because in that tiny second of silence I realized I sounded like a Franklin Chamber of Commerce brochure. A hungry one.

He was still looking at me and smiling.

I pushed the hair off my forehead and tried to look a tiny bit professional. It was time for me to move. To stop speed-talking about fast food. To do my job. "If there's anything else we can help you with, just ask." I turned and started to walk away.

"Wait. Greta, right?"

My heart thudded once and then seemed to stop. He remembered my name? How did he remember my name?

"Greta," I repeated. "Right."

He might have tossed his hair a little. "Thank you, Greta."

"My pleasure."

He reached into his jeans pocket and pulled out a piece of paper, about the size of a business card. As unexpected as that was, I wasn't going to reject any piece of paper this guy wanted to give me. He might be giving me his phone number. He handed it over, but when I took it, he didn't quite let go. We stood there for a couple of Very Meaningful Seconds, each holding on to this little card. Then he let go and took half a step back.

"That," he said, "is for you." When he smiled this time, I felt my knees buckle. "He said you'd know why."

He said? Who said? There was a cartoon drawing on the paper. A picture of me, holding library books and grinning, standing next to a huge wrapped gift. It was unmistakably drawn by Will Marshall.

I laughed. "Wait. Where did you get this?" He didn't say anything. He stood beside me, smiling and exuding confidence and perfection. "You know Will?" My brain tried to bend around the probability of this gorgeous, library-visiting, poetry-reading man knowing the guy who'd been my best friend since second grade. Without getting any explanation, I turned the card over. On the other side, in practiced block script, were the words, "Happy late birthday. I always deliver."

The birthday wish. This? Him? No way.

My eyes went from card to gorgeous stranger and back. It was dizzying, honestly. And I might have had my mouth open. As soon as I realized that, I reinstalled my polite smile.

"Thank you very much for bringing me this," I said, waving the card. "I love it."

It wasn't like he'd stopped smiling at me, but there was some kind of reset to it since it now blazed in a way that managed to be charming and not at all aggressive. He had very nice teeth and very, very pretty lips, and I wanted to see more and more of that mouth. I mean *smile.* I wanted to see more of that smile. Then it occurred to me that he could absolutely tell that I was staring at his mouth. I had to look away. My eyes landed on his shirt, and I read, "Do you have a map? I just got lost in your eyes."

He saw me look. Or maybe he didn't. Oh, yes, he did. His eyes went down to his own shirt and back to my face. Was he gauging my reaction? He looked pleased.

A small, nervous laugh escaped my throat, and I realized that I was on the brink of a twenty-first century swoon. *Pull it together,* I told myself.

"I should get back to work. It was good to meet you."

"You, too, Greta."

I had never, ever loved the sound of my own name so much.

"Are you going to check those out?" I asked, pointing to the books in his hand.

He looked down, and back up at me, and I was completely lost. "Sure," he said. "Help me?"

I nodded, and he followed me to the circulation desk. "You said you were new in town. Do you have a library card?"

He let out a breath of a laugh. "Oh. No. Is that bad?"

"No problem. I'll get you set up." I pulled up the right screen and tried to act like a professional as I asked for his name.

"Mac. Mackay Sanders."

Mackay Sanders proceeded to give me, in the world's most professional manner, both his phone number and his address. Turned out he lived right by the university.

"Are you a student?" I asked, pretending

it was information I needed for his account.

"No. I'm in management."

No. He's in management. Sigh. I wrote that — all of it, including the sigh — in the Notes section, which only I ever used, then I finalized his application and printed him a card. He spent those two minutes checking his phone and sending a couple of texts, allowing me to steal glances pretty much whenever I felt like it.

"All right. You're all set." I slid the books and the card across the counter.

He put his hands on either side of the little stack and leaned toward me. "Now that we know how to find each other," he said, "I hope to see you again soon." He picked up his books and walked away.

When I returned to reality, I looked around. The circulation desk was quiet. Nobody needed anything. I pulled out my phone and texted Will.

What just happened?

He answered so quickly I could tell he'd been holding his phone.

To me?

No. Here. Someone called Mackay Sanders just made my day.

That's Mac.

Yeah. He said. Mac. Mackay. Where did you find him?

He's the cousin. Mac.

I may have inhaled a tiny gasp.

Will Marshall, you've been holding out on me.

I stashed my phone to help a young mom check out a pile of picture books. Then the mail-delivery guy, Stan, who was at least ninety years old but didn't look a day over a hundred and fifty, dropped off the post and wanted to talk. Rumor had it Stan had been delivering mail in Franklin since Harry Truman was the president of the United States. I didn't know how big his route was these days, but it couldn't have covered too much ground since he wandered into the library every day and stayed to chat for at least twenty minutes. Today it was something about bugs in trees. I did a lot of smiling and nodding, and when he looked particularly serious, I ditched the smiling.

Before he left, he patted my hand, shook his head, and said, "You never know."

I agreed, because what else could I do but agree?

After Stan left, I pulled out my phone and tweeted, "You learn something every day, if you try. #GoToTheLibrary"

CHAPTER 2

When the clock bonged for closing time, I went around and checked all the windows, stuck my head (or at least my voice) into the bathrooms to make sure all was clear, turned off the lights, and shut down the computers. It meant I left at 5:10 instead of the actual 5:00 closing we promised, but Julie wanted to make sure people didn't feel rushed out of the building.

I didn't mind. In fact, it was something I loved about the old-fashionedness of the Franklin library. If we wanted a door to lock, we had to go lock it. If a light was on, we flipped a switch to turn it off. It was personal. And I liked it.

And now, at 5:10, I stepped outside and pulled the wooden door closed behind me, locking up until Monday morning. I pushed the metal flap over the book drop, making sure it wasn't stuck, and shivered when it screeched. After all these years, I still wasn't sure if it was a shiver of discomfort from the noise or of delight that I knew the screech was going to happen.

I heard a voice behind me. "Oh, wait, don't lock up the library yet. I need to come in and get something."

I knew it was Will, so I pretended to huff in frustration. "Seriously? Don't you know that everything you might possibly need from a library is already on the internet?" I turned to see him standing in the walkway, grinning and holding his arms out like he'd enjoy a little applause.

I clapped. Loud and slow.

I cleared my throat like I was going to make a declaration. "Will Marshall. You are hereby the greatest friend in the universe. If this whole high school teaching thing doesn't work out, go into Birthday Wish Fulfillment." I stepped around a broken brick that had fallen onto the path and walked into his arms. He hugged me tight and picked me up off the ground. Will was more than big enough to enfold me until I almost disappeared. Will was more than big enough for pretty much anything.

"You didn't make it easy this year. If I remember, you required single, clever, good hair, and what was the last part? Skin-melting hotness? Something like that?"

Pulling out of the hug, I wobbled my head back and forth, not quite agreeing, but certainly not disagreeing. "Something like that."

"So far, so good, yeah?"

"So far, pretty close to perfect." It seemed like he already knew what had happened, but Will never minded hearing me overexplain things that I found relevant. And this was relevant. I spared very few details as I explained my Mac Encounter while Will and I walked to Happy's. When we'd ordered and sat down and I had run out of adjectives to describe the run-in, Will picked up his water cup, swirled it around, and drank it all down.

"This birthday thing was easier when you wanted polka-dot socks," he said, not quite looking at me. "Not that I've regretted any of the work required to procure your gifts. Or the 'ask for what you want, get what you want' rule. Don't misunderstand me. I'm just saying, if you continue to get increasingly picky or demanding, your gifts will continue to come later and later." He set down his cup and picked a napkin out of the tabletop dispenser. "Some of these things take more than twelve months to procure."

I nodded and hummed in agreement. I

drained my water, then said, "Worth the wait."

Our waitress brought a tray full of cheeseburger goodness and slid it onto the table. "Mr. Marshall," she said with a big smile, "good to see you on the outside." She gave him a high five before walking away.

I shoved three fries into my mouth, enjoying the burn and the salt and the grease. "Is she one of yours?"

He nodded behind the single fry he nibbled. Such manners. "Last year. She's a great improv speaker. Very funny. Very confident." Will always complimented his students.

"And possibly harboring a mad crush on her debate coach."

He shook his head, and I watched a blush creep up his neck. It always freaked him out when I talked like that. So I always talked like that.

In a graceless but effective effort to change the subject, Will said, "So, according to your stated demands, you are now in possession of the world's best twenty-fourth birthday present. Don't break it before you have a chance to really enjoy it."

"Seriously, Will, you've outdone yourself. Good work. Thank you. Have I mentioned thank you? Because thank you." I shoveled in more fries, unwilling to let them get cold.

He shook his head. "I deliver, but I can't guarantee any satisfaction once you've accepted the gift."

I ticked off a list on my greasy fingers. "Single? I can take your word for it. Clever? For real, you should have been there to hear him. 'Now that we know where to find each other . . .' Yeah. Clever. Check. Good hair?" I closed my eyes to call up the picture of him I'd locked into my mind. "It's dark and curly and it honest-to-goodness tumbles across his forehead. Did you hear me, Will? It tumbles. And, let me see, what was the last one? Can you remember? Maybe I've forgotten the last one. Oh, wait. No, I haven't. Crazy handsome? That will speak for itself. Loud and clear." I only stopped talking to shove a huge bite of cheeseburger into my face.

Will ate normal-human bites and smiled at me. With his mouth closed. Because manners.

After I finished eating, I swiped at my fingers and mouth with a blue napkin and reached across the table to take his hands. "Seriously, Will. You're a wizard."

He shook his head. "I just told him to go check out what the local library had to offer. You did the rest, just by being perfectly irresistible."

I smiled. Will was the most generous guy with compliments. "Okay, but did I say about the T-shirt?"

He hauled himself out of the booth. "You said. Twice. Get me out of here." He dropped a generous tip on the table and waved to the kids who hollered hello to him on our way out. I left Happy's full, giddy, and hopeful. Will always delivered.

CHAPTER 3

As I sat behind the desk in the nearly silent library on Monday afternoon, I heard the door open. How was it that every time I heard the door, it felt like salvation? There was something threatening about an empty library. I shook off the drama and told myself to stop reading news stories about branches closing. Not helpful.

Glancing up at the door, I saw a girl about my age, messenger bag slung over her shoulder, butterfly sleeves and wavy hair fluttering in the breeze from outside. If I were casting a movie about a girl who wished she'd been from the late sixties, I'd make her the star. I quickly checked her shoes to see if they might be made from discarded car tires. Of course. Elbow fringe? Check. Flared pants? Check. She was adorable, in a weird and slightly discomfiting way.

She looked around for a few seconds and

caught my eye.

"How can I help you?" I asked as she made her way to the desk.

She put her hands and forearms flat against the counter and leaned across. Looking right at my face, she raised one arm and almost touched me.

I rolled my chair backward and tried to pretend I hadn't.

"Wow." She said it like a breath, and I stifled the world's most nervous laugh.

Shaking the blonde waves away from her face, she pushed several hemp bracelets up her wrist. She stood up straight, hands out like a cartoon zombie, mouth hanging slightly open over perfect teeth. She swept her arm over the air above the counter and leaned toward me again.

I stood up out of the rolling chair.

Her eyes, blue and huge, slicked over like she was going to cry or something. But the open mouth turned into a smile when she touched my arm. "I've never seen such a strong orange."

And we had a candidate for the Card. Even as I mentally filed the words away, I knew Kevin wouldn't believe me.

"I mean it. Never." She was still inclining toward me.

I nodded, reached up, scratched my nose.

This was my place, I reminded myself. And she was weirding me out. Part of me wanted to bolt. But the professional part of me demanded I stay. She was in a full lean now, nearly ninety degrees, the top half of her touching the counter. I stood firm, forcing myself not to back into the workroom.

She raised herself up and breathed in like she was smelling the difference between me and the rest of the library. Her hand floated up toward my face, and I backed away again. She didn't touch me, exactly. More like her fingers swept the air away from the side of my face.

"Is there something I can help you find?"

She started talking as though we'd not just taken part in a weird ritual-smelling moment. "Hi. So. This place is remarkable. Don't you love this building?"

"I do." Truth.

She nodded, as if we'd solved a crucial problem. "I'm Marigold."

Like the flower? That was a person's name? "Really?" I didn't snort. Nearly. But I didn't.

"I'm glad I didn't freak you out. You know. Just now. Before."

Okay, well. She had, and I think it would have been clear that she had to anyone nearby who was speaking the same language. She called me a strong orange. That was weird. But there was something in her smile that seemed sincere and endearing. "Mmm," I said noncommittedly.

"I just saw so clearly the essence of pure dedication in you. And I was sure you were going to be important to me."

What? "Well, I'm not really that important."

"We both know that can't be true." She tucked her long hair behind an ear. "Have you got a name?" It didn't sound confrontational when she said it, not really. Interested, I guess. Curious. As if perhaps I might not.

I nodded once. "Yes. Greta."

"As in Hansel and Greta?" Her eyebrows arched, ruffling her slightly pimply forehead.

"That was Gretel, so no, not really," I said, but her weirdness was disarming and her smile contagious. I found myself smiling back at her.

Marigold. I was talking to a person named after a flower.

"I bet you give great gifts." She said it like it wasn't a bizarre conversational segue. As though, maybe, we had been talking about anything remotely associated with giving gifts.

Weird, but amusing. And possibly true.

She kept going. "That's the orange in you.

You've got the strongest orange aura I've ever seen, and I can tell a lot about a person whose aura is so strong."

Oh. Aura. Right. Was that less weird than being a literal strong orange?

As Marigold rambled on about my aura of helpfulness and my obvious spiritual need to fix the unfixable and make things right, I began to hope someone would come in the door and need something. This was fun and everything, but I probably needed to do something useful today.

Marigold continued to talk about auras, and I gave an occasional nod as I sorted through some mail on the desk.

I had almost completely stopped listening to her when she said, "Things are going to get tricky for you when you lose your work."

She spoke more words, but I stopped her with my waving hands. "Wait. Why am I losing my work?"

She made a trying-patience face and then smiled. It looked like a practiced move, and I wondered if she randomly told fortunes to everyone who stood in public buildings' reception areas. She seemed to have a handle on it.

"Well, some people would say libraries are dying. And there's the bond, of course. And in general, technology puts a lot of people out of work. It's been an issue for decades. This town is not immune to the ravages of modernism. Do you want to talk to me about your mother?"

The laugh came out before I realized it was going to. "Wow. Auras to fortune telling to therapy. That's a nice set of tricks you have."

She didn't look offended or even surprised. "Oh, I'm no therapist. Not at all. You're a young professional woman, so I assumed you have issues with your mom, and sometimes it helps to talk about it. You can release some of your negative energy and replace it with soft, golden . . ."

I stopped listening long enough to watch a couple of middle school-aged kids skulk in and head toward the comfortable chairs in the nonfiction section. I was certain I knew what they were doing there, and it had nothing to do with nonfiction.

"Of course, orange people do tend to make rash decisions, so watch out. You don't want to do anything you'll regret." She nodded as if she agreed with herself.

"Well. Thanks." What else could I say? I gestured toward where the kids had gone. "I should go see if I can help those people while I still have a job."

She nodded, tucked her hair again, then

leaned on her elbows. Hands folded together under her chin, she smiled as she talked. "Orange people tend to be friendly so I think you are perfect for a job where you interface with a lot of people. Also, you are emotionally available. That suggests you could help people connect with products that they'll become attached to. Library work is perfect for you. It's a natural fit."

I couldn't help it. "My master's degree agrees with you."

She nodded. "Of course. This is clearly where your heart lives. It's going to hurt you to lose this."

"Oh, no." I smiled and shook my head. "I'm not getting fired. Nobody gets fired from the public library. And I'm second in command around here. Someday I'll get to run all this."

Her smile looked genuinely happy, as if I'd made her day. "You're so easy to talk to." She sort of shook her head, her careless waves tossing around her face. Combined with her bright smile, she looked like she couldn't believe her good luck.

"So, Marigold," I said with an indulgent smile, "is there something I can help you with today?"

"I think you've done it. I needed to choose a project for my political science class, and you're it. Well, your library is it. I have to choose an issue — a current bond issue on the ballot — to research. Local or national. Something that has the potential to make the world better. That part's not the assignment, but it's what matters to me. Can I use you as a source?" All of this came out through a bright and, as far as I could tell, sincere smile.

"Sure."

"That's wonderful." She pointed to me. "Greta." As though she was reminding us both of my name. "Thank you." She adjusted the strap of her bag and waved as she walked toward the door. "We're going to change the world, you and I."

I loved how those words made me smile. Rash promises always amused me.

Whatever the political science project might be, I was actually looking forward to crossing paths with the crazy flower hippie again.

I pulled up the librarian Twitter account. "Supernatural things happen in libraries — and not only in books. #WeirdAndWonderful #GoToTheLibrary"

Looking around, I saw that the middle school kids hadn't resurfaced, but I could give them a few more minutes. There was nothing pressing to do and nobody to help.

I sent a text to Will.

This library has magical properties.

When he didn't reply right away, I continued.

Strange and beautiful creatures make themselves known within these walls.

I put my phone down and straightened a pile of mail. Then I texted him.

Did you send the flower girl, too?

My phone buzzed with a reply.

Dear Miss Elliott, on our team we have a three-strikes rule. Once three texts come in during practice on any one phone, the teacher sends a reply. Mr. Marshall is busy teaching Parliamentary Procedure so we are sending this reply in his behalf. Please don't expect an answer until after practice. Have a nice day. (Advanced Debate.)

Ten minutes later, Will sent me a text.

Sorry about that. Rules apply to everyone. I'm glad you work in a magical place, but I didn't send you any flower girls. Any wedding planning will have to be done by more capable hands. I delivered Mac. That's my only trick.

An excellent trick. And not that kind of flower girl. I'll tell you all about her later. How about you bring your cousin to dinner Sunday?

Are you cooking?

Shut up. There will be delicious foods there. Promise.

You provide dinner. Plan on men. I will make it happen.

You? The best. Coming to the library after practice?

We have a tournament Friday and Saturday. Impending overnight hotel stay. Many hours on a bus. Much practice every day. You'll have to live without me.

Impossible.

Have a nice day, library lady.

Thank you, Mr. Marshall.

Six days and Mac would be in my house. Perfect beautiful Mac, who was "in management." Swoon. He would be sitting near me at a tiny table. With Will, who absolutely didn't fit near, around, under, or beside any tiny table. When we were younger, Will had been a chunky kid. Now he wasn't a kid anymore, and "chunky" didn't really do justice to his form. He was huge. Not in the weight-lifting, tackle-sport-playing way. Huge in the way that nobody really wants to be.

Some people were horrible to him when we were growing up. More in junior high than in high school, of course, because in every way, junior high was more horrible. The teasing never seemed to bother him. Will had always been cool. Relaxed. Confident. My best friend, who delivered me gorgeous, poetry-reading men as birthday presents. Who could ask for more than Will?

CHAPTER 4

The next Saturday, I was heading to the break room that doubled as the workroom where we taped falling-apart paperbacks back together when my phone buzzed. I pulled it out of my pocket hoping it was Will. No such luck. It was my mother.

Call me when you have a minute. Really important.

"Really important" to my mother could mean anything from "Someone we know and love is currently undergoing emergency surgery" to "I can't remember which brand of microwave popcorn leaves the fewest kernels unpopped." There was no easy way to ignore a text like this.

But I wanted to. Texting with my mother was way too much like talking to my mother. She was the queen of what she imagined was subtle subtext, but once you knew that her mind had exactly three tracks, it was easy to know which track she was on.

Track One: Single Men are everywhere. Abundant. And I am not looking hard enough.

Track Two: Will Marshall does not count as a Single Man.

Track Two has a corollary, which is that people need to grow away from their high school friends before they get into a rut and go ahead and marry them which is all fine and well until the guy decides that life has more to offer than the town he's always known and the girl he's always loved and leaves her wrecked and divorced and dealing with a teenage daughter all on her own, not that *you* were ever difficult, dear. The Track Two corollary is exhausting.

Track Three: Come home, Greta.

I shot back a text as I passed the circulation desk and squeezed past the workroom table.

I'm on break at work. What's up?

Want to talk?

Kind of running, Mom. What do you need?

I sprawled on the lumpy pink couch

43

shoved into the corner of the room. I put my feet up against the wall and rested my head on the couch arm. Comfortable? No. Reasonable? Sure.

I cleaned out the closet in your old room. So spacious! A way better closet than mine. Or the one in your apartment.

Translation: Move home. Track Three.

That's great. Way to be organized.

Come see! Stay for dinner!

Translation, per Track Three: Stay forever! Pass.
Countering with a Track One.

Thanks, but I'm making dinner tomorrow for Will and his cousin (who is both handsome and single), so I'd better not make any non-grocery-shopping plans. I don't want to overload.

Of course. You're so busy. Maybe you should cut something out of your schedule.

Translation, as per Track Two corollary: Don't make dinner for Will.

Not too busy. Just-right busy. It's a lot of work to be an adult, you know.

Oh, I know. And when you're an adult, you have to let go of some of the things you held on to when you were a child.

Translation: Ditch Will.

Right. So thanks for getting rid of my teddy bears and pony dolls. Good job cleaning! Got to run back to work.

I dropped my phone on my stomach and covered my face with my arm. The Mom-and-Will dynamic always made me tired.

Short version? Will loved her. And she loved Will when he was the cute chunky neighbor kid. She loved him when he was my best friend in middle school. She loved him right up to the second year of high school when my dad decided to "make a change" in his life and took off. Then, suddenly, the boy-next-door-plus-best-friend was a dangerous Sign of Things to Come. The number of times we'd had the "Broaden your friend horizons" versus "Will is not Dad" talk in all its varieties, well, it was a miracle we ever had time to talk about anything else.

Not that there was never anything else. In

fact, my mother was a professional at talking about something else. Specifically, anything that fit into Track One — single men looking to settle down.

It is possible that no one else of her generation talks like her or thinks like her. But my mom is a woman obsessed. In a few short minutes, she can say all the following things:

"Next-door neighbor's got a nephew visiting. I believe he's single, but I can't be sure."

"Come home and see."

"Did I tell you about the handsome bank teller? I noticed he was not wearing a ring. If you moved back home, that bank branch would be convenient for you."

"You had a dinner date? Are you going out again?"

"When are you bringing him around to meet me?"

For a late-forties divorced woman, she was steeped in the business of connecting humans to one another. Specifically me to any man who wasn't Will Marshall.

Obviously the short version of any story leaves out details and nuances. And it would be unfair of me to neglect to admit that Mom was working from what she thought was a reasonable premise.

But she was still nuts, and there was no

way I was either letting her set me up with anyone *ever* or moving back into her home. No way.

My number one reason to be an employed adult? Not living with my mother.

Saturday afternoon at the library was busy, at least in contrast to pretty much any other day. It was raining, so there were small bands of middle school kids lurking in corners. I kept walking past one particular couple because they made me laugh. The girl, a pretty redhead with loads of freckles, was at least two heads taller than the boy who was slowly making middle-school moves on her. First there was the lean. It was subtle, but there was leaning. Really subtle. In fact, I was certain the girl didn't know the lean was happening. The next time I passed, she had a book in her lap with her hands placed awkwardly on her thighs, totally in his reach if he wanted to hold her hand. As I walked past a third time, a stack of books in my arms, I saw him perched on the side of her chair, his arm over her shoulders. They were looking at the book she was holding, their heads close together. Adorable.

Today's tweet brought to you by middle school romance. "Fall in love — awkward, awesome, swoony love — with a good book.

Ask a librarian & find your perfect match. #LibraryLove #CheckOutTheLibrary"

Far less adorable was the high school couple at the top of the stairs, right in the picture book section. Three moms had come down the narrow staircase to the desk to complain. Kevin had been up twice to warn them to knock it off. It was hard for Kevin to make a dent, because although he never stopped talking, people rarely listened to him. He was a bright guy, he just said really weird stuff. Really, really weird. It was my turn to handle the lovefest. I jogged up the stairs, avoiding the piles of books someone had left. I'd clean it up later.

They were on one of the beanbag chairs, and neither of their faces was visible. I walked over and kicked the boy's shoe. He didn't notice.

"Excuse me?" I kicked his shoe again. "Guys?"

No answer. I tapped the girl on top of her head. "Hello?"

She came up for air. She was wearing one earbud; he had on the other. They looked annoyed.

"Yeah. Hi. Sorry to bother you, but maybe you need to take this activity outside."

The boy had the decency to blush, but the girl huffed at me and said, "We're not bothering anybody."

I motioned over my shoulder to the lineup of small kids watching them make out. "No, I'm sure this is exactly the kind of education these kids came to the library for. Let's go. Up and out."

I followed them down the stairs and to the door, waving good-bye with a big grin on my face. I pulled out my phone and texted Will.

Debate topic for the bus ride home: The library is an excellent place to make out.

He answered after a few seconds.

I take the affirmative.

All the preparations were made. Salad? Check. Meat, potatoes, things made of chocolate? Check.

I had texted Will half an hour ago.

Do not dare be late. Everything is coming out of the oven at precisely 4:05. You will be in your chair by then.

Yes, ma'am. In our chairs and prepared to be impressed.

The knock came as the microwave clock

flashed 4:00. I stuck my head in the bathroom and checked my reflection. Lipstick on mouth, not on teeth; hair slipping across the forehead, but short hair doesn't allow for ponytail fallbacks; Central High basketball hoodie that I'd used instead of an apron (because who has an apron?) chucked into the closet.

I pulled the door open with a prepared smile on my face. Then I saw Mac and the smile turned so real. It had been eight days since I'd met him, and I had not, in fact, misremembered his face. He was precisely as perfect as I'd thought. The dark curly hair really did tumble over his forehead. No kidding. It tumbled. And his eyebrows were the stuff of legend. I wanted to reach out and touch one. I refrained. His mouth and his jawline matched perfectly.

It occurred to me that I was standing in my doorway staring at my guest.

Oops.

"Hi, guys. Thanks for coming." I opened the door wide, and Mac handed me a bouquet of flowers. He had on a black T-shirt that said, "Do you believe in love at first sight? Or should I walk by again?" I felt my brain clicking, trying to find a proper response to that shirt. Nothing. My only thought was "Yes, please." Which, no.

I moved my eyes back to Mac's face. He was smiling. "Thanks for having us. You have a great place."

It was a nice thing to say, if totally untrue. It was a cheap apartment decorated mostly in cast-off furniture my mom couldn't stand anymore after my dad left. The living room couch was newish, though — fake leather with a bunch of colorful pillows piled on it to hide the fact that I didn't know how to decorate.

Mac walked in. It's possible I checked out the back of him for a fraction of a second before I met Will's eye and made a face of shock and awe. Just in case there was any confusion, I pointed to Mac and then to the flowers.

I mouthed, "Is this for real?" and held out my arm.

Will nodded and gave me a tiny pinch so I could be sure I wasn't dreaming.

"Dinner's ready," I said. "Grab a seat at the table."

The tiny bistro table wasn't really big enough for three, especially since one of the three was Will, but the guys pulled out chairs and sat. Will poured water from the pitcher into the glasses while he told Mac the story of how I got the signed book jacket that was framed on the wall above the table.

"When we were in high school, Greta skipped class to sneak into a lecture at Ohio State."

He kindly didn't elaborate on the fact that I was the kind of nerd who only skipped school to sneak into other schools. "She waited in a two-hour line to get that book signed."

I grabbed a glass vase from the cupboard and put the flowers on the table. There was almost room for plates around it. I served food from the stove onto plates and handed them over. The guys made appropriate noises of satisfaction.

When I sat down, I realized I'd been holding my breath. I unfolded my napkin onto my lap and looked up through the flowers. Mac offered to say grace. I glanced at Will again.

"Please bless this wonderful food and the beautiful hands that prepared it," Mac said.

I looked down at the "beautiful hands" in my lap and tried not to laugh. Not that it was funny, really. Except it was. Because my preparation consisted of taking the food out of Ruby's containers and putting it into the serving dishes my mother had once shoved into my cupboards — "just in case."

Will bumped my leg with his knee. As close as we were all sitting, that could have been an accident. But it wasn't. "This looks great, Greta."

Ruby's Diner takeout did not disappoint. The food looked good, it smelled better, and it tasted amazing. Will held up most of the conversation telling us stories about the weekend's debate tournament and how proud he was of the super shy kid who had won his first round. My contribution was laughing and nodding in the right places and staring at Mac.

When Mac stepped outside to take a phone call, Will leaned back in his chair and raised his eyebrows. "So? Can your boy deliver?"

"We're talking about you now? Not my boy Felix who brought dinner?"

"Right. Me." He locked his hands behind his head in an exaggerated relaxation pose. "Tell me I'm the best friend you've ever had."

"Let me count the ways. When I told you what I wanted for my birthday," I glanced at the door to be sure Mac wasn't coming back right away, "I had no idea you could actually make him come true."

"You should have learned by now never to doubt my ability to come through for you." He put all four legs of his chair back on the floor and leaned across the table. His voice lowered. "You wanted the package. I've delivered the package. Good looking, perfect hair, blah, blah, blah. But here's your bonus. Soul of a poet."

"Wow," I said. He was really proud of himself. "I didn't even ask for that part." At least not lately.

When we were in college — both in state schools, but not the same one — we'd constantly compare dating notes. Will almost always had a girlfriend, which was not a shock to me because I knew how awesome he was. But it was a shock to him.

He'd not been super desirable in high school. Even though he was amazing and fun and perfect in nearly every way, he didn't look right. Too big and too awkward. And all those silly, stupid, shallow high school girls had made sure he knew how they felt — and why. They were horrible. He stepped back from them, and in solidarity, I stepped away from them, too. Will and me. Me and Will.

But in college, Will hit his stride. The girls he went out with didn't seem to care about him being heavy. When he'd tell me about dating, about the number of available girls who were everywhere, he always seemed stunned by his good fortune. I kept reminding him that it was the girls who were lucky.

But I didn't have quite as much luck. Not that I didn't date. I did. But the guys who were interested in dating me never measured up to what I wanted. They were nice but not interesting, or interesting but not nice, or handsome but not intellectual. I told Will I realized that maybe I was asking for too much, that maybe I was being a snob. Will laughed at that because of course I was being a snob. I was well aware of my personality flaws. He told me to be patient.

I'd been patient long enough. Because hello — Mac.

Will grinned. "And this poet's soul is really going to impress you. But it might take him a while to get comfortable enough to show it to you." He took a drink from his glass of water. "And, the best part, you didn't even have to settle for Howard Villette."

"Who?"

"Option number two. He lives in my building. He writes music and paints. He has remarkable eyebrows, very expressive. In the way Einstein's eyebrows are expressive. Also, he's seventy-three."

I laughed. "So what you're saying is that maybe there isn't a flood of handsome, charming, brilliant, poetic, available, employed men under thirty who would be interested in dating me?"

Will grinned. "You only need one if he's the *right* one."

I started to get up, looking toward my tiny living room.

"What do you need?" Will asked, standing, ready to help me.

"I think my mom stitched those words on a pillow for my couch."

56

CHAPTER 5

I slid behind the circulation counter and dropped my bag under the desk. That caught Julie's eye, and she smiled at me with teeth showing, her eyes crinkled up — an aging hipster with groovy glasses and spiky hair.

"Morning. How's it looking?" she said, slipping into the rolling chair next to mine.

I pretended to scan through the non-existent crowd waiting for our help. "Looks like another record-breaking busy day."

She usually laughed, but today it came out like a painful little grunt. I could actually see the smile evaporate from her face. "Huh."

I should have said something else. Something about the weather, or politics, or war in the Middle East, or a hostage situation. Anything less charged than the empty library. "Sorry."

"Hm." It was all grunts now.

I pulled out a packet of gummy bears from my pocket. I offered her the package, and she rooted around until she found a green one. She put it in her mouth, but didn't chew. It was a let-the-gummy-dissolve kind of moment, apparently.

After a few minutes, she swallowed. "City council meeting was Thursday night."

Oops. "Was I supposed to go?"

"No. I didn't tell you about it."

Was there an implication there? Should I have gone without being told? Navigating the change from being the kid working in the library to being the second-in-command librarian was still occasionally a mess.

"So, how was it?"

"The city would like very much to keep the library open." She said it while looking out the window, past the beech tree's yellowing leaves and arching branches.

"That's good news." I thought about celebrating with a gummy of my own, but she was clutching the package. Tightly. In both hands.

"Hm."

The grunts were back. Not a great sign.

"Isn't it? Good news, I mean?" I stared at the gummies, using mind powers to make her hand the bag back. No good.

When she spoke again, it sounded rehearsed, mechanical. "They would like to keep us open, but they don't see how it's possible without a tax increase."

"So, let's have a tax increase. How much could it really cost to spit shine this old house?"

She eyed me sideways, her silent way of calling me out. "There's a proposed increase on the ballot for November. But the bond is for a lot of money — an entirely new facility — plus the school district's bonding for a new elementary school and playground, and people don't want to spend more money on anything. So it's not looking good."

That all sounded vaguely familiar, like it was information I should have known. And maybe I did, but I hadn't planted any of it in my memory.

The baggie disappeared in her clutch, all the air pressed out from inside. I imagined she felt similarly squeezed. Something in me felt like taking her hand, or patting her back, or saying something sympathetic. But she never really seemed like someone to touch, so I didn't.

I put on my master's degree voice. "Libraries are an American institution. Every community needs one."

She gestured out the window at Pearl

Street in front of us. "Family farms used to be an American institution, too. Things change." I knew she was thinking of the tract house developments that had replaced acres of fields only a few blocks away.

I nodded, like we'd come to an agreement about something. "We'll be great. We'll find the money to fix up this place. Or the bond will pass. People will stand with us."

My mind shifted from the theoretical to the practical. "What about our monthly anonymous donor?"

During all the years I'd worked in the library, and probably for a hundred years before that, we got a money order in the mail at the beginning of every month. It didn't have a name or return address on it, but it was always two hundred dollars, and it always arrived with a typed note. Typed. On a typewriter. Like the Cards. The note always said something about the privilege it was to have such a lovely library in town and then suggested one or two book buying possibilities. Whoever our donor was, he or she hadn't adjusted for cost of living increases. Or publication cost increases. It was the same amount every month. Two hundred dollars may not seem like much, but every single month? For years? Decades? Someone in Franklin was sharing a whole lot of cash with us.

Julie looked confused. "What about our donor?" she asked.

Wasn't it obvious? "We have a fan. Someone thinks we're doing something great here. So chances are good that other people think so, too."

"Okay," she said, still sounding like she didn't understand.

"Can't we ask for more donors to come forward? The zoo does it. The community theater does it. People hustle donations all the time."

Julie sat up straighter in her chair. "We will not hustle donations." She frowned like the idea was unspeakable, or at least uncouth.

I shrugged. "Maybe we could put up a sign."

She shook her head. "No sign."

"A jar?"

She put herself between me and the counter. "I absolutely forbid you to put a donations jar in this library or anywhere else." She almost made it to the end of the sentence before she started to laugh.

"Fine. No jars. I'll think of something else."

I stood and grabbed a rolling cart of picture books that needed to be reshelved.

Parking the cart at the bottom of the staircase, I lifted a plastic crate of books into my arms and walked up the stairs to the children's section.

Halfway up the narrow staircase, I felt my phone vibrate. It would be imprecise to say I'd been obsessively checking for messages from Mac since dinner on Sunday. Imprecise, but not incorrect. Knowing I should get the crate of books up the stairs before I pulled my phone from my pocket did not stop me from leaning the crate against the wall and checking my texts.

Him. It was him. Were those angels singing? (In fact, it was not. It was the ice cream man driving by on Pearl Street.)

I've been thinking about you. I hope we see each other again soon.

Cheeks? Flushing. Heart rate? Elevated.

How should I reply? When should I reply? Wait — *should* I reply? He didn't ask me a question. *Don't be eager,* I told myself. I put the phone face up on top of the pile of books in the crate so I could keep reading the message over and over until the screen turned dark.

Focus, Greta. I took the last few stairs at a jog. Upstairs, the picture books lived on short shelves, theoretically so that any small person could reach any book. In reality, that translated to small people tossing books off every shelf at the least provocation. And strange as it sounds, I loved picking books up off the floor. I loved finding piles of books next to chairs. Knowing these books were getting loved up by kids made me glad.

A little boy in plaid shorts and an orange shirt sat on the floor looking at a book about soccer.

"Hi, buddy," I said. "You like soccer?" Because they paid me to make conversation with four-year-olds.

He shrugged. "Soccer's okay," he said. "I like blue books." Sure enough, several inches of blue-spined picture books were stacked beside him.

I sat on the floor near him. "I like blue books, too. Which one is your favorite?"

He looked at me for a second, possibly assessing my intentions. He must have found me harmless because he pushed a book toward me with a snoring dog on the cover. I picked it up and turned to the first page.

"I love this one. Have you read it?"

He looked at me like I had missed the obvious. "I just did."

"Oh, but this one's special. You really have to read it out loud."

He rubbed his nose with his fist. "I only know how to read inside my imagination."

"Lucky for you that I'm here, then," I said, scooting a couple of inches closer. "Would you like to hear it?"

He nodded. I read.

After the first book, he handed me another.

"I'd love to read to you all day, buddy, but I have to work. How about this? I'll put away these books, and then I'll read you another story. My favorite from when I was a kid."

"Okay. I'll help you." He clambered up off the floor and shoved his entire pile of blue books on the shelf in front of him.

Inside my head I rolled my eyes, but out loud I said thanks. And suggested a system.

He grabbed a book from the pile, I read the spine, and we shelved it together.

As I made space on a shelf for the next book on the pile, I started to realize the weight Julie was carrying. What if I was being naïve? What if the majority of people in this community actually didn't care about the library? What if they weren't willing to pay for it?

When we finished shelving the last of the pile, I tweeted: "Communities that read together succeed together. #KeepLibrariesOpen #GoToTheLibrary"

Then I led the kid to the R stack and pulled a battered copy of Eleanor Richtenberg's *Grimsby the Grumpy Glowworm* off the shelf.

"Do you know Grimsby?"

He wrinkled up his nose. "That looks like a baby book."

"Yeah, it looks that way. But sometimes looks can fool you. This is my favorite funny book. There are seven Grimsby books, but the first one is the best."

By the time his mom came to find him, we'd read the book through twice, and he asked to check it out and take it home. It wasn't even blue.

CHAPTER 6

Saturday morning I watched the sunlight filter through my tiny bedroom window. My mother did not approve of such small windows in a bedroom; she thought it felt like a prison cell. I loved it because I didn't have to think about buying things like curtains. Decorating with curtains was way above my pay grade. Blinds. The end. I put cool old film posters on walls and cool old books on shelves. Sometimes I found funky bookends in antique shops. I had read about half of the books that decorated my apartment. Three of the last five years, my birthday wishes had been for rare or interesting books, and Will had come through. Which, of course he had.

As I watched the sun patch move across the wall, I thought about how to spend the hour before work. I could go for a run, but then I remembered who I was. Running was excellent for people who liked pain. I liked lying in bed. Or yoga and rock climbing gyms.

Also, ponytails seemed to be required for running. I couldn't grow hair long enough without it looking like a Dr. Seuss bush had sprouted from my head. I stayed in bed, pondering my hair situation and inspecting the job-hazard paper cuts in my fingers. I also thought about ways to make money for the library. Crazy ways and simple ways and likely ways and impossible ways. Just like that, I'd wasted all my extra morning time. Shower, food, and off to work.

I loved Saturday mornings at the library. Maybe it was because there was more action then. Maybe it was because Will was almost always there.

His job teaching at our alma mater, Central High, allowed him all kinds of weekend freedom, provided there wasn't a debate tournament or he'd done something weird, like assign long papers he'd have to grade. Part of the reason he was Central's favorite teacher was that he didn't do anything too weird very often. Another part of the reason was that they don't come any more awesome than Will Marshall.

He showed up on Saturdays to help me with my ongoing venture that had started as a summer project but kept growing in scope and depth. It was called Local History. Before I became the library's resident expert on digitizing previously analog source materials, I knew exactly three things about the local history section: one, most of the collection got dropped off after someone's grandparent died and no one knew what else to do with all the random papers left in desks; two, said papers were stored (i.e., shoved) in a closet behind the bathroom; and three, said closet was a mess.

Within the past four months, I'd commandeered a table in the periodicals room that — surprise! — nobody used, and set up shop. A month digging into the piles in the storage closet, and I'd made excellent progress. Then Julie unlocked the door to the basement, which was full of boxes, skittering critters, and impending doom.

As much as I loved organizing and scanning and rearranging all kinds of photos, newspapers, recipe books, and journals, the basement was enough to kill me, probably. I'd read Stephen King; I knew what could happen to me in that musty, dank place. I had a policy to never go down there alone. Enter Will, every Saturday morning.

Here is an illustrative difference between Will and me. When I went through a box, I dumped out the musty and mold-stained contents, spread out every paper and book and photograph, tossed the ones that looked too manky or unreadable, and stacked the rest in the queue for the scanner. But Will, the one of us who was not getting paid, picked up each photo and scrap like it was a treasure. It was exciting to him, like obscure Hungarian short films or articles about 3-D printing replacement body parts.

He went about his task like it was an archaeological dig. He'd pick up one tattered folder stuffed with pictures, papers, tax statements, handwritten family stories, and probably shopping lists and names of the farm animals. He'd carry the folder to his table in the corner of periodicals, then pull out one sheet of paper at a time, read every legible word on it, catalogue it in my nerdy spreadsheet file, and box it up.

Between the two of us, hundreds of hours had gone into this project since June, and now there were three big plastic bins full of hanging folders with what used to be someone's garbage, carefully organized and labeled.

I watched him lean over a scrapbook full of blurry, damaged photos. I loved the way he focused on the details of a person he'd never meet. But, I thought, who knows? Maybe the woman in that fifties dress was the grandma of one of his students. I pulled out my phone and tweeted "Libraries — making connections through the generations with people both real and fictional. Make a friend. #GoToTheLibrary"

At hungry o'clock, I stretched my arms over my head and said, "I feel lunch. Are you feeling lunch?"

Will was literally up to his elbows in local history/garbage. His arms were both inside a ratty cardboard box. "Yes. I am feeling lunch. You choose a place while I put this treasure back in the closet."

Ten minutes later, we walked down the sidewalk, me on the outside when we passed the Greenwood place. We didn't even have to discuss it anymore. For years, he'd stood between me and my fear of that terrifying house.

A guy drove by in a beater car with the windows rolled down, and I could hear his music get higher and then lower in that moving-sound Doppler effect. The music settled in to my brain right next to the crazy thoughts I'd had lying in bed. I didn't know I had even made a connection between the things until I said, "I'm going to hold a battle of the bands as a library fund-raiser. Tell me that is a brilliant idea now."

Will rubbed the side of his nose. "That is

a brilliant idea now."

"Thank you." I patted his arm. "But is it?"

He thought for a minute before he answered, which I hated, because it meant maybe not, but which I also loved, because it meant he was actually thinking it out.

He made a "hmm" noise. This could go either way.

"It's a great idea. People love music. They love competition. They love you, obviously. And if they remember they love the library, all problems could be solved." He looked around at the people wandering around downtown on a Saturday afternoon. "People of Franklin," he said in a voice that was too loud to be ignored, "you see before you a brilliant tactician." A few people smiled at Will. More people studied the sidewalk, the shop windows, or their phones. He was not deterred. "Ladies and gentlemen, I present to you — the library rescuer." He started to slow clap.

I grabbed his hand and dragged him around the corner. "That was a lovely speech, but my lunch break is disappearing fast."

He patted his stomach. "Mmm. Lunch break. One of my favorite breaks."

"When I said lunch," I said, "I meant

cupcakes."

He shrugged, as if cupcakes were a given. "Nutrition is overrated."

"I want to try this new coffee shop I heard about."

Will looked uncomfortable. "Coffee shop?"

"Coffee shops are not only for breakfast. They're for all the time. And for pastry, obviously. Because pastry is delicious. So, speaking of neither coffee nor pastry, I really like your shirt. It's a good color on you." I didn't let him respond before I went on. "Also, not speaking of coffee or pastry or shirts, how come Mac only texted me once this week?"

My random conversational leaps didn't faze him. "Maybe he thinks it's wise to keep it slow." He kicked at a rock on the sidewalk.

"Huh." I wondered if Will had told him it was wise. "Or maybe he's not that interested."

"I'd definitely go with the first option."

I stopped him and made him face me. "Why? Did he say something? What did he say? Did he tell you he was interested? Tell me. Tell me. Tell me tell me tell me."

Will laughed and started to walk down the sidewalk again. "You're cute when you're overeager."

72

"That is not an answer."

He shook his head. "True. It's not. And we're not in seventh grade."

I sighed a giant breath. "Fine. Turn right."

We turned. "Where are we going exactly?" Will asked.

At almost the same time, I heard someone yell, "Hey, Greta the library girl!" I turned and saw Marigold. I waved. She glanced at Will and hurried over to me. "Hey. I already said that. Hi. What are you doing?" She stood close to me and did not look at Will. I knew that kind of studious avoidance, and I hated it. But I thought I'd give her a chance to overcome it.

"My very best friend in the world and I are going to get cupcakes for lunch." I stepped back so she couldn't ignore Will beside me. "Marigold, this is Will. He's brilliant and funny and charming and a seriously great kisser."

She stopped with a look of complete shock on her face.

"Want to join us for lunch?" I said.

"No kissing, though," Will added. "Nothing personal, I just don't know you that well yet."

She didn't seem to have any tools for dealing with us. "Um," she said.

"Come on," I said. "I promise we're good

company."

When we resumed walking, she followed. I smiled, pleased. "So, how's the library project?" I asked. Before she could answer, I pointed at Will. "He studied political science, among other things. I bet he has great thoughts on your assignment."

Will laughed out a quiet breath. "Aggressive much?" He knew the drill. People were simply not allowed to discount Will in my presence because of the way he looked. The end.

"Okay, here we are. Beans. Isn't it the cutest?" I opened the door to the narrow coffee shop. An old-school metal bell rang to announce us. Inside, round tables crowded together, surrounded by mismatched chairs. Coffee and sugar smells combined with all the baked goodness. The brick walls held art deco posters and blank chalkboards for people to write messages.

"Wow. Not bad," Marigold said. But she wasn't looking at the décor. She was staring at the counter. Specifically the guy taking orders. More specifically, Mac. Mackay Sanders. Standing behind a coffee counter wearing a black T-shirt and a white half-apron.

I spun around and faced Will. "What? How? Isn't — ?"

He looked ashamed. "So, didn't I tell you? This is Mac's shop."

I almost laughed. Almost. "No, in fact, you didn't tell me." Then the words sank in. "You mean, like, he owns it?" Well. That was impressive. The place was obviously doing pretty good business.

Will shook his head. "Not owns. Manages."

"I'm in management." Oh.

Don't be a snob, I told myself.

"Don't be a snob," Will whispered into my ear. "It's a good job. Which is a big improvement over the last guy."

I followed Marigold up to the counter. Mac greeted her, then his eyes jumped to me. "Greta. Hi." He smiled.

Physically I smiled and possibly offered a wave that I'd like to think was cool and breezy. Emotionally I melted into a puddle on the glazed concrete floor. I reached behind me and grabbed Will's hand. He gave me a tiny squeeze and let go. He put his fingers on my back and pushed me forward.

I talked way too fast. "Hi. We're hungry. What's good?"

He leaned over the counter and stared into my soul. Marigold and Will were probably still there, but I didn't actually care anymore.

"Are you more a cookie girl or a cake girl?" Mac's arms were close to me, and yet again, he wore a black T-shirt with words printed in white. "Are you Wi-Fi? Because I'm feeling a strong connection." Huh.

"Are those things mutually exclusive?" I asked. He looked at me like he didn't know what I was talking about. It was possible I'd missed some crucial part of our conversation. "Cookies or cake — do I have to choose?"

"Of course not. There's enough of everything to go around."

I was pretty sure he was talking about pastries. I ordered a few things and paid. Will stayed at the counter to talk to Mac while Marigold and I got a table.

"So, that guy's your best friend?" She nodded toward the counter.

"Will. Yes. Will is my best friend. The other guy? That's Mac. And I'm working on making him the love of my life. But Will is a given. And he is great."

"Did you really kiss him?"

A rather forward and personal question, but then again, I'd brought it up.

"I did. Will Marshall taught me how to kiss. He's an excellent teacher, if you're in the market." If any of his students — or, heaven forbid, their parents — were around, Will was so getting fired.

Marigold squinted at me. She was trying to figure out if I was for real, I think. "I'm good. Thanks."

"So how's the political science scene? Are you prepared to change the world?" I asked her, assuming she was ready for a change of subject. I was right. She talked about her project while I watched Mac and Will talk over the counter. Mostly I watched Mac listen to Will talk. I decided that if a person's library career suddenly fell apart, that person could probably make a job out of watching Mac Sanders make coffee.

Will pushed his way to our table with a tray full of yummies. He sat down midway between Marigold and me.

"You can't sit there," I told him. He looked at me sideways. "You're in the sight line."

He didn't even sigh. He just scooted his chair away from mine. The metal legs screeching against concrete floor sounded like a wounded animal. I knew I'd handled that wrong.

"No good. Come this way." I pulled on Will's arm until he screeched his chair toward me instead. Our chairs were touching. I could feel the warmth of his leg beside

77

mine. I loved feeling him close to me. He made me feel protected. I kept my hands on his arm until I was sure I'd made my point, which was, I'm pretty sure, clear to everyone: I needed to be able to see Mac, but I needed to have Will in all kinds of proximity. Then I let go of his arm and attacked the plate of pastries, cutting everything into quarters so we could all try each treat.

When I'd tasted two kinds of cupcakes (raspberry-vanilla and German chocolate), a peanut butter cookie, and a blueberry scone, Will told me I should go get drinks.

"What do you want?" I asked.

"I don't want anything. But you should definitely go get drinks." He pointed with his eyes.

I glanced over at the counter. There was no line.

I walked casually over to the counter in about half a second.

"Can I get you something else?" Mac asked. "Muffins? Pound cake?" He gestured to the glass case between us.

Tempting, but no. "I think we have enough treats to last forever. But we need some water. Please."

I watched him turn away and reach into a little fridge behind him for water bottles.

There was a tiny piece of my brain functioning enough to tell me I was capable of being more than the most shallow woman in the world and that my interest ran deeper than his hair and his arms and his face and that I shouldn't be staring at the way his shoulders pulled his T-shirt tight, but I chose not to hear it.

It was a very, very tiny piece of my brain.

He set the water bottles on the counter, and I reached for them. He didn't let go of the bottles. My fingers touched his hand, and I felt a shock run up my arm. It was a literal static electricity shock, but that didn't make it any less, well, shocking. He ducked his head and looked at me with those dark curls totally tumbling, and I knew it was the second he was going to say something perfect, something romantic, something to make a moment of this moment.

"So, you like food?"

Ahem. I tried to make those words something else. I tried to make them mean that he was considering intellectual mysteries or fundamental connection in the human condition. It didn't work. Any way I thought of it, he was just asking me if I like food.

I swallowed, nodded, and managed, "Yes." Okay, that was something. I tried to salvage what should have been our moment. "I do.

And you?"

He nodded and smiled this confident, fantastic smile, and I realized that maybe I was overthinking it. Maybe I was expecting too much. Maybe Direct was the new Sexy.

"Want to get some food with me?" he asked.

I glanced behind me at the table full of pastries and saw that Will was watching us. And I could tell he could hear us, and was trying not to laugh.

"I've kind of already eaten." The words were falling out of my mouth even as I realized Mac was asking me out. He was asking me *out*. And our fingers were still connected around the water bottles.

He didn't give up. "Right. Not today. Not now. Monday?"

"Monday." I nodded. Monday was now my favorite word.

"Great. I'll pick you up at your place at six."

"Do you remember where I live?" Oh please, please, please, remember where I live.

"I remember everything." The words meant exactly nothing, but they felt like a declaration. Maybe it was the way he looked at me. Those eyes. And lashes. And eyebrows. I felt dizzy. He gave my hand a squeeze and let go.

I lurched back to the table and set the water bottles down in front of Will and Marigold.

"You're glowing," Marigold said. "Your aura is brighter than I've ever seen it." She moved her hand in the space around my head as though she could touch the atmosphere surrounding me.

The way Will looked at her, it was clear they hadn't been discussing auras while I was at the counter. He politely ducked his head and didn't laugh. After a second, he was back in control and able to look at me without smiling. "You're swooning." I couldn't tell if he was accusing me of something.

"Oh, I so totally am." I slid into a chair and leaned my elbows on the table. "He asked me for dinner. I forgot how to speak English for a minute."

"You? Unable to speak?" He was laughing at me without actually laughing.

Marigold brushed scone crumbs off her fingers and stood up. "I have to get to my study group. Good to see you, Greta." She grinned at me. "Good luck with that." She turned her eyes in Mac's direction. "Bye," she said to the side of Will's head.

He stood. "Marigold, it was lovely to meet

you. I hope your project is a great success." He gave her the patented Charming Will smile, and she took it in, accepting it and smiling back. She took his hands in hers and said, "You're a pure soul." She nodded at her pronouncement and waved at us both.

"Bye," I said. "See you at the library?"

She nodded and walked out the door.

I turned back to Will. "I forgot what we were talking about."

He laughed and shook his head. "Mac."

"Right. Mac." I smiled. "This was a happy mistake, showing up here. I had no idea."

Will pinched up a bite of raspberry cupcake.

"But you knew?"

He did a little shrug, pretending there was way too much cupcake crumb in his mouth to speak. I waited. He cleared his throat. "Well, I didn't know we'd be here for lunch today."

So, yes. He knew that "in management" was code for "in an apron." It shouldn't have surprised me that he knew. After all, they were cousins. Mac moved here to Will's hometown. So maybe, possibly, I was too much of an elitist to choose "barista" from a list of acceptable jobs. But that was before I met Mac. I decided to let it go, knowing that Will hadn't mentioned the details of

Mac's employment because he was protecting Mac from my snobbery, or me from myself, or something. It was enough. It was a tough economy out there, and we couldn't all have awesome jobs when we were in our twenties. Certainly Mac had other impressive qualities that made up for whatever else I might consider he lacked.

Will bumped me with his elbow. Apparently I was in a lingering reverie about Mac's impressive qualities. Oops. "What time do we need to head back to the library?" he asked.

I looked at the clock over the counter, and then at the guy behind the counter, and then I had to look at the clock again because seeing Mac may have made me forget what time it was.

"I forget what time we left." I put my hand on my neck. "I'd forget to inhale today if it wasn't a reflex response to being alive."

Will smiled and pretended he didn't know exactly what I meant. "Why?"

Without looking exactly like a stalker, I glanced Mac's way. Will didn't take the bait. He waited for me to form words.

"Look at him," I commanded.

He nodded. "Yeah, I've seen him. He's a nice-looking guy."

"This guy, as you call him, is the most

beautiful human being of our generation."
It was hard to make my point in a whisper,
but I was doing my best.

Will looked. Shook his head. "Disagreed."

"Overruled. He's perfect."

He shrugged. "I'm not going to talk you
out of using that word, am I?"

"Not today."

He shook his head and slid the plate of
treats in my direction. "Perfect implies he's
good in ways other than personal hotness."

"Gross for you to mention it."

"No, it's not. I'm quoting you."

I sighed. "Don't ruin this moment, please.
A person who looks like that, who brings
flowers, who looks like that, who texted to
tell me he was thinking of me, and who
looks like that has asked me to dinner. Allow me to absorb it."

"Don't dive off the side right here. You'll
hit your head."

I pretended to be offended. "Are you sug-
gesting that I'm being shallow?"

He didn't bother to answer. He just looked
at me with his knowing look — a tiny smile,
a patient face — until I looked away. Because obviously I was being shallow. And
why not? Everyone deserved a dip in the
shallow end now and then. It was warmer
over there.

CHAPTER 7

I unlocked the library Monday morning just before ten. Letting myself inside, I took a deep breath of the over-the-weekend smell. I loved the library when it was busy, but I also loved the library with no people in it. There was a feeling of history there first thing on a Monday morning, like the sensation of permanence that doesn't have anything to do with how many people are crowding around. I loved how the morning sunlight hit the angles of the soft wood around the doorways. I liked to imagine all the lives this building had seen before it was the library.

Bonita walked through the door and chirped, "Good morning," the same way she always did. The way she always had. I loved how she always carried herself with class and grace and quiet beauty.

"Happy Monday," I told her. "Indeed," she said, like she always said.

Within ten minutes, a couple of families with small kids had come in and thundered up the stairs. I went through the usual Monday morning checklist — it was an actual paper checklist, a fuzzy copy of a memo that had originally been printed before I was born. When Julie decided to retire, or move on, or give up her place as head librarian, I would get to pass the checklist duties on to someone else. This was something to look forward to. The checklist was a symbol of, well, if not my childhood, then at least childishness. I looked forward to bigger responsibilities.

When the list had been checked and everything pressing taken care of, I returned books. This was an excuse to walk through each shelf section before I landed at the stained glass windows.

When I got there, I found Bonita dusting the plants. Which was exactly why I went back there. I loved hanging around when it was plant-dusting time. She picked up each dinner plate–sized leaf and rubbed it with baby oil. She'd been doing this task for the decade I'd worked in the library, and I imagined for a long time before that. I picked up a book that had been shoved through to the back of the shelf and reshelved it.

"What's the scoop today?" she asked. Bonita loved to "chat" while she dusted. I was totally in favor of this plan. For years I'd pretended to help her with her dusting, but we both knew why I was there.

I didn't bury the lead. I came right out with the good stuff. "I have a date tonight. With someone I met here. In the library."

Her eyebrows disappeared into the wrinkles in her forehead. "Really? Do tell."

I did, though I might have glossed over the parts where I looked like a snob, and I certainly didn't tell her that Mac was a birthday present from Will. I also didn't mention that I'd accidentally run into him serving coffee. So it was a short story, is what I'm saying.

She nodded in approval. "What did you find when you Googled him?"

My laugh may have been louder than library laughs should be. Sometimes the words that came out of Bonita's mouth surprised me. That wasn't exactly a phrase I was used to hearing white-haired women say. "I didn't Google him." I tried to sound amused. I think I managed to sound both affronted and defensive.

Bonita put down the cloth and the oil. She turned all the way toward me. "Are you joking?"

"Of course not. That's prying. Spying. It's weird."

"It's not," she said, wagging her finger in my face like a proper grandmother figure. "It's safe."

"He's safe."

She was not convinced. "You're no dummy, Greta. You'd really go on a date with someone you'd never Googled?" I could tell she was trying to believe me — and not sound totally judgmental.

"He's Will's cousin." That should do it. Bonita loved Will. Everyone loved Will.

"Hmm," she said, turning back to the plant. "New in town?"

"Yeah."

"Student?" she asked, not looking at me.

"No. He's in management." I almost got the words out before I laughed. So then I had to tell her the story. "Well, that's what he told me. And it's true. But I pictured a tie-wearing management position, and the reality is a little more the 'black T-shirt and apron' look. He works at a coffee shop."

She glanced over at me. "Good thing you like treats."

"Exactly. It's serendipitous."

She grinned.

"I'm going to straighten newspapers." I made this announcement seem like something exciting.

"You're going to Google the coffee shop guy, aren't you?" She asked it without turning around, but I could hear the grin in her voice.

"Maybe. After all the newspapers are straightened." But I knew I wouldn't. I wanted this to unfold on its own.

I passed the circulation desk on my way to periodicals. Julie thought I couldn't see her, standing there at the corner of the office. If she knew she was in view, her back would straighten, her smile would slip around her slightly crooked front teeth. She would march out to the desk and boss someone around in her friendly way, staring over the tops of her funky glasses, pushing her favorite books on kids who pretended to be afraid of her. Nobody was really scared of her, though.

But she didn't know I could see how her shoulders slumped when she rubbed the back of her neck. Seeing her look so pitiful sparked fear in the hollow in my stomach, a flash of heat that traveled up the back of my neck. I wasn't afraid of her, but afraid of what was going wrong. Things with the board and the city council and the vote must be worse than I'd thought. She looked defeated.

And I didn't have any tools to help her. I stood behind a shelf and watched. I wanted to help. To fix. But what could I do? I was practically still a kid. At least around here, that's what everyone thought of me. So what do you do when there's nothing you can do? You file newspapers. Obviously.

Newspapers rested on long bamboo sticks in an organized row, most recent closest to the front. I pulled the latest stack of papers from the pile on the circulation desk and walked back into the periodicals room to cycle them through.

The periodicals room was both a vast overstatement and a tiny, out-of-the-way corner of the library. Racks leaned against a wall that led nowhere, and the few small tables sat mostly empty almost all the time, except for the one I'd commandeered for digitizing local history. I scanned the tables for something to straighten or clean, but the section looked unused and unnecessary. The bamboo sticks made almost musical rattles as I pushed the last one out, the next one back, and the next one back. Sunday's *The Wall Street Journal* unfolded.

Ditto for *New York Post*.

Then *Los Angeles Times*.

Then came the *Herald-Tribune,* the weekly paper here in Franklin. There was a top-of-the-fold photo of the library, in full color, with a woman in a wheelchair. I pulled the paper back out of the bamboo stick and looked at the article. "UNJUST" read the headline.

Cool. Someone was standing up for the library. They thought it was unfair that people wanted to close it. Then I scanned the article. Not cool. It was ranty. The article told the community that the library was morally, legally, and ethically responsible to retrofit the building for the differently abled. I was totally on board with the sentiment, but the syntax was stabby.

Someone named Lydia Allen spoke for the woman in the picture. "If the people who run this institution think they can win a bond election without making the building universally accessible, they have got to get their nose out of the books and look around. Quit hiding behind your outdated building and your reverse-technology book stacks and see your patrons."

I let my eyes slide over paragraphs of legal-talk and looked for actual words from the woman in the photo. I couldn't find any.

"We've talked to the city council," Allen added. "They've agreed to have an exploratory inspection done. We can expect to see details and even architectural plans by early next month."

Architectural plans?

Then there was a quote from Ms. Marnie Blum, attorney. Apparently she was a city council big shot. "We intend to search this issue from all angles and make the best decisions for everyone involved." Which, obviously, sounded exactly like the kind of political spin that says lots of comforting words and means absolutely nothing. There was no best decision for everyone involved.

I'd heard the phrase "I'm of two minds about this" before, but I'd never actually felt my brain split in half over an issue. Of course I wanted our library accessible to everyone; I'd love to have a new, modern, wide-open, accessible building with elevators and wide enough spaces between shelves to actually accommodate a wheelchair. But I also wanted to keep this library. The one I'd grown up with. The one my parents had loved as kids. The one I loved.

I looked up at the tall ceiling, the wooden moldings, the white window frames that had been painted over so many times I could make a dent in the paint with my fingernail. I loved this crazy place.

I read the article again. It seemed like the Allen woman was saying that people should only come to the library if the county promised to rebuild. She was upset, obviously.

I looked up at the chandelier hanging in the periodicals room. It looked like it belonged in a ballroom. Probably since this room had once been a corner of the home's ballroom.

How could a cold, impersonal, metal building be better than this — even with wider walkways? I pulled out my phone and tweeted "There's room for everyone in the library. But maybe not all of us at the same time. Hey, we can stagger entrances and exits. #GoToTheLibrary"

I took the *Herald-Tribune* back to the circulation desk. I slid it in front of Julie. "Did you see this? Is this what the last council meeting was about?"

She glanced over to see what I was talking about. Nodding, she said, "The council decided that the bond should be big enough to build a new building."

I nodded. "I get it. So if the vote goes through — new library. But if it doesn't — we keep this one?" I was comfortable with that.

"Not exactly."

"Exactly which part not?" I asked, feeling something like dread.

"The second part not. If the bond doesn't

pass, Franklin won't have a library."

"Wait. What?"

She didn't answer. She understood I wasn't really asking her to repeat herself. She knew me well enough to know that I needed a few seconds to process the news.

I used to think I was smart, but now I was second-guessing that, too. Why was this so hard for me to grasp? The reality started to settle in on me. I took a quiet breath. "So, either way, I lose my library?"

She shook her head. "It's about more than a building," she started to say, but I shook my head and picked up the newspaper. "Greta? Are you okay?" Her voice was concerned.

I waved the paper over my head. "Cleaning up," I said, trying not to cry. Of course the library was more than a building. But this building, my building, was integral to the feeling of the place. The whole package — shelves, people, magazines, musty scents, books, computers, stained-glass windows, creepy neighbor houses — all worked together to make this place I loved. There had to be a way to keep it and still make everyone happy. There had to.

I walked fast to the periodicals room, grateful that nobody else felt the need to look at a newspaper. Me and my stupid tweets, trying to modernize the system by making dumb jokes. What would any of it mean if the city council took away this perfect, shabby, wonderful place? How could I have not understood what was at stake?

It's not like Julie had been unclear. She'd probably said the same thing several times. Sooner or later, this building I loved would not be my library anymore. I worked on breathing in and out for a minute. Then I thought of all the great arguments I'd make in favor of keeping this building as the library, just in case anyone ever bothered to ask me what I thought about it. Then I breathed some more, grateful for the comfortable silence surrounding me. I'd have to find a way around the financial decisions of the county.

Or else I was in trouble.

This building was more than a workplace for me. It represented my livelihood, my career path. And all the plans I'd made since I was in junior high. I'd gone to college and gotten a master's degree in library science. *Library science.* If I didn't have a library, I didn't have a job. My stomach lurched at the possibility of finding a non-library job. I wasn't useless, but without a library, my degree was. I'd have to leave town. I'd have to leave Will.

Never.

I couldn't move.

But if I lost my job, I'd have to move.

Home.

With my mother.

My knees started to sweat at the thought.

I needed something good to happen. Fast. Now. Evening could not come soon enough. I watched the clock.

Of course, that meant the day dragged on and on. I planned fund-raising proposals in my head. And I went on a pre-date fantasy date with Mac. For the uninitiated, a pre-date fantasy date consists of imagining all the best things that could happen on the date that's about to happen. Nobody claimed it was rocket science. I imagined Mac knocking on my apartment door, wearing a tux. (Why? Well, why not?) I was in a hoodie and yoga pants. Because comfort. Fantasy-Mac also had an Australian accent. Again, why not?

The other fantasy date details would not be of general interest. No, really. Having tried to explain these details in the past has taught me that other people really don't care. Even Will. Maybe especially Will.

At six o'clock, Bonita and I both clocked out and walked to the door together. In her gentle way, she reminded me I was nuts to not do a thorough online search of any person with whom I was planning to get into a car. I waved good-bye as she got on her bike and sped away. I was still laughing to myself as I passed the Greenwood place. I peeked toward the window and saw something that might have been the face of the old man. In fairness, it might also have been a reflection of a car in the window, or a bird, or nothing at all. Whatever it was, it gave me the chills.

I got different chills when Mac came and picked me up. Much better chills.

But before he got there, I sent my mom a text.

I have a date for dinner.

The speed with which she replied might have qualified her for a record.

Who? Where?

Track One.

He's Will's cousin. I told you about him. New in town. Very handsome. He's taking me to his favorite place. Maybe Happy's? Maybe a place I've never been?

Great. Wonderful. Enjoy.

No more questions? No instructions to bring him over on the way home? Well. This was a pleasant derailment from Track One.

It's not like Franklin was backward, restaurant-wise. We had plenty of restaurants, if you didn't mind ordering while standing up. There were also super hipster places with tiny portions and enormous prices. So I wasn't all that surprised when we drove away from town. I was more surprised when we pulled up to a house with statues of many-limbed, nearly naked women in the front yard. Uh-oh. We parked on the street and walked up the path between the statues. Mac touched the tip of one stone woman's hat with his finger.

As we approached the door, a gorgeous woman with café au lait skin and black shiny hair opened it and led us inside.

"Welcome to Bengaluru," she said, in a musical voice so soft we both leaned toward her. Well, I leaned because of her voice. Mac might have had different reasons to lean. Her Indian accent was so lovely, hearing her speak was like listening to a song.

"Table for two?" she said, her voice sliding all over the words like they were a melody with way more than four syllables.

If I was going to say something about my Indian food issues, my chance was slipping away fast.

Mac nodded, and the woman let us through a silky curtain into a good-sized dining room with candles on tables and spices floating in the air. Every table, set with plates and bowls and silver and glasses, sat empty. This was concerning because I generally chose my restaurants by how long the line was to get in. The longer the line, the more likely it was worth the wait.

I already had opinions on the "worth the wait"-ness of this place.

She gestured with a lovely, graceful hand to a table near a curtained window. "Will this be comfortable?"

"Perfect. Thanks." Mac pulled a chair out for me. I gulped, smashed my knee into a table leg, and fell into the chair. He pretended not to notice and scooted me close to the table.

I loved that Mac was polite. I loved that Mac was present. I loved the fact of Mac, in all its ramifications.

It was my turn to say something. I was totally keeping track. "This place looks great." Strange and exotic smells hovered around us, spicy and smoky, making my nose itch. And my memory of the first —

and up until now, last — time I'd eaten Indian food made my stomach jump.

"You've never been here?" He didn't sound surprised, really. More like pleased that he was the one introducing me to the magic or something. "Everything's good."

I doubted that I'd agree, but I didn't want to say so. It's not like I'd had a major food disaster. But a minor food disaster could be just as disastrous.

Short version: College. Dinner with a blind date. Cozy Indian restaurant. Ambiance? Charming. Scents? Delightful. Food? My face melted off and everything tasted like dust. Spicy dust.

I wasn't about to tell Mac that my taste in exotic food ended at cheeseburgers and pizza.

"How do you know everything's good? You haven't even lived here a month. This is a big menu." I looked at the menu because it was hard to keep eye contact. My bones were soft, my muscles mushy. I felt like I might slip out of my chair.

He shrugged and grinned. "It's my favorite."

Be brave, Greta, I told myself. "Want to order for me then?"

"What do you like?" He was talking about food, I had to remind myself.

100

I tried to remember. "Naan. I really like naan. And I drank something like a mango smoothie once in a place like this." That pretty much summed it up.

He laughed. Oh, his laugh. "How do you feel about trying new things?"

Were we still talking about dinner? "Totally up for it. Bring it on."

He grinned again, and I resisted the urge to reach across the table and stroke his face. Barely.

When the gorgeous exotic lady came back, he said words that sounded like "ticky-tocky" and something else that had lots of *S* sounds in it. He also said "curry," which I understood, and remembered, and feared.

When she had the order, she bowed and backed away from our table, silent footsteps in an almost empty room.

He handed me a basket covered with a linen napkin. "Take one."

Warm, delicious, safe naan. I bit off a garlicky chunk and felt grateful for white bread familiarity.

He broke a piece off and put it in his mouth. After chewing for a few seconds, he checked his phone. On a date. Which was weird because everyone knows you Don't Do That. When he put it down, he put it on his leg, not the table. Not that I would have tried to read his texts, but now the possibility was gone.

"How's work?" he asked.

I suppressed the urge to unleash a political, historical, or financial rant. "Great," I said. "We're going to do a book jam — a bunch of bands playing songs to raise money for the library."

The beautiful woman came back and handed me a creamy orange drink. "Mango lassi," she said.

I took a sip. It was like heaven through a straw. I slurped on it for a few seconds and stopped when I realized it was half gone.

"So," he said. "You've got this battle of the bands."

It sounded so violent when he said it that way. "Not a battle. Just a jam. You know, a gig everyone can come play in."

"Cool." He smiled. "How does that make you money?"

"Oh. Ticket sales? And the bands pay to play." I ate more of the yummy, warm naan.

"A lot?"

I reviewed in my head to get context for what "a lot" might mean. Oh, right. A lot of money.

"Fifty dollars for each band." As soon as I said it out loud, it seemed ridiculous. Nobody would pay that much for the privilege of doing what they could do at home for free.

He seemed to agree because he grunted out a "huh" sound and took another drink.

I nodded. "I know. It seems rough to ask them to pay fifty bucks to play. But if you've got five guys in your band, that's only ten dollars each, and they get to watch a concert for ten bucks. Not so bad, right?"

"Right. I'd do it." He tore off another bite of bread. "If I had a band. And fifty bucks." He made a little shrug like he was asking "What can you do?"

"I know, right? It's so hard to save money when you have to drive out of town to eat dinner." As soon as I said it, I wished I could hide. I mean, what kind of dumb do you have to be to talk about spending the guy's money on a date when you're actually *on the date*?

He smiled, though. "Totally worth it. Promise."

Did he mean the food was worth it? The drive? Me?

When the beautiful lady brought the food, she slid each dish onto the table and uncovered it. My nose itched with the scents. The first one was sort of brown and stewy-looking. So was the second one. And the third. In fact, they all looked exactly like lumpy, saucy, orangey-brownness. With rice.

Mac's eyes glittered in the candlelight as he served food onto my plate. He told me what each dish was called, and I nodded. I was going to do this. I was eating Indian food again after five years of studious avoidance.

"You're getting the real deal here," Mac said. "The good stuff."

That was promising. Maybe the time I'd tried it before, I'd been eating sub-par curry.

I waited for him to serve himself before I put anything on a fork. Just in case I did it wrong. I would have, apparently, because he picked up a spoon. He scooped up a big bite of something brown and — wait for it — saucy. When he put it in his mouth, he made this delighted yummy-face. That was a very good face. I may have previewed in my mind what I could do that would cause him to make that face again. I may have blushed.

I managed a little scoop of what may or may not have been the same food and ate it. Then my eyeballs started to melt and run down to my chin. Trying to hold it all in, I choked back a fire-breathing roar.

I couldn't inhale. I couldn't see.

I hadn't imagined it before. It wasn't a bad curry experience in my past. Apparently there was something wrong with me. I was lacking the gene that made people like Indian food.

No coughing, I told myself. *No coughing at least until you swallow. No.*

I pushed down all my physical reflexes and swallowed. Honestly? I felt it the whole way down, the fire settling somewhere south of my collarbone and probably planning to stay there until it was time to die. Which, you know, could have been any minute.

Water. Water. I clutched my glass with both hands, vaguely aware that I'd be embarrassed if it spilled. Mostly, though, I didn't care as long as some of it went into my mouth and followed the path of destruction that used to be my throat.

Gasp. I blinked away some of the tears and swallowed the rest of the water, ice bumping against my teeth. Only when every drop of water was slurped out of my glass did I place it back on the table.

Mac grinned at me, chewing and smiling like this was completely understandable behavior. "Good, right?"

"I can't feel my tongue."

He laughed, so I tried to smile and pretend I was joking. Meanwhile, I couldn't feel my tongue.

I pushed a spoonful of rice into my mouth.

Lovely, bland rice.

"Try that one." Mac gestured to a slightly yellower saucy pile on my plate. I dipped the edge of my spoon into it and let it touch the tip of my tongue. It tasted like dust.

"It tastes like dust."

He squinched his eyebrows together, like he wasn't sure what he was looking at.

"I mean, it has a dusty sort of flavor, you know?" But I was no longer sure I could taste anything. Maybe the dusty business was the byproduct of the incense burning in little pots around the room. Or my damaged tongue.

"What about this one?" He stabbed something with his clean fork and held it over my plate, totally looking ready to put his utensil in my mouth.

I was terrified.

For a million reasons.

Or at least three reasons.

1. What if the bite was coated in that fiery, face-melting spiciness again?
2. What if he poked the fork too far into my mouth and I choked/gagged/broke a tooth?
3. What if I ate it, hated it, and he walked away, never to look back?

Be bold, I told myself. *Try it.*

I opened my mouth, and the fork went inside. Just far enough — no broken teeth or gag reflexes. I chewed. It was a potato. I had never met a potato I didn't love. Potatoes made fries. And chips. And, you know, potatoes. This was something potato-esque, covered with a dusty-tasting sauce. I nodded, hoping that was all Mac needed. I tried to smile while wondering how to swallow dusty-sauced potato bites.

I chewed that bite into oblivion, and noticed a whole lot of other flavors that I'd never tasted before. If I'd liked the dust, maybe I could have loved the rest. Maybe. I kept nodding and chewing.

Mac kept watching. And eating.

Come on, brain. Think of something true and positive to say.

I couldn't do it. I kept chewing, and, when I remembered, smiling.

Altogether, this date was not a great success. I felt inexperienced and silly. I mean, who doesn't like Indian food? What self-respecting woman gets teary over tikka masala? And why in the world couldn't I have said something before we got inside?

But I knew why. I wanted to have a perfect first date. I wanted to like what Mac liked. I wanted him to be impressed. I wanted him to ask me out again.

All I could think about was eating a cheeseburger at Happy's with Will. I'd had that feeling many times before, and I knew it was not a great sign. I shook off the feeling and focused on watching Mac enjoy his dinner.

CHAPTER 8

Mac brought me home after dinner. But dinner had lasted hours. Every few minutes, I'd been able to eat another bite of naan or sip on my mango drink. And every few minutes, Mac checked his phone.

I got it. We're the screen generation. Whatever. Every time it happened, I would feel a tiny bit jealous, or ignored, or just lame because what was happening on the phone was more important than what was happening at the table. But then he would say something so sweet. So charming. So funny or thoughtful or interesting that I would forget to be annoyed.

I wanted to remember all the things he said to me, but I was way too focused on making it look like I totally understood the allure of Indian food. Not easy for me. But since it was Mac's favorite, I decided to make it look like I was still eating.

In the car on the way home, he told a

funny story about playing baseball when he was in school. It wasn't clear if he was talking about high school or college, but it really didn't matter. He laughed when he told the story, and he looked over at me and smiled like he was happy to be there with me.

He walked me to my door. He thanked me for a fun evening. He put his hand on my arm — between my shoulder and my elbow — and turned me to look at him. For a second I thought he might kiss me, which would not have been objectionable, but there was the food-breath thing to consider. Instead, he slid his other hand around my waist and hugged me. I could feel all kinds of muscles engaged in the activity, and I enjoyed that. I said thanks, and he said good night.

Inside my apartment, I checked my phone. Two messages. Both said, "How was it?" One from my mom. One from Will.

I answered Mom first.

It was fun. Thanks. Good night.

Then I answered Will.

He was a perfect gentleman.

Within a minute, I'd gotten a huge drink

of water and started brushing my teeth. I was scrubbing when he replied.

Is that a good thing or a bad thing?

After my hands were free, I answered.

Good, obviously. We ate curry.

Really? You haven't eaten curry in years.

Yeah. I know.

And?

It was unchanged. I am uncool. I don't like Indian food.

Need a pizza? Or a burger?

I laughed. Will knew me so well.

I think I'm good. It's after ten. Thanks, though.

So, it's your move, right? Are you going to visit him at work tomorrow?

I hadn't even considered it, but now the answer was obvious.

Of course.

Good. That's good. Text me when you can and let me know how that goes.

Will's evening social life was limited by his need to be at school by seven in the morning.

Sure. Night.

At 9:40 the next morning, I was at the window of the coffee shop. I wasn't staring inside so much as I was examining the length of the line. Medium-long, but if I waited outside, it would only get longer. I stepped in. My timing was, for once, excellent. Nobody came in after me, and the people in front of me knew what they wanted. The line moved quickly.

Mac gave his attention to every customer, and I wondered if they all felt lucky. When his eyes landed on me, I felt more than lucky. Chosen. Blessed.

He breathed in as though I'd brought springtime into the shop with me. "Greta, I was hoping you'd come."

I wondered if he knew what happened to my knees when he said my name. Speechless, I focused on keeping my mouth from dropping open. I tried to smile and hoped it looked right.

"I've been thinking about you," he said.

Are there five more swoon-worthy words?

"I've been thinking about you, too." I told him I needed a minute to think about what I wanted. I bet we both knew I was lying.

I stared at his face until I realized I wasn't breathing. Then I read his T-shirt. Again, black with white words. "I've rearranged the alphabet to put U and I together."

"So the shirts." I pointed to his chest, in case he didn't know what a shirt was or in case he didn't know I was talking about his.

He grinned, but didn't offer any response.

"What's the deal?"

He did big innocent eyes. "What deal?"

"Why," I tried to be completely clear, "do you wear pickup lines on your chest?"

Did I just say the word "chest" to a man? I crossed my arms in front of me so he wouldn't think I wanted him to notice mine.

"Why do you think I do?" he asked as he slid the glass door closed behind the pastries. He gave me one of those Man of Mystery smiles as he ran his white cloth over the glass countertop.

I pressed my thumbprint into his clean counter. He didn't wipe it off.

"I think," I said, "that you have a standing

arrangement to flirt with every girl who comes in that door." I pointed over my shoulder.

More big, innocent eyes. "Oh, no. Only with you."

I laughed because when a guy you've been out with once says words like that, you're supposed to laugh. But then I hoped, too. And I wasn't sure my face would hide my hope.

I stared into the tip jar, which held three crumpled one-dollar bills, a bunch of change — mostly pennies — and a Post-it Note that said Raven on it, with a phone number. Ick.

He shrugged. "It's just my thing."

"Like libraries are mine?" When I smiled at him, he grinned again, and that grin made me feel like a soda can that's been shaken up — ready to explode with giddiness. In my head, I expanded my little commentary: *Like* you're *mine*? But of course, I couldn't say that. Never. Out loud.

He stood. He waited. He smiled. He didn't even have to say anything.

But when he did say things, even though they seemed to be short replies, he seemed to know exactly what to say. When he said swoony things, it was flawless, like he'd practiced. Oh, I hoped he hadn't practiced on all the pretty women in the shop. I hoped he'd only practiced in his room, in the mirror, with his mom. Or a cousin. But not Will. A girl cousin. A much younger, unattractive girl cousin.

"Know what you want?" he asked.

I didn't know how to respond, exactly, since what I wanted was for him to keep looking at me exactly like that. "I think a small hot chocolate, please."

He nodded and pulled down a mug. "Staying?" he asked.

I checked the giant clock on the wall. "Actually, work calls. Can you make it to go?"

He nodded and put the mug back on a high shelf, effectively displaying every single muscle in his arm. He filled up a smallish cardboard cup. Before he handed it to me, he checked his phone. I wondered who was sending him texts. And what they said.

He cradled my cocoa in both hands. I held out some money and said, "Trade you."

He shook his head. "This is on me."

I may have stood and stared, holding money across the counter like a surprised person. Trying to process this moment of generosity resulted in my next impressive conversational addition: "Huh?"

He set down the cup and put his fingers

on my money-holding hand, barely pushing it back to my side of the counter. Every place his hand touched mine, I swear I felt tiny neural explosions. It made me want to try paying him again, so he'd touch my hand again. But I didn't. I acted the way I assumed a woman would act who had gorgeous men buy her hot chocolate to go.

I shoved my money back in my pocket and put my hands around the cup. "Thank you. That is very . . . Thank you." I was grinning. Not smiling with some demure, grown-up smile. Grinning like a little kid with a cup of free cocoa. I tried to smarten up. "Thank you."

He didn't say anything, but he placed his hands around mine over the cup. I grew roots into the floor. If the fire alarm had started to ring right then, I wouldn't have heard it over the thudding of my heart in my ears.

He leaned far enough over the counter that his face was near mine. I started to sweat. Oh, no. Gross. "Thank you for stopping by," he whispered. I tried to remember if that was what he said to the other people who bought things at this counter.

A man had come into Beans and was standing behind me. He started ordering over my shoulder, so I yanked my feet out of the floor and walked away. I glanced back when I got to the door. Mac looked at me. He *looked* at me. I walked out into the morning with gooey thoughts of golden light and falling leaves. Then I hurried and slurped down my cocoa so I could text Will.

Melting. Melting.

There was a short pause before his reply came in. I'd caught him at class break.

Like an ice cream? Is it hot outside?

No, dummy. Like a girl.

Melting's good?

Very good.

What happened?

He bought me a drink.

Kind of early in the morning for that.

Right? And he touched my hands and I can't think in sentences.

You sound perfectly literate to me.

That's because you don't make me nervous.

That's because I don't make you melt.

There was no reply that was both true and kind, so I didn't reply.

What do you like about him? I mean, other than the looks.

I hadn't thought too much about him beyond that. Obviously, the looks were enough right now. Will sometimes teased me about my tendency toward shallowness. I'd prove I was looking deeper — or at least longer.

He's generous.

That's true. He's always been like that. When we were little, he was good at sharing. I was not. Really not.

Good. I'd landed on something real. That was helpful in creating the illusion of depth. This whole train of thought made me distinctly uncomfortable, so I determined right then that I would seek out other likeable (nonphysical) character traits. There had to be millions, right? I could think of so many in Will, so it wasn't like I was blind to them in general.

I changed the subject.

I'm saving the library.

I didn't know I was thinking it until I keyed it in.

Right now?

Starting now.

I meant it. Starting right that minute, I knew what I had to do.

Bond won't pass. No way. So I'm going to find the money we need to stay open and make the library work for everyone.

How much is that?

IDK. More than you and I have.

We're not really in high-paying industries.

But I already saved $ today. Remember? HE BOUGHT MY DRINK.

Oh, did that happen? I forgot.

119

Liar. You never forget the important things in my life.

Truth.

I realized I'd made it to the library.

Look. I'm at work. Come in and see me this afternoon.

OK. After classes.

Make it sooner than later. If you hurry, you can watch me come back from floating several inches above the ground.

I'll see what I can do.

When I got inside and swiped my card, I went to find Julie. If she were in a particularly good mood, maybe I'd let her in on my brilliant plan — the plan that, so far, had few details and no specifics. So maybe I *wouldn't* let her in on the plan. But I could see if she had something awesome for me to do.

I found her around the corner from the bathrooms, bent over with her head in another closet.

"Hello?" I wasn't sure interrupting her

was a great idea.

Pulling her head out of the closet, she brushed off her arms. Dusty in there, apparently. "Greta, I'm glad you're here."

I would never get tired of hearing her say that.

I looked around her and tried to find a respectful way to ask. No such way occurred to me. "What are you doing?"

She smiled and motioned to the dusty closet. "I don't think I've ever opened this door before. Looks like more local history. Will you help me carry some boxes to the periodicals room?"

I tried to be casual about how not fun that looked to me. "You don't want to wait for Kevin to come in after he's done with school?"

She didn't answer, just looked at me with a face that couldn't hide the fact that she was desperate for Things to Do.

Right. Got it. "Yes, I mean. I'd love to move boxes."

She nodded and her upper half disappeared back inside the closet. When she resurfaced, she was lugging a cardboard box. She handed it over, and I immediately sneezed. In fact I sneezed my way past the bathrooms, the staircase, the circulation desk, and the fiction section. After setting the box on an empty reading table in the periodicals room, I sneezed three more times.

Dusty boxes — a successful antidote to the floating/ melting sensation one gets when Mac buys one a beverage and then initiates physical contact. Who knew?

I went back for the rest.

Will would love this, I thought as I sneezed.

CHAPTER 9

Will stepped back from the cardboard box he was emptying and scratched his face. "Where did these come from?" He'd come right after school let out because I'd told him we'd found something he'd love.

"Closet behind the bathrooms. You know, one of the secret doors that nobody's ever opened." In an old house like this, there were plenty of tiny rooms and cupboards nobody ever got around to using. I pulled another leather-bound scrapbook out of my box.

"This is beautiful," I said, risking a sneezing fit to smell the leather. I untied the straps keeping it closed and flipped through it. All the entries were penned in German.

I pulled out my phone and wrote a tweet. "Every word of every book was written by a person like you. Will people read YOUR words? #WriteSomething #ReadSomething #GoToTheLibrary"

"These journals are probably awesome if you could read them." Will ruffled the pages of a small book. "What if there was a law that we all had to keep a handwritten journal? I might be jailed. My handwriting is the worst."

"Probably not the worst-worst," I said, "But, yeah. You have bad handwriting."

"This is why I live now — when the important things I have to say can be said digitally." He tapped his shirt pocket where his phone rested.

"Right? What a relief that someone invented Technological Advancement."

"If I lived in this guy's time," Will said, waving another journal at me, "I'd have written everything on a typewriter."

"You'd need bigger pockets."

We dove back into the boxes.

He flipped through folders and stacks of photos before putting them back in his box. "This is a whole lot of Civil War-era stuff. Cool guns," he said, tipping a framed photograph toward me.

I nodded and tried not to sneeze. Unsuccessful.

He loaded the last of the stacks back into the box. "Okay. Write 'Civil War' on this one." He slid the box across the table to me. I marked it with a sticker label.

He pulled open another box and started sorting piles in silence. That didn't last.

"Look. Here's Central." He slid a brittle, crusty newspaper in my direction, a black-and-white photo on the front page of the school we attended, the same school he worked in. I almost pushed it back, but then I noticed the picket signs.

The photo showed what was probably a typical sixties American high school integration mess, but it was happening at our school. Our town. This completely uninteresting Midwestern place. Had our school been the setting for something important?

"Ohio wasn't a segregation state, was it?" The high school civics teacher knew the answer to that question. "No." He flipped a few more things over. "Wow."

"What else are you finding in there?" I kept my hand on the crumbling edge of the newspaper, while Will pulled out a few yearbooks and a thin black book. He handed over a rubber-banded pile of photographs. I slipped the band off and flipped through. Lots of pictures of a tall, thin man in a suit and a hat. He looked at the camera with a serious face and sad eyes. Handsome. A little mysterious. When he smiled, his face completely changed. Still handsome, but now mischievous instead of mysterious.

Cheeky. Sassy. I was hooked.

"Why don't men wear hats anymore?" I asked.

Will grimaced at me. "There's this dude in my debate class — Cade Llewellyn — who wears a trilby every day."

"I guess that answers that. A trilby? How do you even know that's what it's called?"

He tapped the side of his head, as though it was some kind of impressive repository for hat-name wisdom. Which, obviously.

I flipped over a photo of the tall, suit-and-hat man. On the back in smudgy some kind of pen that leaked ink were the words "Dr. Silver, 1966."

"Who is this guy?" I waved the picture at Will. "I might be in love with him."

He rolled his eyes. "You might fall in love too easily." Then he smiled so I knew he was kidding, and pointed to the box. "This one seems full of him. Look." He handed over another stack of photos, this time with frames.

"So who is he?" I asked again.

Will kept checking photos, and I started reading the newspaper article. We were quiet for a few minutes, and then we both said, "Wow."

I knew my story was more amazing, so I said, "Listen. In the sixties, segregation in schools was totally forbidden in Ohio, which you already seemed to know. Right? But the schools were totally segregated anyway because of where people lived and where they were willing to go to school. So this guy, Dr. Joshua Silver — the charming and utterly handsome guy in the hat — was the principal of Central High. Young. Maybe a bit of a maverick. He announced that his school was going to be the leader in integration."

"Greta," Will tried to interrupt me. I didn't let him. This was too good.

"So he rents a school bus. He gets behind the wheel and drives over to the Hancock neighborhoods. He picks up a hundred kids and brings them to Central. He walks them into school, past throngs of screaming white adults. He directs these kids into classes and walks the halls all day, watching to make sure teachers teach them stuff. And he does this every day for an entire semester."

"Greta."

"Not done yet. Then he gets put on probation because all the white parents are freaked out. So he organizes the kids at school — white and black — for this rally." I pointed to the newspaper. "The kids said, 'Hey, adults, don't be jerks. We all belong in school together. We all deserve access to awesome educational opportunities.' And the kids all marched together in big circles in front of the school singing songs about equality and freedom."

"Greta."

"Yeah, okay, but don't change the subject, please. I'm totally falling in love with this hat-wearing man, and it's no longer because of how he looks. This is the coolest. Can you imagine being there? This happened here. Where we went to school. A rally, right in front of the building where you spend all your days." I shook the paper at him — gently — to remind him where I'd gotten this excellent story. I was stunned that I'd never heard it before. How was that even possible?

Will met my eyes with a patient expression. He nodded, and then held up his hand in a stop-talking-now gesture. "Greta. Yes. Completely amazing. Will you please look at this?"

I finally tore my eyes away from the newspaper story and looked. Will was clutching a framed photo to his chest. It showed Dr. Silver, smiling this time, shaking hands with . . .

"No."

"Yes."

"That can't be."

"It totally is."

Dr. Silver and Martin Luther King Jr. standing in front of the Franklin library.

I ran to the front desk. Julie wasn't there. I ran up the stairs. I couldn't find her. Running back down, I skipped past a pregnant woman and her toddler.

"Sorry," I said over my shoulder.

The front door creaked open, and Stan the ancient postman wandered in. I intercepted him on his way to the circulation desk.

"Stan!" I said in a very non-librarian voice. "Did you know that Dr. Martin Luther King once visited Franklin? He was here in this very library. On the steps. There's a picture."

If I was hoping that Stan would know that story and tell me his version of it, I was disappointed. Instead, he gave me a list of all the famous people he'd met in Franklin. Most of them were famous only by some nebulous Stan standard. A golfer from the sixties. A war hero that maybe I should have known. Third-rate movie stars, minor pop culture celebrities, and possibly one Beatle — but he was in disguise, so Stan couldn't be certain.

"Who knew we lived in such a hot spot of

fame?" I said, delighted by Stan's adorable standard for celebrity status. "I'll see you tomorrow."

I found Julie in the bathroom. She was scrubbing a batch of indeterminate slime from the wall below the paper towels.

"Hi," I said to her back. My voice echoed around the bathroom. "Historical people won't let anything happen to an important building, right?"

As Julie turned around and looked at me, I got the distinct impression that I'd been unclear.

"I'd like to try that again, please."

She almost nodded — a tiny dip of her head.

I cleared my throat and forced my words to come out clearly. "If something of national historical importance happened, let's say, at a building, would someone from some kind of historical society be interested in keeping that building from being demolished or becoming, for instance, a Taco Emporium?"

That made her smile. "I think that is probably the case. Why?"

I showed her the framed photo. Her eyebrows disappeared into her hair. She spoke slowly, as though she had to create each word in a new language. "Wow. Greta.

This is very interesting. What do you know about the situation represented here?"

I answered without any such care. My words tumbled out, filling the tiny, echoing bathroom with increasingly squeaky chatter. I could hear my words bounce through the room.

"Doctor Silver. Doctor King. Integration. Protest. Peaceful. History. Important. Relevant. Evidence. Change. Everything."

"We're going to save the library," I finished in triumph. "We're going to keep the library."

Why did her smile look sad?

CHAPTER 10

Mac sent a text asking me to dinner on Wednesday.

Wednesday's my late night at work. I'll be here past 8. Thursday?

It took him a minute to answer — maybe to decide if it was worth it to reschedule his plans.

Thursday is too far away. Tuesday? Please say yes.

Apparently it was worth it.
I may have stood staring at my phone for longer than was technically required.

Tuesday sounds great.

I managed to remember to keep my squeal to myself.

I have another favorite place to take you.

But even though I asked three times, he didn't tell me where this place was. I decided to brave it.

Tuesday dragged on at work, but I spent the time when nobody needed me (translation: most of the day) working on poster ideas for the upcoming Book Jam fundraiser concert. I'd fleshed out the idea with Will, and he was a total star. He suggested all kinds of great details that would get kids from the high school to sign up — details like donuts and laser lights. Julie was on board, even if she seemed hesitant that my concert would bring in enough money to make a dent.

I put on my most confident face. "It's a step. This journey may take a lot of steps," I said.

She nodded and said that all important journeys did. I showed her a few mock-ups for the posters.

She held the poster at arm's length, looking at it over the rims of her funky glasses. She made some "hmm" noises. "These look great. So, anyone can perform if they pay the fee?"

"Right, but their song has to have something to do with a book or a story. It's a literary musical celebration," I said, pointing to the words LITERARY MUSICAL CELEBRATION on the poster.

"Got it." She smiled.

I loved to see her relax and grin, and realized that it had been a long time since that was normal. "This is going to help," I said. "We're going to keep our library."

Her smile fell a little, like it was too tired to stay in place. "It will be wonderful," she said, but her voice didn't carry too much conviction.

I'd show her. I'd deliver the best book-related rock concert Franklin had ever seen. Which was probable, as I was pretty sure this would be the first and only of its kind.

That afternoon, right about the time my body called out for a nap, I looked up from the circulation desk to see Marigold come in the door.

She did a big-arm wave and then seemed to think better of it. Holding her back straight, she cleared her throat and said, "Hi, Greta. I'm here on official business."

I did not laugh. "That sounds very official and businesslike. What can I do for you?"

She reminded me that she needed to research and write about a bond on the November ballot for her political science class. "I want to put a grassroots spin on my paper about the library bond." Then she leaned in across the counter and mock-whispered, "I didn't actually know what a grassroots spin was until my TA told me I should have one for my paper. But now that I've looked it up, it seems like a perfect idea. So," she said, still leaning close, but back to her regular voice, "what grassroots things are you doing to save your library?"

"What makes you think I'm doing anything like that?" I asked.

She huffed out an amused breath and gestured toward me. "Orange," she sang out. "You are going to make some joyful and possibly rash decisions to make the world you occupy a whole lot more awesome."

Obviously.

I told her about the book jam concert.

"That's excellent. How are you advertising?" She actually licked the end of her sharpened pencil, as if she was a newspaper reporter in a 1940s film.

"Twitter. And these, all over town." After I showed her my poster mock-ups, she asked if she could keep one. I ran her a copy, and she offered to talk to the advertising manager of the Franklin paper to see if they'd put it in their "Upcoming Community Events" section.

"That would be great. And if you want, you could come to the show and write about it. Maybe the paper would publish it."

"Would you really let me do that?"

Eager smile-lines creased her face. Her look of pure joy almost made me regret that I was about ninety-two percent kidding.

"Absolutely. I'll make you a press pass. That will get you into the show for free."

She scratched some notes on a piece of paper. When she finished, she looked up and grinned. "This is so fun. Let's save the library."

I nodded. "Yes. Let's." When she left, I allowed myself a laugh. Marigold was certainly crazy, but it was a happy crazy. I took a picture of the ad and tweeted it. "Rock out with Book Jam. You could be a star! #SongsAboutBooks #SaveFranklinLibrary #GoToTheLibrary"

Mac met me at the library at the prearranged time of 6:00. He had on another black T-shirt: "Tired? You've been running through my mind all day."

He came to the circulation desk and smiled at me. "I need to return a book."

"Okay," I said, and held out my hand.

"I didn't bring it with me." He did this face, this unbelievable face that looked ashamed and proud at the same time. It was a full-throttle flirting face, is what it was.

I took two seconds to remember where I was. "Would you like me to renew it for you?"

"You can do that?" He angled himself closer to me. My face flushed.

"Sure." I pulled up his account and re-newed the Rilke he'd checked out the first day we'd met. "Need anything else?"

He put his hand across the desk. "Actu-ally, do you think you could remind me where that book came from? I'd love to get another." He gestured back into the stacks.

"You bet." I had this feeling that if I let it, this little jaunt back to the 831 shelf might yield more than another book of translated poems. I was absolutely planning to let it.

When I led him around the corner, I slowed down enough that if he'd been fol-lowing me really closely, he'd have bumped into me. He didn't bump. I couldn't decide if that meant he was keeping his distance or he was paying attention. I chose to believe the part about attention.

I pointed to the shelf of poetry, but instead of scooting to the side, he leaned around me, his arm reaching over my shoulder to pull a book off the shelf. He didn't even look at the title.

"You look especially lovely today," he said, making all my brain cells melt. "Have you been doing something that makes you happy?"

I made a mental note of another excellent personality trait I could tell Will about. Who doesn't love someone complimentary? And he had great conversation-starting skills. I thought about all the poster-designing and concert-planning I'd done and nodded. Then I turned on the bravery. "I've been looking forward to seeing you."

A single syllable of happy laugh came out of his mouth. "Nice," he said, which didn't really match the rest of the conversation up to this point. So, the conversation-starting skill was stronger than the conversation-continuing skill. I absolutely didn't care.

I leaned a bit against the bookshelf. The smell of musty paperbacks made my head spin. His arm was still on the shelf behind me. He leaned in, and I felt my stomach do an anticipatory lurch. I couldn't have taken my eyes off him for any conceivable reason.

His face got very close to my face, and I readjusted my feet so I wouldn't fall over. He stared through my eyes directly into my soul. His hand moved from the shelf to my shoulder, and I felt my smile expanding. He moved closer, even though that seemed impossible, and I knew it was totally happening. My hand started to move up to touch his arm.

"Hungry?" he said.

If this had been a movie, that would have been the second where the soundtrack screeched to a stop. "What?"

"I'm starving. Ready for dinner?" He didn't wait for me to answer, which was just as well, since I literally had no words at my disposal. He put the book back on the shelf and took my hand. "Let's go eat." He turned away from the stack.

Right. Eat. Good. And we were walking through the library holding hands. I took a second to enjoy the giddy flutter that always came with holding hands. When we passed the desk, I slowed enough to reach my free hand over the counter to grab my bag from the chair where I'd left it.

Ponytailed high-school Kevin caught my eye, glanced at Mac, and made a face of wide-eyed impressed-ness.

I grinned at him and waved good-bye.

We walked out the door and to the left. I didn't say anything about the old Greenwood house. Creepy old men and possible haunted houses weren't really date conversation material.

But then again, conversation wasn't actually happening. Mac seemed perfectly content to walk down the sidewalk holding my hand and smiling at me every few steps. Maybe he was messing around with me. Maybe he was trying on personalities. Maybe he was just trying to keep me on my feet.

We'd walked a few blocks when I asked, "Where are we eating?"

He squeezed my hand. "It's a surprise."

I forced a smile as I remembered the feeling of my throat burning under the power of some other food-borne surprise.

We crossed a street and turned a corner and — surprise! — Mac opened the front door of Happy's, Franklin's best burger place. I felt my face relax into a sincere grin.

"I love eating here," I said, aware that it was neither fashionable nor traditionally feminine to admit to eating cheese fries and milk shakes.

"I know you do." He walked up to the line at the counter.

Following closely, I asked, "How do you know?"

He looked at a few spots around the dingy dining room, probably unchanged since the 1950s, and said, "Spies."

I laughed. Funny. I added it to the growing list of depth-giving characteristics.

"That sounds exactly like something Will would say."

"Does it?" he asked, but not like he wanted me to answer him.

After we ordered and sat down, I watched him get comfortable in his chair. Usually I came here with Will, who always sat with his back to the wall so he could smile and wave at his students who filled up the place. Today I could see people all around the room looking at us and double-taking. Women took several glances at Mac. I felt a weird combination of defensiveness and pride.

Hey, ladies, I wanted to say. *Back off. He's here with me.*

But also, *Hey, ladies. Check it out. He is here with* me.

It was a strange sensation, one I'd certainly never experienced coming here with Will. I spun the plastic pyramid that had our order number on it for a second, uncomfortable at what felt like a disloyal thought. Then I looked up and Mac was looking right at me, and I forgot all about disloyalty.

I wanted him to keep looking at me, but I was having a hard time thinking of something to ask him. So I just stared. He appeared to stare back. There was a tiny smile

141

on his face — just enough to curl up the edges of his mouth. Honestly, it made it hard to focus on words. On anything but his lips.

A guy walked over and slid our plates onto the table. "Need anything else?" he asked as he walked away, clearly not anticipating an answer.

I could not speak, but I could eat. I reached for a fry and consciously picked up only one. Well, one at a time.

After a minute of eating fries and staring, I realized I would have to say something.

"So aside from the Book Jam concert I'm organizing, I want to schedule an author visit." I'd mentioned to Julie at work earlier that I would keep my mind open to other ideas in case the concert wasn't enough to cover our expenses. Sitting here reading the cheesy posters on the walls of Happy's and staring at my date, the idea sank into my brain. "I just thought of it. Right now. An idea inspired by our meal together. I think it will be awesome."

Mac nodded and dipped a fry into his ketchup. "Cool."

I waited for him to say something more. Something to prove that he knew what a big deal this could be. He didn't say anything. But maybe that was because he didn't have any experience with this particular kind of big deal.

"Have you ever been to an author reading?" I figured that would require some moments to answer, so I took a bite of my cheeseburger. Heaven tastes like Happy's cheeseburgers, I'm pretty sure.

He shook his head and ate more fries.

After I swallowed, I dug a little deeper. "What about a poetry reading? You're really into poetry, right?"

"Oh, yeah. I'm totally into it. But I just, you know, read it myself." When he picked up his burger, I could see his muscles moving in his arms. I wondered if I had visible muscles, and then I remembered that of course I did not.

I started telling him about a website I liked that had video and audio files of poets reading their own work. I expected him to pull out his phone and look it up, but he just glanced between me and his burger and smiled that amazing smile. So I stopped trying to make conversation and enjoyed the meal and the view. I reminded myself of a quote Bonita had printed out and mounted next to the phone at the library: "You don't have to say everything you know." I wasn't sure if that was there for her own benefit or someone else's, but it stayed in my mind.

We finished eating, not saying too much, but it wasn't uncomfortable. He smiled a lot, joked a little, ate everything. Occasionally his leg touched mine under the table. I spent some moments wondering how that possibly sent as much electricity through my body as it did. I felt like my hair was getting longer through the energy his touch was delivering. Which was silly, so I didn't mention it.

He stood up and cleared our table mess onto a tray. I excused myself and told him I'd be outside in a minute. I went into the ladies' room and washed my hands in the frigid water that squirted to the left instead of straight into the sink and checked my reflection in the mirror.

Hair? Fine. Lipstick? Gone the way of cheeseburger and fries. No big deal. Clothes? Free of Happy's residue (not always a given).

I made my way out to the patio and saw Mac leaning against an empty table. His phone was in his hands, and he was concentrating on whatever he was reading. I hoped it was the poetry reading website, but when I walked up, he quickly stashed his phone in his pocket.

"Would you go for a walk with me?" he said. "It's an almost perfect evening."

"Sure."

He took my hand and gave it a squeeze. "Closer to perfect now."

I felt myself blushing. We walked to Burton Park and sat on a very particular bench under a huge and very familiar maple tree.

"Want to sit somewhere else?" I asked, but Mac shook his head.

"This is a good spot. I like this tree."

I nodded, deciding my hesitation was not worth explaining.

He put his arm over the back of the bench. "Did you play here when you were little?"

I had, of course, but the real memory of this park was always as the place Will and I kissed. This park. This bench. Under this tree. I was sixteen years old, and Will and I had made an agreement: If I reached my sixteenth birthday without kissing anyone, he would give me a proper kiss. It was the wish of the year.

The day after my birthday, he'd brought me here in his car — a benefit of being several months older — and had led me to this bench and sat next to me. I'd scooted close to him and inhaled the yummy scent of clean shirt and manly deodorant. I told him he smelled nice and batted my eyes hard enough to make me dizzy.

"It's a miracle," Will had said, "that you don't get kissed every single day."

I laughed. "Are you making fun of me right now?"

He smiled but neither confirmed nor denied.

"Well?" I'd asked. "Are we doing this?" I rolled my shoulders and cracked my knuckles.

"Seriously, Greta. You are an Olympic medalist in ruining the moment."

"Sorry. Sorry. Okay. I'm ready. What do I do? Where do I put my hands?"

Will had shifted on the bench so he was facing me. "You have all kinds of options. I am going for the prime spot." He put one hand on the back of my neck, his fingers warm under my hair.

"Am I supposed to close my eyes?" I asked.

"If you want. I'm going to stare at you for a minute, if you don't mind."

I squirmed. "Are you psyching yourself up to do this?"

He'd leaned in so his mouth was close to my ear. "I'm enjoying the view," he said.

With his hand on my neck and his voice so low, I forgot about Will's size. All the high school stuff about toughness and hotness and what a guy should look like melted away. I felt the warmth of his hand and the tenderness with which he moved closer to me.

He whispered into my ear again. "You are my favorite person in the whole world. I'm really glad you didn't get what you wanted for your birthday." And he kissed me.

Even sitting down, my knees had gone weak. He knew exactly what he was doing.

My hands found the sides of his face, and I felt him smile. His other arm came around my back. For the first time, I noticed things about Will's body that were exactly right. His mouth was the perfect combination of soft and warm. His hands held on to me just enough so I felt connected but not overpowered.

He broke away. "Well?" he asked. He had that shy-boy look that I loved about him.

I pretended to think about it for a second. "I think . . . I definitely think we should do that again."

We did.

I straightened up and shook out my hair. "How do you know when you're done?" I asked him.

Will laughed. "You're never really done, you just pause for a while."

"How long does the pause last?" I said.

He smiled, and he'd never looked so

handsome. His brown eyes sparkled with reflected sunlight. I'd always loved making him smile, but now I looked at his mouth differently. That mouth had just delivered an excellent kiss. He looked happy and confident and very satisfied. He really did have a great face.

"I hope not very long," he said, and leaned in again.

After the kiss, I jumped up from the bench. "That was fun. Really fun. Thank you." And then I thought of something. "Is it always that fun?" I stood in front of the bench waiting for him to answer me.

"Kissing," Will said, in the voice he always used when he was imparting great wisdom, "is like pizza. Even when it's not that great, it's still pretty good."

I pulled him off the bench. "I don't know. I realize I don't have anything to compare it to, but I think you might be really good at it. In fact, I feel sorry for any girl who learns how to kiss from anyone else."

He'd laughed then. "That's nice of you. But we both know that without any real data, your conclusion is invalid. How about we discuss it again when you have some further comparative evidence?"

"Deal." We'd shaken hands on it. And we'd kept the deal. I'd met Will at the bench under the maple tree to discuss every kissing experience I'd had. And I was honest with him — he was still the best.

And now, here I sat on the same bench. With Mac, hoping a great hope that I'd have another experience to add to the list. And that maybe this one would top all the rest.

"Greta?" Mac asked. "Did you?"

"Did I what?" I asked, aware that I had gotten distracted.

"Play here? When you were little?"

I pointed to the playground. "When I was a kid, I used to run up that slide and turn around and slide down again. I'm pretty sure the slide was much taller back then. I bet I couldn't do that now."

He stood up from the bench and took my hands, pulling me up. "Try it."

I shrugged. "Come with me. You can catch me if I fall."

We walked over to the playground set. The slide looked tiny now. I jumped onto it and ran up a few steps. At the top I spun around and sat, sliding down a much narrower space than I remembered. About half a second later, I reached the bottom. Mac held out his hands and pulled me up. In the same motion, he put his arms around my waist and drew me close.

The space between us was so different

from the space between Will and me. I put my arms around him, and my fingers touched my elbows. That never happened when I hugged Will.

When Mac kissed me, I forced myself to stop thinking about Will. It might have been too easy to compare, and I knew this was a kiss I wasn't going to discuss, at least not right away. It wasn't hard to let myself dissolve into the moment and stop thinking about much of anything except mouths and hands and a warm autumn breeze.

CHAPTER 11

The next morning, I stopped at Beans on my way to work.

"Hey, Greta," Mac said, setting down a load of boxes and dusting off his chest. His T-shirt asked me if I had any plans for the rest of my life. "I'm happy to see you." They were innocent enough words, but as he said them, all I could think of was standing in the park, holding on to each other, ignoring the rest of the world.

I'm not saying he caused it or anything, but I had a tiny episode of amnesia, so I stared at him until I remembered why I was there. Oh. Right. "I need three peanut butter cookies, please, and the name of your favorite author."

He smiled and put the cookies into a brown paper bag. "Today is your lucky day. The prettiest girl to walk in today wins three free cookies." He handed the bag across the counter. My whole body squirmed. Was that shock? Surprise? Pleasure? What do you even call it when all those things happen at once? Distraction, apparently, because I thanked him and walked out without getting an answer to the author question.

Walking to work, I clutched the bag of practically stolen cookies and texted Will.

What living writer would you want to meet?

It was his prep hour at work so he answered right away, as if he'd been holding the phone in his hands already.

You know who. Same as you. Obviously.

Obviously.

Good call. This is why I love you. Also — free cookies to the prettiest girl to walk into Beans. That was me. He's good.

He is very good. I'm so proud. Enjoy your spoils.

I'd walked about half a block when my phone rang. "Wait. Living author? Are we doing an event?" Will laughed, knowing the answer.

"Hi," I said.

"Hi. But, are we? Are you bringing in an author?"

Leave it to Will to get squeaky with excitement at the prospect. "I'm thinking about it. What do you say?"

"It's the best idea in the history of great ideas. You're a genius. I could not be more into it. Tell me what I can do to make it happen. I want in. I want to be a part of this historical awesomeness." The excitement in his voice made me laugh out loud.

I breathed in the perfect morning, the happiness of the conversation, and the possibility that lay ahead. "Thank you, Will, for real. Thank you for being so excited with me. You are my favorite."

He laughed. "Are you kidding? What kind of cretin wouldn't be stoked about this? Okay. I have to go teach school. But do not — I repeat — *do not* leave me out of this. Text me all the updates. You're a genius. And I'm so proud of you."

When I got to the library, I swiped my time card and tossed my bag under the desk. I handed Julie a cookie and started talking to her as if it was normal to eat cookies at ten in the morning, and as if we'd ever actually started this conversation. "What about a reading? With a picture book writer. What about someone who adults loved when they were little and now they love to share with their kids? What about" — I paused for effect — "Eleanor Richtenberg?"

Julie opened up her mouth and showed all her teeth and laughed out loud, in a non-library-approved way. "I love it."

"Really? Because I think it could be perfect. I think it's the way to draw the biggest crowd. I think she will be the most accessible because kids and adults and teens — everyone — can connect with her. I think this is the one."

She closed her mouth, but couldn't stop her smile. "You sound like you're defending your thesis."

"I'm pretty excited."

"No kidding. Me too." She pulled the bag of gummy bears out of the desk drawer and handed it to me. I took a green one and pulled off its head.

"Okay. How do we find her?" Julie asked.

I sat down at the computer and Googled her. Website? Grimsby.com. Oh, yes. A squirming glowworm glared out of the screen, alongside a photo of the author that must be twenty years old, at least, judging from the hair. And the outfit.

I flipped through the digital bookshelf, and each *Grimsby the Grumpy Glowworm* book flashed up on the screen. I was giddy. These were the favorite books of my kidhood. I had permission, and I was determined to make this happen.

Take the following steps to arrange an author's visit to a community library:

1. Search author's website for contact information. Find none.
2. Google author to see if, by some chance, her phone number is listed.
3. Find that, in fact, it is not.
4. Discover a hidden website page, behind a particularly grumpy glowworm drawing, that contains a link to author's publicist.
5. Contact the publicist, who has a polite assistant who assures you that your call will be returned (at work) as soon as possible.
6. Wait, staring at the phone, for eleven days.
7. Moan.
7.5. Send polite reminder emails to publicist every thirty-six hours.
8. Receive a phone message (at work) from publicist, who, as it happens, returns calls in the middle of the night.

9. On a Saturday.
10. Do a giddy dance.
11. Engage in a game of pro-level phone tag with publicist.
12. Erase several community events from library calendar to clear an entire week for author's possible visit.
13. Accept (without reading) publicist's list of requirements for author's comfort.
14. Hear these words: "Congratulations. Eleanor Richtenberg will be at your library on October twenty-sixth."

"Save the date: Beloved author E. Richtenberg @ Franklin Library 10/26. Reading, reception, & signing. #Grimsby #Save-FranklinLibrary #NotAJoke"

CHAPTER 12

At the library, I pulled the stack of fresh newspapers off the desk and walked to the periodicals room. Replacing the big papers first, I tried to pretend I wasn't completely eager to get to the Franklin paper. *Journal, Times, Post.* There it was. I pulled the half-sheet of grocery store ads out of the fold, because they'd only end up on the floor.

Front page had an article on the football rivalry between East High and Central. Pass. I turned to the arts section, and there was nothing about the library. Ditto for metro. I almost gave up, because the only other thing I really wanted to do was dive into the Dr. Joshua Silver collection, but Julie had asked me to save that until the weekend. I went back to the front section and turned each page.

Near the back of the first section I saw an ad for our Book Jam concert. Marigold seemed to have worked her magic. The ad looked great in black and white. The graphics were cool and readable and totally unlikely to find an audience among the newspaper readers of Franklin. Maybe somebody would tell her grandchildren about the concert over Sunday dinner or something.

On to the sports section, not to be confused with the front page sports article. It's not like I actively expected anything in that section, but the publishers of the newspaper were often creative with their article placement, so I looked. There was a shuffleboard tournament on Saturday in Burton Park. Nothing about the library.

Editorials. The opinion page. There was a column of letters under the headline "Library Controversy" that filled up nearly half a page. It was too much to take in all at once. I let my eyes bounce from letter to letter.

"This is proof that we need a civic center far more than an outmoded building full of books."

"A library will always have a place in a community that values learning."

"Welcome to the twenty-first century. We've been waiting for you."

"I loved the library as a kid, but I can

see how it's become more trouble than it's worth."

"Dr. Martin Luther King visited our library in 1966."

I did a little cheer inside for that one. Someone else knew.

There was a letter from Mayor Cutler's office voicing support of the bond. Was that normal? Could that be a good sign?

The last letter was the weirdest one.

"The library is a historical piece of Franklin, and the community has grown up with it. But once it becomes exclusionary, we need to look at better options. A public building should be accessible to every member of the public, and if any institution should be all things to all people, a library should."

I read that line over a few times and then glanced at the end of the letter.

Ms. Marnie Blum, Attorney, City Council

I went back to the letter.

"Interested parties should feel confident that their opinions matter. Any letter, phone call, or email directed to the city council containing viewpoints about the options for dealing with the library matter will be carefully considered."

I read the letter again. Ms. Marnie Blum, attorney, seemed to say everything and nothing. Like she held every opinion at the same time.

I straightened up the periodicals room and went back to the front desk.

Bonita was filing papers. Kevin taped covers back onto falling-apart paperback books. Julie sorted a stack of mail straight into the recycle bin.

Nobody was waiting for any help, so I sat down at the computer and searched Ms. Marnie Blum, attorney. She had a couple of websites, clean and boring. I found her campaign site and snorted out loud. "Your agenda is my agenda."

Julie heard me, of course. "Are you finding the internet funny this afternoon?" she asked.

I didn't want her to think I was wasting time, so I hurried to justify myself. "A lady from the city council wrote a long letter to the newspaper. I was doing some research. Look. This is her campaign. And she got elected." I pointed to the screen, and Julie leaned over the monitor. She looked with me at the photo of Ms. Blum's metal yard signs. I made a gentle scoffing noise. At least, I'd like to think it was gentle.

Julie nodded. I thought she was agreeing with the scoff, but then she said, "You know her."

I looked up. "I do? How?"

"She brings her mother here to senior activities. She's the one who does laps around the building instead of coming inside." Julie drew a looping circle in the air in front of her to demonstrate the path, I guess.

I scrolled down the site and found a photo. "Oh. Yeah. I do know her. She sometimes comes in," I said, feeling like I needed to justify her. "She sits by the stained glass if it's raining."

"And she probably reads," Julie said. "Something with every opinion at the same time." She gave me a smile and went back to the stack of mail she was mostly throwing away.

"Did you write the letter in this week's paper about Dr. Silver and Dr. King?" I asked Julie.

She shook her head and pointed across the desk.

"I did," Bonita said.

I wasn't sure how to ask the next obvious

161

question without offending Bonita. So I went ahead and asked. "Were you here then?"

"In Franklin? At the library? In 1966?" She glanced at Julie and smiled, like they were adults and I was a precocious child. Well, they *were* adults.

"Sorry." It was automatic.

She didn't turn around from her filing, but she laughed to let me know she wasn't offended. "You don't need to be sorry. And no, I wasn't here then, not in Franklin or the library. I moved here in the seventies, when I got married. I wrote to the newspaper because the story needs to be told."

"Right?" I said. "How is there not a Dr. Joshua Silver book on display around here?" I pulled my latest collected cardboard box out from under the desk where I'd stashed it. "I've been reading through this stuff, and I can't find anything at all about him after he left Central High. It's like he disappeared. When you Google him, there's only a tiny mention of him in an article about Midwest school integration."

"You've caught the research bug," Kevin said over his shoulder. "It's highly contagious." He kept going, but I stopped listening. Kevin had the ability to appear seventeen and sound sixty. He said everything with a weird pomposity that was totally at odds with his ponytail and eyebrow piercing. And he didn't seem to know when to stop talking. I was sure high school was a disaster for him.

"It helps when the subject of your research wears a hat in almost every photo," I said.

Kevin laughed. "Do you have a historical crush on Dr. Silver, Greta? That's cute."

I laughed too. "Yeah, okay, but it's strictly an educational crush. Like my thing for Hawthorne. Or Euclid. I love a man of mystery."

Bonita made a noise of agreement. "Maybe Dr. Silver decided he wanted a private life. Maybe he left education and political activism to become an accountant or a shoe salesman."

"Maybe," Julie cut in, "you're looking in the wrong direction. Maybe in order to understand what he did after he left Central High, you need to know who he was before he got there."

I felt like I was suddenly in a social history class, and Julie's suggestion sounded like homework. But also like permission. "I'm not giving up on you, Dr. Joshua Silver. You can run, but you can't hide from me forever."

I pushed my chair away from the computer. "In the meantime," I said, clutching the cardboard box, "I'm going back to my scanner to digitize all the pictures of this extremely handsome man and his hat."

CHAPTER 13

Mac called and asked if he could come over to my house. I didn't know why that made me nervous, so I suggested the park again. Maybe I was hoping for a recurring kissing-in-the-park theme to this relationship. I could think of a lot of worse ideas.

I walked over to Burton Park. The parking lot, shaded by a bank of sycamores, held a few minivans and a stack of kids' bicycles all tumbled together in a tangle of handlebars and chains. I hoped the gang of little kids would play in the other end of the park from where I was meeting Mac. I walked past the duck pond and on to the paved path that ran through the park. The fountain had been turned off for the season, but a couple of girls were sitting on the edge of the stone, backs to the dolphin that wasn't spitting any water.

They appeared pretty deep into a conversation about something that made them gasp and shake their heads and say, "No way" and "Shut up" over and over. I wondered if, when the weather got cold enough to force them indoors, they'd come into the library for this kind of conversation.

I checked the time and made my way across the park toward the bench under the maple. The kissing bench. My bench. Mac wasn't there yet, so I pulled my feet up and wrapped my arms around my knees. I got out my phone and opened the book I was reading. A couple of minutes in, I was interrupted by a text from Will.

She loves orange juice. Take her a bottle when you meet her.

I finished my paragraph before I texted back.

Was that for me? Because I don't know who you're talking about.

His reply came quickly.

Sorry. Nope. That was a work thing. Someone wanting to butter up the principal.

I hope it works. It will probably work. OJ always works for me.

I know.

A few minutes later, I looked up and saw Mac walking in the dappled shade of the afternoon. He moved with confidence across the grass. He waved, one arm held behind his back. I waved too. His black T-shirt said "This shirt is made of Boyfriend Material."

I put my phone away and slid my feet off the bench and shook out my sleeping legs. He sat on the bench beside me, sliding across the slats until our shoulders touched. I wished I wasn't sitting down. It made the whole how-do-we-greet-each-other awkwardness more painful. I mean, here we were on The Bench. Did that mean we should start with a kiss? Or was that way too familiar? But it seemed really weird to hug sitting down.

"I have a present for you," he said, still hiding one hand behind his back.

I clapped my hands. "Is it a puppy?"

He looked worried. "No. It's not. Not at all."

"Not even a little bit a puppy?" I was teasing, but I wasn't sure he could tell. I had to keep reminding myself that he really didn't know me that well.

Nervous? Confused? I wasn't sure what his expression was expressing. "Is that what

167

you want?"

"Thank you. No. I don't want a puppy." I smiled, trying to change from a bizarre-girl vibe to a flirty-girl vibe.

He put his free hand over my eyes and placed something cold in my hand. When I looked, I saw a plastic bottle of orange-colored juice-type drink. The kind made of not-fruit.

I waited for him to say something. He didn't. But he looked pleased, so I thanked him.

"You're welcome. Drink up."

I smiled and told him I'd save it for later.

And now I sat on the bench next to Mac while I held a bottle of juice-flavored drink that I would never, ever drink. An awkwardness settled over us.

Mac seemed immune to such weirdness. He sprawled out on the bench and put his head down right by my knee. "Perfect day," he said. Then he looked up at me. "Perfect view." He reached up and touched my elbow and ran his hand down my arm to my fingers. "Are you using this?" he asked.

"Not at the moment."

He smiled and closed his eyes. "Good." He took my hand in both of his and held it against his chest. I stared at his amazing face for a minute, until he opened his eyes.

168

"Tough day at the office?" I asked. Then I wished that I could bite the words back. We had never talked about his job. Because, really? What was there to say? *Oh, yeah. Big day for ordering chocolate chips and Styrofoam cups.* No. Just no. *Don't be a snob,* I told myself. *And don't make Mac uncomfortable.*

He stretched his arms up and sighed. "Nah. It's a great job. Totally chill. No worries. People come in hungry and leave happy."

I didn't know if I was supposed to reply so I said nothing, just gave in to an urge I'd been fighting since the day we met. I brushed the hair from his forehead and wrapped a curl around my finger. My other hand was still held in both of his. He let go with one of his hands and spread my fingers across his palm. He traced my fingers, and I squirmed from trying to hold in the giddy shivers. Lucky for me his head pinned my knee to the bench because I almost leaped off when he put my hand to his face and kissed my fingertips.

If I had ever thought about being kissed on the fingertips, I would not have expected it to feel so good. While I was remembering how to inhale and consequently how to exhale, he was thinking of something to say.

"You are the prettiest girl in Franklin," he said.

My brain wanted to argue that he didn't actually have enough evidence to make that claim. Had he even seen all the girls in this town? Wait. He stood behind a glass counter all day serving coffee and pastry. It was entirely possible that he had. I chose not to fight it. "Thanks. That's sweet." I wrapped my finger in a different curl.

"You have excellent hair," I said. This was entirely true, and I had ample evidence to support it. Maybe I could teach him by example how to give a sincere and deserved compliment.

He reached up and brushed mine across my forehead. "I like yours, too. Do you ever grow it long?"

Huh. I started analyzing subtext. Was that code for "I prefer long hair"? Were we really going to sit on this bench and trade small-talk compliments? I shrugged. "I like it like this," I said.

I tugged on his arm. He sat up.

"I know — play me your favorite song. On your phone," I clarified in case he thought I'd meant on the piano I had (not) rolled in behind the swing set.

"Favorite? That's hard." He looked confused, like I'd asked for something tricky.

170

"No way. Play the one you play the most often." I reached for his phone to pull it up myself. He snatched it away.

All right. No touching his phone. Got it.

He typed in his pass code and clicked through, keeping his face to me, and his phone facing away. When music started playing, I admit, I had to work to appear unsurprised. It was a total teen music Top 40 radio song. From six months ago.

Again, not what I'd anticipated. Maybe because Will and I were obsessive about finding amazing bands with weird and unexpected sounds, I assumed Mac would be the same. But nope. A bubblegum pop song. About kissing.

Okay. Kissing was a thing I could get behind. I leaned over and put my hands on either side of Mac's perfect face. The cool October breeze ruffled through the bright leaves and made an excellent addition to the pop-music sound track. So the music was dumb. So what? The kissing was pretty fantastic. I'd still call it a win.

With the First Annual Franklin Library Book Jam advertising well underway, I started taking reservations for bands. It was a high-tech organization that relied on a manila envelope with a piece of lined paper taped to the outside. If someone called the library and asked about the concert, the call was directed to me. If anyone came to the desk, all employees knew that I wanted to handle the transaction.

At the end of the first week, I'd signed up six bands, all of which had assured me that their songs had a literary bent. I found out quickly that "creative control" was a thing, and I wasn't supposed to question the band about any kind of detail. So I worked out a reminder system: I'd thank them for their interest, solidify the date, verify the name of the band and the number of songs they planned to play, and then casually mention that all bands would be singing songs that had something to do with books or stories. People were all for it.

Will was advertising at the high school. He told me he was offering extra credit to both his debate students and his civics classes if they signed up.

When a pair of blue-haired girls came in and told me they wanted to play in the show, I ran through the list of reminders. They assured me that their song was about banned books. It took effort not to ask if their song was explicit. It seemed a loaded question. Instead, I asked them if they went to Central.

"Yeah. Mr. Marshall promised it would be worth it," one of them said.

I smiled at them. "Mr. Marshall is my favorite."

The other girl grinned and nudged her friend. "That's what he said about you," she told me, leaning against the counter. "Are you guys, like, a thing?"

"Only if best friends is a thing." Laughing, I gave the first girl her change.

"You should give him a chance. Don't judge based on appearances." She folded up the ten-dollar bill and shoved it in her pocket. "He's really great."

For as much as I teased Will about being the object of a number of student fangirl crushes, I'd never actually met many young women who saw through the physical Will and into the heart and mind and guts of the friend I loved. That had certainly not been our experience when we were in high school. Maybe it only took ten years to change the culture of a place. Or maybe Will only had to be well out of their reach for the girls to see how awesome he was — despite how he looked. Maybe they were more in tune with the Real Will. I felt guilty at how the possibility surprised me. They seemed like bright girls. They were certainly confident and friendly. Did the thought surprise me because I was underestimating them? Or because I was underestimating Will?

"You're right. Mr. Marshall absolutely is great. I'm excited to hear your song. Thanks again for signing up." The girls waved and walked out.

A few minutes later, Will walked in.

"Welcome to the library. How can I help you?" I said in my best public-servant voice.

He leaned over the counter and used his best quiet-patron voice. "I need someone to eat this banana muffin that jumped into my bag," he said, opening his messenger bag and pulling out a paper sack stamped with the Beans logo.

"I believe I know someone who can help you with that."

He handed it over and smiled. "This is why I love this place. Excellent service." He pointed to the Book Jam concert poster hanging behind me. "How's the pre-concert business?"

"Great," I said, nodding. "Two blue-haired students of yours came in to sign up a few minutes ago."

He rubbed his hands together. "Excellent. Girls or guys?"

"Girls. How many blue-haired students do you have?"

"Plenty. It's a trend. I'm thinking of jumping on it. What do you think?"

I didn't answer right away. After a second, I lifted my hands and made a picture frame through which to study him. "I think . . . not."

He looked embarrassed that I was examining him. "I was kidding, you know."

"I know. But your look is too classical handsome boy-next-door for the flashy hair to work."

He ducked his head. "Right."

I shrugged. "You're no Dr. Silver, circa 1961, but you'll do." I patted his arm. "Speaking of my fictional historical boyfriend, want to have a look at the scans I did this morning? I'll shoot you a link to the files."

"That'd be great. I'll go hide out in our private research quarters and paw through the originals."

I handed him the folder full of photos I'd digitized that day. "I'm off at six. Dinner?"

He looked surprised. "You don't have plans?"

"You are my plans tonight."

He smiled and checked the time. "That gives me two hours to do something impressive."

"While you're busy being impressive, I'm going to the basement to search for more

Dr. Silver. Kevin is going to go in front of me down the stairs to keep me safe from crawly things."

We both looked at Kevin, long hair swishing as his head bobbed to whatever music was coming out of his earbuds.

"You're in good hands," Will said, smiling. It was true — if anything attacked, the kid could argue it to death.

Kevin and I were down the basement stairs in record time. Nothing attacked, and Kevin only felt the need to explain one thing he'd learned about architectural subflooring from the late-nineteenth century. I grabbed a box from the nearest corner, and we zipped back upstairs.

When we'd opened the box and discovered dozens of cassette tapes, both commercially produced and home-recorded, Kevin lost interest and went back to repairing paperbacks. I flicked through the cassettes, looking at names of bands and titles of albums I'd never heard of.

"Greta?"

I turned when I heard my name. Marigold stood at the desk.

"Hi," I said. "How's the paper coming?"

"Well, that's what I wanted to talk to you about." She pulled a folder out of her satchel. "Will you look this over for me?"

She looked uncomfortable.

I didn't reach for what she was handing me. "You mean like proofread it?"

She pulled it closer to her. "Kind of. Just go over it and see if you think it's heading in the right direction."

I was not very interested in being her editor for free. "I don't really even know what the assignment is."

She put the folder on the counter and laid her hands on it. She didn't raise her eyes. "I want you to know what I'm finding. It's not looking so good for you. For this place."

"Oh. Well, you don't have to worry about that. We are selling lots of spots for the benefit concert, and I have a great author visit lined up. We are going to be fine. Money will be coming out of the floorboards." I smiled at her. "It's going to be great."

Kevin slid over to my side of the desk in his rolly-chair. "If the traps Julie is setting are any indication, it's not money that's coming out of the floorboards." He paused for a second. When we didn't respond, he went on. "There is an uncommonly large number of uninvited wildlife in the walls of this building."

What I wanted to say was "Shut it, Kevin."

What I actually said was "Thank you,

177

Kevin." I pushed my foot against his chair, and he rolled back to his project, muttering about vermin.

I leaned toward Marigold. "I think he's the only high school student who uses words like 'vermin.' It's cute, right?" When I grinned at her, she seemed to relax.

"Yeah, it's cute. Kid's intense," she whispered, as if maybe anyone in the vicinity hadn't noticed Kevin's leading personality characteristic. "So, will you take a look at this? Let me know what you think?" She slid the folder closer to me.

I didn't sigh. "Sure. I'd love to see what you've got."

Thanking me, she told me she'd be back on Saturday. I told her Will was in the periodicals room, if she wanted to say hi. She pointed with a question on her face, and I nodded. She was headed in the right direction. She turned to go, but came back and stood right up against the counter. "It's going to be okay, right?" She was pointing to her folder, but I knew what she meant.

"Of course. Everything is going to be perfect."

CHAPTER 14

Saturday morning felt chilly — our first real autumn day. I stopped into Beans for a cup of hot chocolate on my way to work. I clearly wasn't the only one who noticed fall had arrived. It was a busy morning, so Mac and I didn't have much time to talk as he poured my drink. His T-shirt said "1+1=<3."

I slurped hot chocolate and read over Marigold's paper. She had pulled the same letters to the editor that I'd read in the Franklin paper. She'd taken a straw poll at the university, and while her conclusions were inconclusive, she was definitely not putting a positive spin on the outcome. I flipped between her argument and her charts until someone asked me if I was almost done with the table. Looking up, I realized how crowded the shop was. When I pushed the door open to leave, I turned toward the counter, hoping to see Mac.

Hoping he'd see me. He looked up. Smiled. Winked.

Winked?

Was that even a thing? Weird. I turned down the sidewalk. Why was winking giving me unpleasant shivers?

I stuffed Marigold's paper into my bag and pulled out my phone.

WILL. Who winks?

He answered right away.

Did you ask me 'Who winks'? Or was that an autocorrect thing?

Just left Beans. Mac WINKED at me. On my way out.

And that was . . .

Strange and borderline creepy. I expect winking people to fashion guns out of their fingers and make clicking sounds with their mouths.

Like Mitchell Grisham?

I hadn't thought of Mitchell Grisham in years. He'd moved to Franklin when we were in middle school, and by the end of ninth grade, he'd managed to grow into this weirdly tall guy with the worst mustache — the kind that looked like an accident born of never looking in a mirror rather than an act of fashion or masculinity. And that mustache mixed with his tendency to wink created this persona of total skeeze. Had he, like Mac, tended to wear pickup lines on his T-shirts, his might have said, "I'm the one your mother warned you about." Eww.

I remembered I was in the middle of a conversation.

Yes. Skeezy Mitchell Grisham. Precisely.

No winking. Got it.

Right. So why did he do it?

Who can say? Maybe he saw it in an old movie or something?

I didn't reply. What could I possibly say to that?

He sent another text.

Maybe when you're around, his nervous system goes berserk and he forgets how to be normal. Go easy on the guy.

181

I love that you used the word berserk. This is why you're my best.

Two minutes later, I got a text from Mac.

When you walked in here, the sun followed you. When you left, it felt dark and cold. Only the memory of holding you warms me again.

Well, that certainly made up for the wink. Poetic and thoughtful. I added those to the list of non-hotness reasons to like him.

Coming around the corner to the library, I caught a glimpse of Mr. Greenwood. I reminded myself that calling him "Old Man Greenwood" was disrespectful and cliché. But the guy was standing on his junk-filled porch, hunched over at what I assumed was the waist, his belted pants up around his armpits. Bushes of grizzled hair pointed aggressively in all directions from his head. His eyebrows covered most of his forehead, especially since they were drawn down in what could have been a perpetual grimace. My arm shot up without my consent and waved to him. He leaned farther over. I worried he'd tip, but he was squinting at me. I slowed down while I was behind the oak tree, but not even my beloved oak tree could hide me for long.

Once I was on the other side, I stared at the ground and told my arm it was in trouble. No waving, arm. Not to the scary old neighbor man who may or may not be cooking up a horrifying scheme starring me as the doomed and unsuspecting maiden.

I scuttled up the stairs and through the library door. Sigh of relief. Tucking my bag under the counter, I swiped my time card and shook off the creepy feelings of Mr. Greenwood, and, if I were being honest, Mac's wink.

Inside the library, I headed straight to my stash of Dr. Joshua Silver photos and clippings. Here was some real comfort. I didn't allow myself hours at a time with Dr. Silver, but I deserved to start each Saturday shift with a couple of hours of firsthand research. And pictures of Dr. Silver. And hopefully discovering where he'd ended up. Looking at him all handsome and hatted was one thing, but reading about his love for his job, his dedication to his causes, his admiration for the youth who were doing brave and difficult things made me kind of crazy about him. Where had he gone? What had happened to him after driving the anti-segregation bus into the sunset?

I pulled up my librarian account on Twitter. "Real people make great stories. What's your story? Maybe it can change the world. #TellYourStory   #SaveFranklinLibrary #GoToTheLibrary"

I was at the circulation desk when Stan came in to drop off the mail. I asked him if he'd always been a postal worker.

"Oh, no. I was a soldier. And a dairy deliverer. We called it a milkman back then, but I know how you young professional ladies like to keep things equal." I absolutely did not laugh. "I taught banjo lessons for a few years. Let's see. I went out West and fought forest fires in the summers for a while."

"Forest fires?"

He grinned. "Sounds pretty macho, doesn't it? Don't kid yourself, sweetie. It was tough-guy work. But it turns out I'm more suited to small town domestic stuff."

"Like banjo lessons?"

"And postal delivery work." He winked. Why was it so cute when he did it, but when Mac did it, it remind me of Skeezy Mitchell Grisham?

When he left, I asked Bonita if she thought Stan might be the monthly anonymous donor who left us checks and purchasing suggestions.

"Can't rule anyone out, but I doubt it.

Stan doesn't strike me as a typewriter kind of guy."

"Is there someone in the universe we occupy who does strike you as a typewriter guy?" I asked. I had honestly never separated people into the categories of "probably owns a typewriter" and "probably doesn't."

She lifted one shoulder. "Something about Stan suggests that he'd rather stand around and talk about it — not leave anonymous messages. Also, those donation notes always have book recommendations. I'm not sure Stan reads books." She said it without a hint of judgment or malice. It made me laugh anyway.

I had a thought. "We ought to have him come to the book jam and play his banjo."

Bonita looked impressed. "That's a great idea. I think you should invite him. Very inclusive. Good blending of the old and the new. Very 'Pass the Bond.' "

I thanked her. "You know me. I'm all about passing the bond at whatever cost. Even postal banjo music."

I made a Card for Kevin: "Stan the Postman used to fight fires. Who knew?"

CHAPTER 15

I hadn't told Will about the kissing with Mac yet. It felt weird. Partly because I didn't know how much was too much information and partly because he didn't ask. And it wasn't like I was only telling him about a couple of pretty awesome kisses. With his cousin. That he introduced me to. It was also the place — the park, the bench. The comparison. And my memories that had absolutely nothing to do with Mac and everything to do with Will. But I had to tell someone, and my mom was not an option. Not at all. I texted Marigold, knowing this was pushing the edges of our new friendship, but wanting those edges to widen.

Guess who is a good kisser?

The fat guy. You already told me.

I thought about throwing my phone, but I

was a grown-up. I had adult relationships. I could set some boundaries to ensure that this thing with Marigold would never remind me of those horrible high school girls.

Don't call him that. And yes, but that's not who I meant. Someone else.

Sorry. Coffee boy? It's about time. Did you read my paper?

Well, it wasn't exactly girlfriend giggling, but she had said she was sorry. It would do.

Read it. Good writing.

I wasn't thrilled with her conclusions.

Does it make you sad?

We haven't lost anything yet. Gotta work. Have to save the library. Come see me?

I was obviously not great at being friends with girls, but I was trying.

The day before the Book Jam concert, Will knocked on my apartment door. He walked in and handed me a piece of white-ish cloth. "What's this?"

"It's a magic shirt."

I unfolded it. "It's not a magic shirt. It's a retro concert T-shirt from a band that broke up before you were born."

He shook his head. "Not retro — vintage. This was my dad's. He bought it when he went to the concert. This shirt represents bravery and dignity and happiness and conviction and persistence. Also, stunningly bad hair."

I angled the shirt for a better look. "I'm totally in agreement about the hair. The rest is a stretch." I pretended to examine the faded picture. "I see no dignity. I promise."

He pointed to the table, and we sat down in the chairs. He spread the T-shirt across the table and smoothed it with his hands.

Leaning closer, he lowered his voice to a super-secret pitch. "It only seems like a stretch because you haven't heard the story."

"Okay," I echoed his whisper. "Can I hear this story?"

"It was the late 80s, obviously." He indicated the shirt again, and I grinned. He backed up decades to tell the story.

"And my dad was, in his words, approaching cool." He did one-handed finger quotes. Finger quotes were so Will. "Some guys from school were going to this concert, and they asked him to be the driver. Because he was famous for his sobriety." He shrugged. "Blah, blah, blah, lots of details about transportation issues with four drunk lacrosse players in a Honda Civic hatchback. They went to the concert, bought T-shirts, and got home again with no problems."

"That's it?"

He nodded.

"Honestly? It's a little anticlimactic."

He turned to face me, straight on, and the smile changed. "The thing is, as you know, the sobriety thing didn't work out for my dad so well in the long run. When I was in high school, he gave me this shirt and told me to do better than he did." Making a throat-clearing noise, he looked down at the table and then back up at me. "I've never worn it, obviously. If he'd wanted me to wear it, he missed his window by about a hundred pounds."

He could probably see the what-do-I-say-to-that panic in my face, because he grinned again. "But the shirt remembers. It holds the moment of when everything went right. Like flesh memory, but not. Cotton memory.

"So now, on the most important occasions, when I need everything to go right, I hold on to the magic shirt." He sat back in his chair, but his arm was still behind me.

"And you're holding it today." I patted the shirt where it lay on the table.

"Only so I can give it to you. Well, not give. Lend. I'm going to need it back."

I picked it up. "Right after I use it to save the library."

"Exactly."

I held it up against me. "What do you think?"

"Stunning. It's never looked better."

"Is it going to work?"

"I can't see how it could miss." He leaned forward like he was going to say something else, but then he shook his head. Pushing himself out of his chair, he walked around the table. Before he opened the door, he put his hand on my shoulder — just put it down and left it there. "It's going to be great. You're going to be great."

I reached up and squeezed his hand. "Thank you."

The next day I spread the shirt out on the foot of my bed. I was deciding if I could wear it to the concert. It wasn't exactly professional attire, but these weren't typical work hours.

He was right. I could use the magic. And the shirt could bring it. I was ready to believe.

Before I went over to the senior citizens' center for the concert, I clipped my hair back. Then I took it down. Then I thought about shaving it right off. This was the part of my life where having a best friend who was a girl could come in handy. Will was no help to me in a hair emergency. I sent him a text anyway.

What should I do with my hair? I'm a disaster.

Curly. And I doubt it.

You've been wrong before.

You keep bringing up that ONE time.

Okay. Curly. See you later.

I put a couple of curls in my hair, and it was still unimpressive. I pulled out Will's magic shirt and dragged it over my tank top.

I closed my eyes in front of the mirror. "I believe in the shirt," I said. "I believe in the shirt."

Opening my eyes, I looked in the mirror again. The hair was still crappy. The shirt was a sham.

My phone buzzed. Mac. *Please,* I thought.

Please don't back out. Please, I need to see you tonight.

> Sometimes when I think about the possibility of seeing you walk in the door, the anticipation is almost as good as the real thing. I stand behind the counter and watch people walk by outside and wonder when it will be you. I smile at everyone in preparation for the moment when I can smile for you.

I may have clutched my phone to my chest. And I may have read the message over and over. And I may have closed my eyes and sighed.

Who cared about messy hair?

Not me — for about thirty seconds. Then I wet my hands and scrunched up my hair until it was wavy. Better.

I chose to take tickets instead of overseeing the "green-room." There was nothing green about the room, in the first place. Also, it was the kitchen of the senior citizens' center, a rectangular cave that smelled of gravy and mildew, where the dripping faucet reminded me of a late-night cable horror show I'd seen once while babysitting. Shudder. No thanks.

I sat behind a folding table fiddling with

printed programs. I'd sent out several tweets over the past few days. People saw ads around town. They might have seen the newspaper. Someone probably heard a radio ad. So where was everyone? Every time the door opened, I launched out of my chair, my aggressively helpful smile wedged onto my face.

"Need a ticket?"

"No. I'm playing. Where do I go?"

I pointed down the hall, and another performer crowded into the spooky kitchen.

"Hi. Can I get you a ticket?" I asked a grinning older man, his shoulder-length gray hair moving as one solid unit as he strolled with eager steps up to the table.

"I'm with the band." He waved his guitar case at me in case I hadn't seen it, which I obviously hadn't. Apparently that was funny, because he laughed.

I nodded. What else was I supposed to do? I pointed to the back.

"Hi, girls. Did you come to watch the concert?" I said to a pack of eleven-year-old kids. One of them popped her gum, her hand on her hip, and rolled her eyes. I wanted to roll my eyes too, but thought I should wait until after she paid for her ticket.

"No. We're doing community service,

which is why we're here." Her little posse snickered, so I guess she was being funny.

I smiled. "Great. That's five tickets at twelve dollars each. Sixty dollars." Holy cow. Would these kids be able to pay for that?

The gum-popper snapped her fingers, and one of her followers pulled a bill out of her pocket. She handed it to me. One hundred dollars? Okay. I handed her back two twenties and five tickets.

"Take a seat wherever you'd like, and thanks for coming. Enjoy the show," I said to their backs.

I heard Will's mom before I saw her. "Hi, Greta!" Everyone in the relative proximity heard Will's mom. I waved from behind my table, and she grinned at me all the way from the door. Will had brought his mom to the library concert.

"Two tickets, please," she said, as though nothing more exciting than this concert could possibly ever happen.

I saw Mac walk in and get in line behind her. He said, "Make that three, and it's on me."

Will's mom turned to see who had come up behind her. "Mackay! Hi, honey." She pulled him into a public hug — something I'd have loved to dare.

He kissed her on the cheek, and I pretended not to be jealous, and he fist-bumped Will. He handed me two twenty-dollar bills and said, "Keep the change." Then he winked.

Again. He winked. Skeezy Mitchell Grisham skulked through my mind. I tried to wipe the image away.

Maybe Mac had a twitch.

Maybe winking was cool and I was behind the times, cool-wise. Maybe it was an allergic reaction to his contact lenses.

I thanked him and looked at Will. He was studying the quarter-page "set list" for the show, trying not to smile. He'd seen the wink.

"Go on in and take a seat anywhere," I told them. As they walked away, Will turned around and did the world's most horrible, unsubtle wink.

I laughed. Then I pondered. This was actually a good thing. Nobody's perfect, and now I'd found Mac's flaw.

He was a winker.

I decided to live with that.

Marigold walked in talking to a guy who looked like he was in high school — and completely stunned that this woman was holding a conversation with him. I checked him in, along with his band, and then I handed Marigold the press pass I'd made her. It was two business cards with their printed sides stuck together. I'd written "Press" on it with permanent marker and then run it through the laminator.

"This is awesome."

"Yes, it is," I said. "Thanks for agreeing to write about this. I saved you a seat in the middle of the front row."

She looked at me with a smile like you'd give a waddling baby penguin — like I was an adorable miracle. "Thank you."

My mom came speed-walking in right at seven. "Am I late?"

"You're fine."

She started fishing around in her bag for her wallet. I shook my head. "No charge for you."

She snapped the bag closed. She didn't appear ready to argue it. "Are you sure?"

"Of course. Go find a seat."

"See you in there," she said, and I nodded and stared out the door.

Kevin, with his long hair and his eyebrow piercing, was the coolest-looking person who worked at the library so he easily won the vote to host the concert. I heard him welcome the community to Book Jam, the first annual library fund-raising musical adventure. Well, at least he *looked* cool. I stared at the door, willing more people to come in and buy tickets. I had gone over Kevin's opening monologue with him, because as cool as he looked, Kevin still talked way too much about things people did not want to hear. All the time. As soon as he went off script, I felt my stomach clench. I kept willing crowds to come and tried to ignore Kevin's opinions regarding the misappropriation of cultural celebrations.

Nobody seemed to notice the power of my will. No one else came.

After two bands played, I locked up the cash box and slipped into what we were calling the "performance space." At any other time, it was called "Bingo Hall."

Kevin had lowered the lights to half strength simply by turning off two of the fluorescent lights. It wasn't exactly moody, but it did make it easy for me to find Mac and Will and my mom, each of whom had an empty seat beside them. Nobody was going to make this easy for me.

I slid into the seat beside my mom.

She pointed at the stage. "Not bad," she whispered, nodding along in time with the music in a very middle-aged way. I gave a nod back.

"Who's the guy with the pretty hair? He seems nice."

I leaned close to her ear. "That's Kevin. He is nice."

"Is he single?"

Track One. I knew it. I knew it was coming, and I didn't even have time to take a breath to fortify against it. "He is indeed single. He's also eighteen. So if I tried to convince him we should go out, I believe he'd find it improper. As would his mother."

She started to say something, but I interrupted her. "Besides that, you heard him speak. He's a little bit crazy."

"You say that about everyone," she whispered. My mother could pack a lot of judgment into a whisper.

I conceded. "I do say that about everyone, and I've never yet been proven wrong. But in any case," I said, "Kevin and I will never be a thing. Sorry."

She shook her head. "I didn't mean," she started to say, but we both knew she totally *did* mean. She folded her hands around her purse, and I rested my elbow on the back of her chair.

"Thanks for coming," I whispered into her hair.

She nodded and patted my knee.

When the next band came out, they took

several minutes to set up. Kevin tried to amuse and entertain the crowd with a story that started out with a dog, then wandered into strange misunderstandings, and ended with "and that's why you should always wear a seat belt!" Three people laughed.

I leaned over to Mom's ear again. "See?"

She saw.

I felt a tiny bit bad that I couldn't even pretend that Kevin might happen so I threw her a freebie. "Mac is here. Want to see him?"

"Who is Mac?" She said it with her eyes wide open, obviously faking ignorance.

I indulged her. "Just this guy I know. He's *single.*" I considered my ability to be nice and mean at the same time as something in which to take pride. "He's sitting two rows behind us on the other side of Will's mom. Wait a second before you look." I would have told her to be subtle, but there were certain things I knew I couldn't control.

She turned and gave a wave. I sincerely hoped it was to Will's mom. When she turned back, she took a second to compose herself. In what was, for her, a slightly subtle lean, she said, "Oh, my goodness. He looks like you won him in a raffle."

"Right?"

She pretended to fan herself. "Wow."

I felt her start to turn again. Putting my hand on her leg, I shook my head. "Don't. You can look at him later."

She leaned close to my hair. "Promise?"

"Gross, Mom."

She laughed.

Kevin introduced Stan's banjo number, an original piece entitled "Happily Ever After." It was a banjo solo, which was a little disappointing since I thought he'd sing. But then he got going, and the man could . . . banjo. There was no actual smoke curling off his fingertips, but wow. He picked? Plucked? Strummed? Whatever he called what he was doing, he did it fast, and it was spectacular. When he finished, everyone cheered.

Half an hour later, Kevin announced the last act, which turned out to be the older guy with the shoulder-length gray hair. He and his band had offered to play out the party, which was apparently musician-speak for "keep singing until everyone left." This sounded like a nice idea, but what it really meant was that I couldn't start stacking chairs, because nobody was leaving. The band played six songs, and I sent mental messages for Kevin to get up there and wrap the thing. Mental messages were useless.

I sent an actual, digital text.

Time to end this.

I saw him read it, and after the next song, Kevin jumped up and took over the microphone.

"Thank you to everyone who came to play and to listen. What a great turnout." I looked around, and when you counted all the people who had played, it actually looked like a lot of people had come. But I knew the truth. We had sold very, very few tickets. The truth was that most of the people in the room had paid some fraction of the fifty-dollar playing fee. They'd paid to play not so much to an audience as to each other. I tried not to look defeated.

Kevin mentioned that the band behind him was planning to keep playing the night away, but that the organizers had promised the senior citizens that we'd be cleaned up and out by nine. People laughed, Kevin sat down, and the old guys started up another song.

A few people stood up and moved toward the door. I swooped in behind them and stacked up their chairs. My mom followed me. The view of the room was more comprehensive from the back corner, and she was much more likely to find interesting single men for me to date from that vantage point.

Some people stood around in clumps, talking, quite a few danced, and a couple of people stayed in their chairs to watch the gray-haired rock stars.

Julie walked over. Sort of. More like she danced over, in a slightly subtle way. There might have been some snapping. She said hello to my mom and told her how wonderful I was. I tried to believe it. As soon as my mom stepped away, I leaned close to Julie so I wouldn't have to yell.

"I'm sorry my fund-raiser was a total fail."

She laughed. "Greta, look at these people." She motioned toward the room, taking in all the laughing, dancing people with her gesture. "They're having a great time."

"Well, of course they're having fun. Almost none of them paid money for a ticket to be here." I knew my voice was sliding into the zone where only dogs could hear me, but I couldn't help it. We'd only sold eleven tickets at the door. Eleven. And three of them were to Mac.

We'd sold fourteen in the weeks leading up to the Book Jam. That made twenty-five. Total. Twenty-five tickets. A nice, easy number. But really? That was it?

"There are over a hundred people in this room, and every one of them is making a memory. Because of the library. Because of you. When they look back on this night, they'll remember playing for each other. Our library will be a huge part of their memory, and it will be positive. I couldn't be more pleased." She patted my shoulder, and I tried to keep my eye-roll to myself. I wanted her to be as upset as I was, to be bothered that we didn't make thousands of dollars.

What good was all her talk of making memories when these people would look back at this night as their last connection with an extinct building?

"You're still fretting." Julie got close to my face and gave me a big grin. "Fret not."

I nodded and tried to find my happy. Walking over to Will and Mac, I smiled. "Thanks for coming to our little party," I said.

Will's mom, who looked like a condensed version of Will but with fluffier hair, grinned and said the concert was great. "Do you want to come out for a treat with us?" she asked. "I've convinced Will to take his old mom for ice cream."

Mac answered for me, which would ordinarily have bugged me but when he said, "Thanks for the offer, but I'd really like to walk Greta home," everything ordinary shot right out of my mind.

"I have to clean up," I stammered.

Julie heard me. "No, you don't. You're off the clock as of right now. Thank you for a great party." She handed me my jacket and pushed me toward the door.

Mac walked beside me. "What's with the T-shirt?" he asked.

"I was thinking that since you've got the market cornered on pickup lines, I'd make a trend of outdated concert souvenirs."

He smiled. "I could get you one like mine."

"That's very nice of you," I said, smiling and hoping we were just flirting and he wasn't really going to buy me a shirt that said "Your first name sounds great with my last name."

He wasn't done. "I could, but then everyone who comes into the library would pick up on you."

No interesting reply came to my mind, so I didn't say anything. Mac waited for me to button up my coat and wrap my scarf around my neck before he stood close beside me and took my hand.

The skin around his knuckles was cracked. Maybe it was an autumn thing. Little sandpaper patches, rough and reddish, surrounded the creases in his hands. I stared at his fingers, his hand, right there holding mine, amazed at how easily it had happened. He'd just reached over and taken my hand, and I'd slid into a joy-induced coma.

How could this tiny thing feel so amazing? I mean, my mom used to hold my hand, but it never, ever made my stomach thump like this.

And it's not like I'd never held another guy's hand. I had. Plenty. Starting in preschool, when Jaden Kingsley and I had to buddy up to cross the street, and in third grade, when Gavin Cousins used to chase me in the playground. When he'd catch me, I'd run away screaming, even though he had freckles and spiky hair and wicked dimples and I adored him. When Gavin and I were partnered up for the spring music concert and we danced a Virginia reel, we totally held hands. For like, minutes at a time. And my stomach didn't react at all. Not at all. Then it was junior high and Taylor Greer and Franklin P. Stratford and Chaz Reese, though all such hand-holding could be described as sweaty.

And Will. Always Will.

It was different now, is what I'm telling you.

Mac walked slowly, as though nothing was more important than spending time with me. He kept my hand in his, and I watched him walking. He looked nervous. He kept glancing around. Like he was watching for something, waiting for a sign maybe.

I squeezed his fingers. "Talk to me."

He might have looked a tiny bit panicked. "About what?"

I looked up. "Stars."

"You want me to talk about stars?"

"Sure. Talk like you text." I nudged him with my elbow. "You've sent me some really excellent texts. You have a poet in you."

He visibly gulped. "You want poetry."

I leaned my side against his side. "I always want poetry."

We walked in quiet for a while, and then the silence became weird silence. Strained silence. Too-silent silence. Pretty soon I realized we were walking faster than before. A whole lot faster. Almost jogging.

He cleared his throat a couple of times.

I waited for my poetry, but also I gasped for oxygen.

"Stars are shiny. Like your hair." The words burst out, loud and fast and so, so odd.

I couldn't. At all.

No response was right. Believe me, I went through every possible one in my head. None was right or even approaching right.

And so I didn't respond.

I told myself it could be worse. He could have said, "Shiny like your forehead." I sneaked a look at his face to see if he was kidding. He looked like he'd been busted doing something Very Bad. (In fairness, it was Very Badly Attempted Poetry, so there was that.)

I was still gripping his hand when we reached my apartment, but our arms were stiff and there was nothing sweet or comfortable about any of it. I realized I hadn't said anything to him since I begged him to compose love-words to me on the spot.

"Thanks," I said. "For coming tonight. And for walking me home."

When he faced me, no sign of discomfort remained. He did the smolder, put both hands around my waist, smiled into my face, and kissed me.

That was where it got weird.

Weirder.

During that kiss, which was not quick, I had time to notice three things: First, Mac was an excellent kisser (which I already knew) and his confidence only added to the goodness of the experience. Second, although there was a difference between being a bad poet and a bad speaker, it was possible that — tonight — Mac was both.

And third, he didn't find it necessary to say anything about the whole mess. Not that I required an apology or whatever, but I'd asked for something in the poetry department and I'd gotten "Stars shine like your hair." Which, obviously, was exactly nothing in the poetry department. And, as a corollary to the third thing, I didn't actually ask much of him. Until tonight. Maybe requesting a face-to-face deeply poetic conversation about stars was pushing the boundaries of our relationship too far.

The second thing and the third thing and especially the corollary to the third thing disappeared behind the first thing.

After a few more minutes, I pulled away, smiled at Mac, thanked him again, and let myself inside.

CHAPTER 16

By morning, I'd gotten over my momentary crisis. So he didn't always talk like he texted. Sometimes he did. I shook off thoughts of the times when his words were, well, weird and focused on the times when he was confident. Rehearsed, maybe. Big deal. Obviously he was a poet who was into revision. Who didn't like people to see his rough drafts. That was hardly a reason to stop making out with him.

I sent him a text after I finished my workout.

Thanks again for coming last night. And walking me home.

He didn't answer for a while. But when he did, it was worth it.

Something about being near you makes my brain grow cloudy. All surroundings dim. You are the only clarity I can focus on. Even my thoughts jumble and my words fly away. After I left you last night, I went home to dream it all again — but this time I could say what I felt. I could speak the words you deserve to hear. Words like stars that glimmer just out of reach and slip away when you study them. I'm sorry I can't make the words come out when I stand close to you.

I . . . He . . . What . . .

I was a puddle. Completely melted.

I lounged on the couch and read his messages over and over. I didn't think about them because thinking was work. I willingly accepted his pretty, pretty words.

A text arrived from Will.

How was the walk home?

After twelve hours, all is well.

Explain?

Nothing bad, he just went mute. All good now.

I've heard he has skills that make up for his silence.

Gross? Clever? Grossly clever? No matter.

You have heard correctly.

So, no big deal if he won't talk?

I wasn't sure if it actually was no big deal. But I was getting there.

He'll talk enough. And he'll send thoughtful texts. Maybe I make him nervous.

That I can believe. You like his texts?

That I do, son.

A lot?

A whole lot. Did he tell you to ask me?

We're not in seventh grade.

Well, that was not an answer.

Avoiding the question?

He did not ask me to find out if you like his texts, Your Honor.

Got it.

But if you had to choose between the handsome, silent, brooding type and the poetic, communicative type, which one would you pick?

I'd pick the hot poet. Good thing I don't have to choose. He's the package, as I may have mentioned before.

Lucky you.

Agreed.

Can we talk about your other crush now?

Dr. Joshua Silver?

Unless there's someone else.

Yes. Let's talk about Dr. Silver.

Is he inspiring great thoughts?

Always.

I want to make something happen like he made happen.

As soon as I typed the words, I realized that was exactly what I wanted. I wanted to make the world more just and more awesome. It was unfair to think that the Franklin of next year might have to live without our library. And I wanted to be the one to rectify that injustice.

And Will understood.

Save the library, and you'll go down in Franklin history.

No pressure. And such a reward.

You can do it. You were made for this.

Thank you. You're my biggest fan. Never get a girlfriend. I want to keep you all to myself forever.

As soon as I sent the text, I realized what I'd said: I can have Mac, but you can't have anyone. You know that moment when you're working really hard to un-press SEND, and it's never, ever worked before, but you're sure that this time — this one time when you really need it to — it will work? Yeah. That.

I saw the sent message. I saw the words "never" and "girlfriend" in close proximity. I couldn't pretend it was autocorrected. I couldn't think of anything I might have meant that would translate to that. I couldn't imagine he'd read it any other way. Obviously, I worried that I'd hurt him with a thoughtless comment like that. He'd never, ever say anything about feeling hurt, and he'd never been a pouter, but he had to be a little jealous that I had Mac and he had . . . nobody. He must think about it. Everyone thought about it. And it must be painfully obvious that he wasn't reeling in the ladies here in Franklin — and why. He owned a mirror. He knew.

What could I do? How could I fix it?

I called Mac.

"Hey, Greta." His voice slid through my phone like some slide-y and gorgeous thing.

"Hi. I need — I can't — What are you do-ing?"

"Working in, um" — I heard him shift his phone — "forty-seven minutes."

"Help me. I did something mean but it was an accident and I regret it."

He cleared his throat. "Well, if it was an accident . . ."

I waited for more. There was no more. "There was still meanness. And, I imagine, hurting."

He didn't say anything.

For a long time.

Many seconds together.

I breathed in and out into the silence and

remembered that Mac didn't like to be rushed into saying things. I changed angles.

"What kind of damage could you do to a vat of French fries in forty-seven minutes?"

He laughed. "Lots. I'll meet you at Happy's in ten. I'll be the one watching the door. Every second. To see if you're there yet."

I tried to keep my sigh quiet. "You're saving my life."

"While eating fries. My specialty."

"Mac?" My voice caught somewhere between throat and teeth, jagged and rough.

"Hm?"

"Thanks."

"No problem."

I put on shoes and a sweater and walked toward Happy's. On the way I replayed my walk with Mac from last night. With Mac's perfection out of my direct line of sight, the whole silent speed-walking bugged me again. Why wouldn't he talk to me?

Then I reread the text conversation I'd had with Will. Oh, Will. I wanted to say "SorrySorrySorry" until he forgot that I ever said anything. Will was amazing and wonderful and funny and brilliant and practically perfect in almost every way.

And now I was hoping to sit down with Mac and talk over how to apologize to Will for the stupid and insensitive comment I made? Really? What did I think Mac could do to help? I could never tell Mac about the conversation I'd been having with Will, because he didn't understand my need to fix the library. And he didn't ever need to know what I'd said about the girlfriend thing, and there was no way to tell him part of it without telling him too much of it.

By the time I got to Happy's, I'd reverted to a state of near-total regret. For everything. There was no way I was going to bring up this Will thing to Mac. He wouldn't know how to fix it. He wouldn't even understand what needed to be fixed. And I couldn't explain it all and then demand quick and thoughtful solutions in the few minutes we had to talk it over.

No.

I stood outside the door and watched Mac as he ate fries at the table across from the fake tree by the door and played on his phone. He made a stack of the really crunchy fries, saving them for me because I'd told him once I loved the crunchy ones. He glanced toward the door once in a while but didn't see me. I stood in a shady spot, away from the sun. Like I planned. His shirt said, "You look exactly like my next girlfriend."

I couldn't go inside.

I walked away.

I put one foot in front of the other foot, over and over until I was around the block. Then I sent him a text.

Something came up. Sorry.

He replied instantly.

Where are you? I have 6 mins before work.

Not close.

I put my phone away.

Wrong. Wrong wrong wrong. I should have done every single thing differently.

Big surprise.

CHAPTER 17

The latest Monthly Anonymous Donor check came with this typewritten note:

I'm pleased to see the library's efforts to work both with and around the system. Keep up the good fund-raising work. And maybe check out Dr. Howard Lampoor's book Effective Moneymaking — it might give your team some ideas.

Bossy. I laughed. And ordered the book.

Pulling boxes of local history from the basement to the periodicals room had become something of a routine for me. I was getting adept at grabbing a box, running things through the scanner for a couple of hours at a time, and clearing things up when I was done. Occasionally even clearing up before I was done, on the rare chance that someone would come in and want to use the room.

One afternoon, I sat in a patch of sunlight coming in through a long and narrow window and sorted piles of handwritten letters into two scientifically ordered stacks: readable and totally unreadable. The unreadable pile grew faster than the other one.

One bundle of letters was tied with a faded ribbon. When I untied it, I discovered it had once been pink, but now it was mostly dust-brown. The letters were written to someone named Evelyn (sometimes Evie) from someone named Walter (sometimes Walt). Walt(er) had lovely handwriting, and for about one minute, I regretted the impersonal device I used to communicate with men. I unfolded the beautiful envelopes to discover gentlemanly words of affection and tenderness. Evelyn had saved all these words. Cherished them. I would have cherished them, too. Whoever cherished a text message? Then I remembered that I was completely unwilling to live without the internet and decided that I'd be fine without handwritten letters.

But Walter was a charmer. I read through the one-sided conversations and wondered if he'd kept all her letters. Where were those letters now? The envelopes didn't have addresses written on the fronts — at least nothing still readable — but the letters inside held clues that pointed to pieces of my town that had been sites of intrigue and romance in 1930. Their story unfolded one envelope at a time, and before long, I realized that Evelyn lived in the Greenwood house. Evelyn Greenwood. I wished for a photo, but I was unwilling to set down the letters to go digging for one.

In one letter, Walter mentioned "sparking" behind Evelyn's parents' house. Sparking! Like antique making out. He said he was sure that the Simmons Spinsters were watching from the second floor of the tall house next door.

The tall house next door to the Greenwood place? That was my library. I was inside that very house this very minute. I felt shivers run through my whole self. I wanted to know who the Simmons Spinsters were. Old sisters? Here? Had a pair of old ladies watched Walt and Evie sparking from the picture book window?

It became easy to understand how someone could get intricately involved with the history of strangers' lives. I read through Walter's side of his courtship of Evie, his decision to go to college, how he hoped she'd wait for him. There was the almost-proposal: "Evie, my life is full of all the important things, but none of them means anything without you. Like taking a photograph of a beautiful sunset, it's all there, but without color. Only gray and white. Will you please consider making my life complete by shining your precious light on everything that matters to me? Would you be the gold to my silver?"

I dug through the box to find more, but the rest of the papers were water damaged and moldy.

I wondered if Google could help me figure out if Evelyn Greenwood ever married Walter. I'd have to check. A tiny voice at the back of my head suggested that Mr. Greenwood would certainly be a better source than the internet, but I told that tiny voice that I'd take my chances with the impersonal web and stay away from the scary neighbor man.

CHAPTER 18

ELEANOR RICHTENBERG
beloved children's author of the Grimsby
the Grumpy Glowworm books will be
appearing at the Franklin Public Library
Thursday, October 26th
5:00 to 6:30 pm
Ticketed reception to follow

The image of Eleanor — my new BFF, obviously — gazed benevolently from the poster, Mona Lisa-esque and slightly mysterious. She had a bad case of 90s hair, though, if I was being honest. I'd done a Google search for a better shot, but every image of her on the internet was the same photo. I guess they call that branding. Grimsby glowered from the borders of the poster, his tail end printed in shocking green.

It was a good job, and I gave myself permission to feel proud of it.

I ran my sleeve over the glass beside the

library door, wiping away a smudge. Slipping inside, I felt a rush of canned air. The warm-then-cold October weather was causing havoc for the air-conditioning.

"Greta, I'm glad you're here." Glasses perched on nose, Julie practically shone with excitement. I would never, ever get tired of hearing her say those words.

"What's up?" I asked her.

"Look at these numbers." She stabbed her fingernail toward the monitor. It was the ticketing website. We'd already sold 413 tickets to the reception.

I stared at her, my mouth open. "Is that right? Can that be right? That many?"

She shook her head, but apparently she didn't mean "no." A little laugh with an edge of panic blew out on a breath. "I know. We're going to need a bigger venue. We certainly can't fit that many people in here at the same time. Even if we moved out all the books." She reached into her desk drawer and pulled out her bag of gummies. Without saying anything she handed me the bag. I put two into my mouth, whole.

"How much — I mean, how many — I mean, will more people buy?" I stammered. This was insane. The tickets bought these people seats to a free event and an hour of mingling, punch and cookies after, with the chance of talking to Eleanor Richtenberg. And now, with that many people crowding around, the chance of any actual talking looked pretty slim. If sixty people came, they could, theoretically, each have a minute of her time. With six hundred people? Six seconds each. Was that right? My brain squeezed.

I felt an insane giggle start to climb up my throat. My nose itched. Cheeks flamed. This part of the plan was working. This was really going to happen. We were going to have to find a new place to hold this party, because everyone — *everyone* — wanted to come.

I texted Will.

Can we use the HS auditorium for Eleanor R?

Two minutes later, he answered.

Asked principal. Sorry. Community ballet dress rehearsal. Stage all full of sets.

When I sat down to make some calls, I had no idea that chair would be my real estate for the next two hours.

When I called a local church, they asked for a three-thousand dollar deposit to use

224

their auditorium. I laughed out loud before I thanked the lady in my most polite voice and hung up.

I dialed the next number. "Hello. My name is Greta, and I'm looking for a place to hold a charity event. How many people does your great hall hold?"

"We're booked every day for the next three months."

"Hello, I'm calling from the library."

"We returned those books months ago. Check your shelves." Click.

Okay.

"Hi, there. If your reception hall is available, would your management be willing to discuss donating it for a weeknight? We're putting on a charity event and need a larger venue."

"Seriously? No."

All right, then.

"Ridgecrest, this is Grant."

"Hi, Grant. May I please speak to a reservations manager?"

"You can certainly speak to me."

"I'm calling from the Franklin public library. We have an event in a couple of weeks, and we've sold a few more tickets than we planned. We need to find a different, larger, place to hold it. Is there any chance we could get a deeply discounted rate on a room rental?"

I held my breath.

"Are you talking about the Richtenberg reading? I bought tickets to that."

"Awesome. I mean, thank you. Yes. We've sold more than we expected, so we need a new plan, but paying for a venue isn't exactly part of our budget."

Grant from Ridgecrest said, "I loved reading those Grimsby books to my kids when they were little. That's a great event you've planned."

"Great. Wonderful. Thank you again. So, can we talk about availability? And price?"

I held my breath again.

"We have a room that will comfortably hold a hundred and fifty people. How does that sound?"

"About five hundred short."

"Wow. Really? That's amazing. Way to go. Okay, well, the Regency Room will hold lots of people, but it's not cheap. What's your budget?"

"Pro bono."

Grant paused. "Pardon?"

"It means free." I think I was muttering.

"I know what it means, I just wondered if I heard you correctly." He cleared his throat and didn't say anything for a minute. Maybe he was waiting for me to change my budget.

Not likely.

"We can certainly talk about giving you a room for free if you make a food order."

"We've already got a bakery set up to deliver cookies and punch."

He cleared his throat. "We could give you a deep discount on the room if we arranged a sit-down meal for your audience."

I hadn't thought about that. "What does that cost?" Maybe we could build that in to the price of the tickets.

He told me his price range. It was so much more than I'd planned to charge for a ticket. Yikes. We were trying to fund-raise, not take out a loan.

"I don't think we can afford this."

"Sorry. I understand. If you want the room, you need to buy the food. It's pretty standard policy in my business."

"Who can I talk to about changing that policy for the one night?"

Grant laughed.

I took a deep breath and hoped I sounded like a non-idiot. "I'd really like to keep talking about this. Is there someone else available now for me to ask?"

"Remind me your name?" he said.

"Greta."

"Okay, Greta. Here's the thing. We can't give you a room for free. But we absolutely support your event. When you find a venue, plan on us donating chairs."

Chairs? I hadn't even thought about that being an expense.

"I really appreciate that. I'll be in touch."

When I hung up, I wanted to crawl into a ball and hide under the desk. Instead, I found Julie, told her we were no closer to a venue (but free chairs!), and took a lap around the fiction stacks.

Julie was on the phone, but standing, when I got back. Battle position. I wondered who was complaining about what.

I walked around the desk and picked up some picture books to shelve. She still stood, her back to me. I wondered why she didn't take the call in her office if it was so private.

"Mm-hm. Mm-hm. I see. No, that won't be a problem. Of course." Her voice was polite, but sounded brittle, like she was in danger of cracking. "I appreciate this information. Thank you very much."

When she hung up the phone, she rubbed her neck, like the muscles had been working really hard.

"How's it going?"

She laughed, but it sounded more like a sigh.

"I've received some information about our

special guest." Her tone was even — maybe too even. It sounded unnaturally free from stress. Rigidly toneless.

"Oh, good. It freaks me out when I don't hear from the publicist for a week."

Julie cleared her throat and straightened the paper she'd been writing on. "Ms. Richtenberg has a few additional requests for her visit."

"Sure. Whatever we can do to make her comfortable, right?"

Was that a snort? Surely I heard wrong.

"Of course. Her comfort is paramount."

That was a weird thing to say. I smiled. "How can I help?"

"Bottled water from Switzerland?" She said it like she wasn't sure she was really asking for a thing.

"Okay. I can find that."

She looked back at her handwritten list. "Green food." She managed to put an audible space between "green" and "food."

"Easy. Is she vegan or something?"

She looked at me and then away, quickly, like I would do if I were trying not to roll my eyes. "Not like that. Actually, not anything like that. Green M&M's and green Skittles. Green sugared cupcakes. Green Jolly Ranchers. Apparently she eats apples, but only Granny Smith, and only in the fall when they're fresh." Her voice got higher with each item on the list. She flushed red, took a deep breath, and blew it out.

"I've had some calls," Julie confessed. "Some helpful calls. And some emails. Quite a lot of emails, actually, from bookshop owners. Other librarians. I've ignored most of them on principle. You know, I don't really do gossip. I don't say it, and I try not to hear it. But I spoke to Ms. Richtenberg's agent and her publicist, and maybe all those helpful people weren't being cruel. Maybe they were being kind. To warn me what we've got coming to us."

She dropped her voice even farther. "They say she's impossible."

I chose to ignore her pronoun. "This isn't impossible. I'll get everything on the list. I'll order stuff online if I have to. Don't worry."

"Oh, Greta. I'm so glad you're here."

Again with my favorite words and the warm flood of relief.

CHAPTER 19

When I went in to Beans the next day, there was no line. My favorite. As soon as I opened the door, Mac made eye contact. My stomach jumped, and I couldn't hide my smile. He waved. It seemed like he was leaning toward me, even though I was practically still outside.

I loved when he leaned toward me.

He took a quick look at his phone in the time it took me to walk to the counter, then he stashed it in his white apron pocket. His shirt said, "Hey, Angle. Did it hurt when you fell from heaven?" Angle. Not Angel.

I laughed and gestured to the misspelled shirt.

He nodded and patted his chest. "I love the angel one." He leaned more. "Is that you that smells so good?"

I believe the word I was looking for was flabbergasted. Partly by the compliment, but mostly by the possibility that he didn't know his shirt was spelled wrong. "No. It's almond muffins." I pointed to the display case.

He shrugged. "Hot chocolate?"

"Yes, please."

He turned and poured. I stared. I thought about bringing up the angle/angel thing, but I wasn't sure what to say. I didn't say anything.

When he handed me the mug, I cradled it in my hands with no intention of moving until I had to. "You don't happen to own a huge auditorium or reception hall, do you?"

He looked at me like I was nuts. Because obviously I was at least a little nuts.

"Drink your chocolate. I have work to do. You're always distracting me. You" — he tapped the end of my nose — "are bad news."

"That's what they all say." I drew in a shaky, almost-laughing breath.

"Go sit at that table over there. The red chair. Then I can see you from any angle behind the counter."

I laughed, pointed at his shirt, and said, "Angle."

He looked confused. I dropped it.

I sat in the red chair where, as it happened, he *could* totally watch me from all around the counter. I felt the back of my neck prickle with happy chills whenever we made eye contact. There was a lot of eye contact. And a lot of happy chills.

The cocoa was gone too soon. I walked back up to the counter before I left, getting back in line. The man in front of me was an adorable old guy, bent over a cane. I heard him order. "My wife likes caramel coffee. Do you make caramel coffee here?"

Mac said, "You bet. What size does she want?"

"Oh, give me the biggest one you've got. She's worth it." He chuckled to himself like he'd let Mac in on the secret of the universe.

After he paid, I leaned over the counter and said, "That guy was adorable."

Mac nodded. "He's my new hero. You're worth it, too. Want a huge coffee to go?"

I made a face.

"Just kidding," he said. "I know you don't like coffee. But you're worth a huge hot chocolate any time."

"That's sweet. I've got to go."

He leaned over the counter and kissed my cheek. "Have a great night."

Well, that kiss helped.

Once I hit the sidewalk, I texted Marigold.

Any chance you know of a big venue for a big event?

There are a few theater rooms at the college.

Free?

I'll check, but I doubt it.

It only took her a minute to respond.

Nothing in education is free. That's a quote. Sorry.

Thanks for checking.

No problem. Don't let this dim you. Keep your exuberance flowing.

Exuberance? Right. Okay.

Thanks.

I sat down beside Julie's chair. "I sent you an email with all the numbers. It turns out that nobody in this town has a venue both big enough for our event and free. The movie theater on East Pearl would consider letting us rent from them, but we'd have to use their concessions and move it to a Wednesday night. Imagine Ms. Richtenberg's response to that. Remember the 'no overwhelming scents' clause?" I laughed.

Julie didn't. I decided to move on. "I know we could always try something in Columbus, but I really want this to be a Franklin event. So here's what I suggest. Let's do it here. Outside. In the lot."

I waited for her to tell me what a bad idea it was. She was silent for a long time.

I felt like I had to say something else. "Somebody could talk to Old Man Greenwood."

She scrunched up her eyes like she was reprimanding me. "Have you ever spoken to him?"

"Are you kidding me? He's like the creepy old man in every kids' movie ever made."

She patted my shoulder. "Exactly. He's probably as misunderstood as those characters, too. But I've burned all my bridges with him over the trash pile that he calls storage. Are you up for it? Talking to him, I mean?"

I was sure I'd misheard. "Me?"

"You're young. You're pretty. He won't be intimidated by you. Come on. Go talk to him." She stood up and pulled my chair out. "Just walk over there and knock on the door. Ask him if he'd be amenable to sharing the lot. He'll probably take one look at you and say yes out of shock."

"Now?" I could hear my own nerves.

"Now." She half-walked, half-pushed me to the door. "I'm sure he'll be thrilled at the company. He'll probably stay calm, but if he does shove you into a closet, stick your shoe into the doorway so he can't close it and lock you in."

"You're hilarious." I reached for an umbrella from the stand.

"I know." She opened the door and said, "Hustle. Don't let the rain in."

The umbrella was a good idea, but the rain was driven sideways by a warm wind. Only my head stayed dry.

I rang the doorbell and waited, staring at the piles of metal objects on the porch. I started counting coffee cans, but then got distracted by rusty tools. They were the same shade of orange as my shoes. How many orange pliers did one old guy need to keep on his front porch? Dozens, apparently.

I heard him shuffling toward the door long, *long* before he actually opened it. I had time to notice that the shrubs growing beside the porch were actually giant dandelions with daggerlike edges on the leaves. Precious.

"How could I possibly help you?"

Well, okay. His growly voice and his crazy-man eyebrows terrified me.

"Hello, sir. I'm Greta. I work at the library." I pointed over my shoulder at the library, in case he didn't know what I was talking about. Totally possible.

He made a noise that I chose to believe communicated understanding. "And? What do you need?"

How hard could it be? I decided to cut to the chase. "We want to use the lot between our properties for an event next month. An author is coming to talk about her books. We'd set up chairs and a sound system. Do you have any objections?"

"Would you clean it up?" He squinted at me like a cartoon pirate, but with less interesting costuming.

I nodded. "Before and after."

His gigantic eyebrows furrowed. "You have to promise not to throw anything away when you clean."

"Absolutely." I nodded once, so he would know I understood his demands. And so he wouldn't think I was interested in standing there talking on his porch for any longer than necessary.

"Agreed." He held out his clawlike hand. I stepped back. I avoided looking at his hands too carefully. If he had long, yellow nails I'd rather not get too familiar with them.

"Really? You're agreeing?"

He pushed his hand closer to me, like he might be eager about this. "I am. You're going to clean up the lot. Twice. I'm going to do nothing. Do you see a downside about that for me?"

"No, sir." I took his outstretched hand and shook it, prepared to scream if he tried to pull me into the dark house.

"Fine, then. Do the cleanup and the setup quietly. Don't throw anything away. Leave me a ticket at the entrance." He turned around and stepped into the house.

"Thank you, Mr. Greenwood."

He looked over his shoulder at me, a little longer than I thought necessary. His mouth moved like he was going to say something, but he seemed to change his mind. He nodded, turned his back to me, and closed the door.

Mac and I sat on a couch in the chain bookstore by the college. He was pretending to scan shelves and I was pretending not to stare at him. This, apparently, was what one did on a date when it was too rainy to make out on a park bench.

He looked at me. His arm went around the back of the couch behind me. "I bet you read a lot of weird books at work."

I tried to remember how to breathe. Maybe I laughed. Maybe I had a tiny explosion of pressure burst through me. "You have a warped idea of what it means to work in a library."

He brushed the hair off my forehead, and I forgot what we were talking about.

He leaned closer, bringing his face near mine. "You said you were reading shelves."

Wow. Those words shouldn't elicit such a spike in my pulse. I swallowed and regained control, after a fashion.

My voice shook for a few words. "It isn't like actual reading. I look at the stickers on the spines to make sure books are in the right place. They usually aren't."

But his hand was in the right place, and honestly, I was finding it tricky to formulate sentences.

"But you have to know what's there, right? What's good? Don't people ask you what they should read?" His finger slid a strand of hair behind my ear.

"I try not to work in 'should.' Book choice is not really a moral obligation." There was a whole lot of breath in those words. Not so much normal, for me. More like I couldn't quite control my respiration. What was the matter with me? This was not exactly a sexy conversation. But I couldn't stop watching his mouth.

He pulled out his phone with his free hand. He thumbed something into the keypad. I stared at his face and tried not to drool. After a few seconds, my phone beeped. I read the text he'd sent me.

I can't stop thinking about the way that one piece of your hair slips across your forehead when you're leaning over a book. I'd never need to read again if I could fill my eyes and my memory with the sight of you. You are all the story I ever need.

"I'm going to kiss you now." I heard the words come out of my mouth, in my voice, at the same time I tried to activate my filter. I tried to swallow them back. But once spoken, such things are difficult, if not impossible, to unspeak. Time seemed to have stopped, and Mac grinned the slowest, most adorable smile I'd ever, ever seen.

He leaned back. Our knees were touching — my right, his left — but his face, that gorgeous face with the flirty smile, was farther away than it had been a minute ago.

What was he doing, moving away? He was still smiling, still looking right at me. Was this some kind of test? Was he checking to see if I'd make a move?

Why not? I reached my arms to his shoulders. He sat straight and still, but that smile stayed on his lips. *Those lips!* Oh. I leaned. All the way in.

CHAPTER 20

Because I'd had the most recent tetanus
shot, I got to clear the lot between the
library and the Greenwood house. Also, I
wasn't sixty. Or a minor. Or in charge. It
was a perfect arrangement, apparently.

Julie had told me to wear something I
didn't mind getting dirty. Dirty didn't touch
it. In five minutes, my clothes were striped
with rust stains from old barrels. I guessed
that there were a dozen metal barrels in the
lot, but when I got closer, it appeared that
I'd underestimated.

A question for the universe: Why in the
world would any person need seventeen
enormous metal barrels? Only sinister possibilities occurred to me. I tipped the empty
ones toward my stomach and rolled them
along the edges of their bases to the space
by the Dumpster. The full ones I'd have to
deal with later because I wanted nothing to
do with emptying them. Anything could be

hidden in those things. Anything. My imagination was filling in the blanks at a rapid, horrifying rate. I'd stick to the empties for today.

After moving the ones I dared, I started on the piles. There were soggy newspapers that smelled like scary varieties of mold. I was grateful again for Julie's insistence that I wear gloves. I lifted a stack of papers, and the once-cardboard box holding them melted into a brownish, sloppish, pulpy mess that mixed with gravelly dirt into what had to be a toxic paste.

But that was nothing compared to what I found in the bottles.

Piled three or four high were stacks of glass bottles with cracks in them. And inside the bottles were "preserved" fruits and vegetables in various states of decline. This would make an amazing science fair project for someone with a steel stomach. One jar held peaches. They looked like ordinary peaches until I turned the bottle around. A hairline crack ran from the lid to the words embossed on the jar. Running inside, following the line of the crack, were dark, wet spores that bloomed like tiny poisonous flowers in the syrup.

I used to love peaches. I would possibly never again even look at peaches.

Under the peaches stood jars of what my grandmother would have called fruit cocktail, but the fruit was bubbling. There was a ring of foam rising from the seal — which clearly wasn't doing its job — and the whole arrangement smelled like a distillery.

Why was he keeping this? Was he going to poison someone?

With every jar, bottle, can, box, and soggy pile of paper, I forced myself to add to the slightly neater piles behind the Dumpster instead of tossing it all inside and slamming the metal lid on the whole mess.

I tried to consider it in a forward-thinking, civil activism kind of way. Demanding cleanup was like censorship, I thought. I might think it's trash — I certainly had every right to think it's trash — but it's not my place to put it in the bin.

Oh, please. It was nothing but trash. Clearly the mold fumes and the rancid fruit smells were affecting my judgment.

I looked at the piles of what looked like clothes and blankets shoved up against the old Greenwood house. Any number of severed limbs, of petrified pets, of *anything* could have been folded within the manky blankets and left there for decades.

"If it's touching his house, I'm not responsible for it." I told myself this enough times that I believed it.

Hours later, I went inside the library for a break.

"Greta, I'm glad you're here." Julie smiled at me but held her arm out straight. "But don't come back here behind the desk. You're a mess."

"Thanks."

She handed me a water bottle and watched me take off my gloves, hovering near enough that she could swat them away if they touched a book.

"So, how's it going out there?"

"I've done a ton." I pointed out the window. "Out of about a million tons of what is left to do."

"Seems like you're clearing a good patch," she said, trying to encourage me. Only problem? I could see the lot out the window, and it didn't look any different — I mean zero difference — than when I'd started.

"It's better from the ground," I told her. "There's more progress than you can see from here."

"Sure." She made it sound so sincere.

I gulped down half the water from the bottle. "I wish he'd let me throw things away. Why would you need to keep decades of Yellow Pages phone books? Who's he going to call?"

Julie smiled. "Some people find comfort in collecting things. It helps them sort through issues of loss."

"I think everything Old Man Greenwood's ever lost is actually moldering in piles in the lot."

"Oh, I assure you, he's lost plenty that he can't keep in his house or his yard." Julie turned away.

She had a habit of tossing out little gems like that. "Wait. You can't say that and then not explain it. Does he have a cool backstory like those creepy old neighbor men do in the movies? Some devastating life story that will make us all feel sorry for him and want to eat Christmas turkey in his dining room?"

Julie looked at me over the rims of her glasses. "Everyone has a story."

"You're not going to tell me, are you?"

"You could research," she said as she walked away.

I shot back, "Not a chance. All my research energy is channeled to the elusive Dr. Joshua Silver."

Librarians. Forget it. I pulled the gloves back on and hauled open the wooden door.

After hours of manual labor and a quick shower, I found this on my phone:

I look at my fingers and they seem barren without your hand to hold. I am only complete when you're with me.

Oh, he was good.

I met Mac the next day at Beans even though he wasn't working. I saw him slouched against the wall as I got close. I looked around for a car, but there didn't seem to be one nearby.

My imagination fast-forwarded to us holding hands, walking to his house, leaves blowing around our feet as we talked about our dreams and plans for the future. Our separate futures, obviously, because it would be freaky to talk about a future together on a random Sunday afternoon in the fall. Much too complex.

He appeared to be reading something on his phone, so he didn't see me coming. I saw his mouth moving as he read. Huh. That was cute in a second-grade way. I decided second grade was underrated.

Close enough to touch his arm, I said, "Hi."

He hurried to click off his phone.

"Sorry. I didn't mean to stop you from whatever it is you're doing," I said, leaning up to kiss his cheek.

He turned his face and kissed me for real.

"I was writing a poem," he said after a minute. Or two. I had to think really hard to connect those words to anything.

"Oh. On your phone? Before?"

"Before I blew your mind?" He smoldered at me and then kissed me again.

I pulled back and laughed. "Yes. Before that. What poem?"

He took my hand, and we started walking. "I just do this thing. A poem every day."

"Like a daily sonnet?" I said, thinking of Rilke.

"Like a little poem."

Well, we couldn't all write a sonnet a day. "About what?"

"Just, you know, stuff."

He leaned in close to my ear. "The wind blows through your / Golden hair, lifting each strand, / and finds the sun's source." He wrapped a strand of my hair around his finger, and before I had a chance to ask him what that line about the sun's source was supposed to mean, he was kissing me again.

And then I forgot about poetry and the sun and the atmosphere and the law of gravity altogether.

CHAPTER 21

Marigold met me at Beans on Monday, during my lunch break and her class break, to update me on her paper and get a few more quotes from me. I didn't mind being a source. We talked about the ads running in the newspaper and the work I was doing for the Richtenberg reading. I'd brought Marigold a printed ad for the reading, and she slid it into her bag. She didn't change the subject, exactly, but she bent it. "What are you wearing?"

I looked down at my zip-front hoodie covering my T-shirt dress.

"No, I mean to your library party."

Oh. "I have no idea. I looked at some dresses online, but I hate that sort of shopping. I'm easily distracted." That was true. I got distracted by another shopping site — a kind totally unconnected to dresses. A site that was full of things I might need for the next step in my Save Franklin Library plan.

One where there was a virtual shopping cart full of super-secret, radical activism stuff waiting for me to type in my password (dr$ilv3r) and click BUY NOW.

"Have you ever been to Sam's?"

I was pretty sure we were still talking about dresses, but I didn't know who Sam was. "I don't think so."

She stood up and swept her piles of papers into her bag. "Come on."

"Come where? I only have forty minutes left on my break."

She looked at the clock, then quirked her eyebrow at me. "Then we'd better do this now. Your guy will just have to see you later."

I stared hard at Mac, trying to force him to look at me by the power of my mind. Which totally worked, by the way. He waved. I waved. Marigold grabbed her huge bag and pulled me out the door.

We walked a few blocks to a shabby little store with a burgundy-striped awning. The painted sign in the window said WEAR IT AGAIN, SAM. Underneath that were the words RECLAIMED CLOTHING.

I couldn't even pretend not to be annoyed. "You brought me to a thrift store? I have a master's degree. I have a job. I can afford a dress."

"Don't be a snob," she said with a smile.

"You sound like Will."

She didn't respond, just nodded.

"Why are people always saying that to me?"

She shook her head as she pushed open the door. "Come on."

The store smelled like incense and mildew. It was strangely appealing, and a little comforting. As I glanced around the shop, I saw dozens of round racks topped with outfits displayed on dress-form dummies.

"Decades," Marigold said. "Are you a twenties girl?" She pointed to a clothing rack. "A fifties girl?" She spun me around the room. "What's your decade?"

I had no idea. "Is this a personality test?"

"I already know everything I need to know about your personality. Passion and light. You're optimistic and vigorous. I want to know if you're interested in any particular time period."

I thought of Dr. Silver. "I like the sixties."

She nodded and pushed me toward a rack topped with a headless mannequin wearing a rectangular dress with huge polka dots on it — only four dots covered the whole dress. She saw me looking and said, "That's late-sixties. That's more me. I'm thinking mid for you."

She pushed a few things out of the way

and reached for a dress. It was stiff; the sleeves hung like arrow points out from the sides. When she held it up in front of me, she shook her head and put it back. The next one was a suit, like Jackie Kennedy would have worn. I said no. The next one was black and knee-length with a round neck and raised flowers on the fabric, like someone had sewn them all on there with thread.

Marigold studied it. "I love the embroidery." She fingered a few flowers. "And this piping." She ran her hand along the neckline and the hem where there was a line of white.

I wanted to contribute something useful, so I said I liked the tiny belt.

Marigold held the dress up to me, pulling the shoulder seams against my shoulders and tucking the waist part around my waist part. She nodded. "I think this is perfect. You're lucky you're not too tall."

I'd never thought of that as lucky, but I could imagine that with Marigold's long legs, dresses that fit might be hard to find.

I held the dress up against me. "Okay. Great. Where do I try it on?"

"Oh, no. There's not a fitting room here. You buy it if you like it and plan for the best."

Weird. "So, if I don't like it, or if it doesn't

fit, I bring it back?"

"I guess," she said. "I've never brought anything back, though. I've loved everything I've ever bought here." She became distracted by a fringed leather vest that looked like someone had dropped a cup of coffee on it. "Do you think I could get this clean?"

"Sure?" I was not in any position to know, but I liked her "plan for the best" mind-set and thought I'd try it out.

She clutched the vest in both hands. "Let's do it."

"I can't buy this. I don't even know how much it costs."

Marigold reached down into the neck part of the dress and pulled up a colored tag. Nothing was written on it. She pointed to a poster at the tiny table holding a cash register. Yellow tags, $10. Purple tags, $14. I peeked at the tag in the black dress — green. Green tags, $7. Seven. Dollars. I snatched the dress from her and ran to the register. At the table, an antique-looking frame held a handwritten notice: CASH ONLY. I loved this crazy place.

The lady behind the counter smiled at my choice. "This is a lovely piece," she said, pushing some buttons on the register, which was old-fashioned, non-electronic, and cute-looking with all kinds of metal scrollwork and round keys.

"Where do these clothes come from?" I asked her, making small talk while Marigold sifted through the sixties rack. I peeled off seven one-dollar bills from the little stack of cash in my wallet.

She smiled at me like we were old buddies. "All over. Estate sales, donations, other secondhand stores. We have a beautiful selection of wedding dresses on the other side of that screen. As well as menswear." She pointed behind her where there were racks and racks of suits. I wondered if they had a suit like Dr. Silver's three-piece number from the picture with Dr. King at the library.

As she wrapped my old-new dress in tissue paper and placed it in a brown paper sack, she said, "I hope you'll come see us again."

I smiled and nodded and managed not to say anything about waiting to make that call until I knew if this dress was going to give me any weird skin conditions. "It's a great shop," I said.

I turned to find Marigold, arms deep in the late-sixties section of the rack. "I'm done."

"I'm never done," she said, grinning at me.

"Got it. Okay. But I need to get back to my job now. Bye, Marigold. Thanks for your help," I said as I headed for the door. She waved without turning around, her attention focused on a shirt that had fluttery, bell-bottom kinds of sleeves. I realized I was clutching the bag in a hug.

I slipped into the library and behind the counter. Placing my new purchase with my purse under the desk, I picked up the pile of Cards. Kevin had added another yesterday afternoon that I hadn't seen yet. "Do whales feel emotions? (across the desk)." I picked up a pink sticky note and wrote a response. "Some species can be sad. That's why they're called Blue Whales." I stuck the note to the Card and hoped I'd be there when Kevin read it, to hear him groan and see him shake his head.

CHAPTER 22

The next few days rushed by in a blur of last-minute event organization. All my extra time was filled with Mac or Will (but not very much Will, because it was debate season, and he was really good at his job) or, when I had time, sleep. Before I knew it, it was Eleanor Richtenberg day.

I stared into the mirror at me in my new dress. I was hoping for one of those startling mirror events. You know, when you're sure you know what you looked like and then somehow — surprise! — you're 75% more attractive than you'd planned on being. This was not the kind of startle I was hoping for. I needed help. Instantly. Mom had a work meeting, so she was out of the picture. She told me she'd see me at the event, but I hoped she wouldn't see me this way exactly.

I could get Will. He could theoretically help me. But I'd have to go outside to get there, and given the current state of my dress — or rather, undress — that might get me in trouble. Or arrested.

For this, I realized, it was time to take the Marigold friendship to the next level.

I pulled out my cell and called her. When I realized I was holding my breath, I forced a few in-and-outs.

"Hi, Greta. Today is your big party, right?"

"Can you come over to my place for a couple of minutes? I kind of have a tiny disaster."

She hummed a tuneless string of almost-notes into the phone, then said, "Sure. Now?"

"Yes, now. Thanks." I told her my address and sat down to stare into the mirror. And to wait. And hope she didn't get distracted on the way over here.

The dress picked up the light and threw it back into the mirror, causing the black fabric to shine and deepen in the creases and folds. Creases and folds it shouldn't have. So much for "buying the dress and hoping for the best."

I decided to stare at my hair instead.

Not the worst. Not the best, but definitely not the worst.

Maybe it'd turned out too curly, but chances were good that by the end of the evening it would sag. Plenty. I hosed it down with a few more shots of hairspray. Makeup? Fine. Nails? Clean. Earrings? Sparkly.

For sure, not the worst.

Except for the small issue with my dress.

Hurry up, Marigold. Please.

I pulled up Mac's latest text just to have something really, really awesome to look at.

When you laugh, all the happiest sounds in the world come together at once: the music on the ice cream truck, the drip of melting snow in the spring, the elementary school recess bell, the sound my phone makes when you send a text. Your laugh brings everything perfect together.

Swoon.

Knocking. I slid out of my chair and ran to the door.

"Wow, look at you. Nice . . . everything. The dress looks good. Maybe a little loose." Marigold flicked a piece of lint off my shoulder. She nodded in general approval, and I let her inside. She glanced around and said, "What's the disaster?"

I turned around and showed her my back.

"You called me over here to zip your dress?" She didn't sound annoyed, exactly, and not quite amused. Maybe she was pleased, but who could tell?

"Not exactly. I broke the zip. The zip is definitely broken."

She tugged on the little metal piece and nodded. "You're right. So? Plan?"

"Sew me in."

She didn't say anything. She didn't do anything. We shared a quiet thirty seconds.

"Are you sure?"

I continued to look at her without saying anything. If I hadn't been sure, would I have suggested it?

Nodding, she said, "All right. Do you have sewing stuff?"

I pointed to the line of threads and a little box of needles on the coffee table. "Do you know how to use those?"

"Please. I'm an adult. I go to *college.* Of course I can use sewing . . . things."

Confidence restored. Or not.

"Thanks. Really, thanks. If you have to choose between sewing a straight line and not poking me with the needle, sew straight. I can take it."

"Relax."

I waited for the first prick.

"I mean it. Relax. I can't do this if you're tense. You're throwing off my chakras." She rubbed my shoulders, which only increased my tension.

She made a sound like a reprimand.

"Greta."

My exaggerated exhale must have convinced her that I was relaxing. She picked up the box of needles and opened it. Staring in there, she might have been communing with the Perfect Instrument or something. She licked her finger and pressed it against the flat sides of the needles. One stuck to her finger, and she lifted it out. Then she stared at the spools of thread.

"Black," I suggested. "There are three black ones you can choose from." I even pointed them out, that's how helpful I was feeling.

When she started stroking the spools, I felt myself losing it. "Please? I'm scheduled to walk out this door in" — I glanced at my phone — "twenty-seven minutes. This is a long zipper. That gives you, like, a couple minutes an inch or something."

She patted me on the head with the hand not holding the needle. "Good math. Keep it up. I'll get it. No worries."

No worries? More like Plentiful Worries. The zipper. Deodorant malfunction. Dragon breath. Zit outbreak. Conversation drought.

At least I didn't have to worry about The Event. Everything related to the event was perfectly in place.

Marigold stuck the needle into the spool

of chosen thread. Then she pinned the dress up my back with the enormous safety pins I'd found in the junk drawer.

"These are diaper pins," she said. "I haven't seen one of these in years."

"I stole them from my mom's house. I don't plan to wear them. Just until I'm sewn up."

"Right. But it's a statement. You might want to consider it."

"Or not."

"Okay, your call."

I told myself to breathe in and out, lightly, so I didn't pull any pins. I felt her hands pinching the zipper together, sliding the needle back and forth. I hoped the dress wouldn't look all Frankenstein's Monster, but was glad I wasn't planning to stand with my back to the crowd much, anyway.

The screen door banged open at the same time as I heard the knock on the frame. "Greta? Are you here?"

"Hi, Will. In the living room."

Marigold snipped a few dangling threads.

Will walked in and saw me. He sort of staggered against the wall. "Wow," he half-whispered. "Just totally wow." He blinked hard and rubbed his eyes. "That's an amazing dress. You look perfect." He coughed.

I laughed. "Did I take your breath away?"

"Something like that. Or I have the flu. Definitely one or the other."

I faced him. "Oh, no. You're sick?"

He shrugged. "A bit. But I'm still coming. Don't worry. I've been waiting my whole life to meet Eleanor Richtenberg. I wouldn't miss it. And you look remarkable."

That was a rather lovely thing to say. "Remarkable?" I hadn't seen him for days, and I'd really missed him.

"Gorgeous. Stunning. You're going to steal the show. Nobody will even look at Eleanor Richtenberg." He walked toward me and reached out to touch my sleeve. He held the fabric between his fingers. Then he looked into my face and moved his hand to my shoulder, right below the hem. The heat from his hand nearly burned my arm. I looked into his eyes and saw some new and different depth there. He looked like he'd been searching for something, and then he'd found it. And that was weird.

But more weird was that I felt it, too. The searching. The finding. The depth. I reached over and clutched the hem of his shirt. I don't know how long I stood there holding on to his shirttail, how long we looked at each other's faces. Somehow I managed to recognize that this was strange, but I didn't care. I felt his hand on me, his eyes on me, and I had never been so safe. I didn't let go. I didn't want him to let go.

"Will."

He pressed his hand into my shoulder. "Greta."

I stared. He stared back. I looked at his mouth and remembered the way he'd kissed me when we were sixteen. I craved his arms around me and his lips on mine. I almost staggered under the weight of my own understanding. I wanted Will Marshall to kiss me. Now. Right now.

Then I heard, "And I'm Marigold."

Spell broken. I laughed. Will coughed.

"Nobody's even going to see Eleanor Richtenberg," Will repeated.

Arms shaking, I stepped away from him. "I am completely sure you're wrong, but that's nice of you to say. Go home and sleep for a couple of hours. I'll see you at the party."

"I'm coming to help set up." He coughed again.

I talked as I pushed him out the door. "Bad idea. You're sick. Sleep it off. Get over it. Feel better."

He waved from the doorway, and I went back to Marigold. "Thank you for saving me."

"Yeah. That was weird." She had her

eyebrows scrunched, looking at the door Will had walked through like she was searching for an explanation.

"I meant for saving my dress."

She nodded, looking through the window. "That too. But seriously? Something very strange," she started.

I cut her off. "I know. Strange."

She shook her head, but whatever she had been about to say remained unsaid. And all the things I was thinking also remained unsaid.

"Okay. Thanks again. I've got to go make a party," I said as I waved her out the front door. Then I sank onto the couch and breathed until I regained control of my heart rate.

Chapter 23

I was nervous to even go over to the lot. Partly because I feared that all the garbage and mess had reappeared overnight, but mostly because the thought of the event made me crazy with feeling things. Excited and scared and eager and worried and anxious. What if Eleanor Richtenberg wanted to be my friend? I'd loved this woman since I was able to grasp the idea that books were written by people.

Walking past the Greenwood house, I held my breath. Well, I tried. I had to gasp in some air just past the mailbox, and then again at the giant tree. But when I came around to the lot, I let the air slide out in relief. The big white tents provided perfect shade and drew attention far away from the piles of things stacked against Mr. Greenwood's house. A pretty little wooden podium stood beyond the shade, warming in the sun but ready to be shaded in two hours, as instructed by Ms. Richtenberg.

Before I stashed my purse under the podium, I checked my phone. Just in case.

I'm going from work to home and imagining what you're doing this very minute. I bet you've put on a dress that makes you look as confident and gorgeous as you deserve to look. I see your hair picking up glints of light from the sun, but I can't decide if it's straight or curled. This is a big day, so probably curled. And you've put on some makeup, but only enough to highlight your perfect face — not enough to hide the freckles scattered across your nose like stars emerging at dusk. I love those freckles.

He said *love.*

Well, he texted love anyway. I gulped in more air and decided not to freak out about texted love. Especially if it was just texted freckle love.

The phone went back into the bag, and I moved toward the truck parked across two spaces in the parking lot. Julie stood pointing to a spot of lawn not already holding something. A guy came down the truck's back ramp and set the speaker equipment on the ground.

"You ladies got a perfect day for your party," he said, checking the truck one more time and finding it empty. "What great weather."

"Thanks for delivering everything. You're sending the truck back in the morning?" Julie asked.

"Right." He checked a list on a clipboard. "Have chairs, tables, tents, sound equipment, and plant stands ready for loading. Good luck," he said. He got in the truck and drove away.

Julie took a visible breath and surveyed the area. "Greta, I'm glad you're here. Ready to unfold?"

"So ready."

She looked me over. "That's quite a dress. Are you sure you don't want to change into something more work-friendly for the next couple of hours?"

"Changing out of this dress and back into it again is not actually an option," I said, choosing not to explain any further. I picked up a white folding chair and carried it to the lot. Then I did that again several hundred more times.

I heard a familiar coughing sound after the first hundred chairs or so. I turned around.

"Will, what are you doing?"

He looked from one side of the row of chairs to the other. He didn't answer, but he smiled that smile that meant he was pleased with himself.

"You're sick. Aren't you supposed to be resting?"

He shook his head and then coughed into his elbow. "Powering through it."

Two hours later, Julie pushed her arms out in front of her, rounding her shoulders and stretching. "If I never open another folding chair again, I will be the happiest fifty-something divorced librarian in the history of the universe."

We checked our work. Rows of chairs under the huge maple tree canopies, and rows of chairs under the white tents. It looked like a wedding, but without flowers and that netted fabric stuff lining the aisle. The podium, bordered by two ferns, as directed, stood twenty feet from the nearest row of chairs. That way, even if someone stretched out long legs, there would still be a fifteen-foot buffer of airspace.

A glass bowl (no etching) holding only green jelly beans and a separate glass bowl (also no etching) holding only green M&M's candies flanked the microphone. The water bottles from Switzerland sat in the break room's freezer, accumulating a perfect layer of ice. I checked the position of the sun against the chart on my phone. Perfect. When Ms. Richtenberg stood at the podium, the sun would be at an acceptable angle — no chance of blinding her or of any embarrassing backlight.

Will rolled the last of the folding-chair carts behind the library and out of sight.

"Want to go over the intro again?" I asked.

Julie shook her head, patting her pocket. "I've got it right here. I don't want it to sound too rehearsed."

"You have it completely memorized, don't you?"

She grinned. "Thirty-three years ago next month, the world met Grimsby for the first time, and the nights have never been quite as dark as they used to be. We are thrilled to welcome the esteemed Eleanor Richtenberg to our community this evening, since she's lived so long in our hearts. Want to hear the rest?"

"That's not what her publicist sent." I pulled out my copy of the official biography. "This is all about her education and awards."

"Which nobody cares about. Let her hear what we love about her. It has to be a relief from hearing the same over-flattering, repetitive, dry —"

I nodded and she stopped.

"Sorry," she laughed. "Nervous criticism."

"I get it. Don't worry. Everything is going perfectly. I mean, look around. It's gorgeous. This is going to be the best night ever."

Bonita was posted at the ticket table, smiling at people and nodding them toward the seats. She gave me a thumbs-up when I waved at her. She did not look concerned that anything might go wrong. That was always a good sign.

After making a final check of the book sales table and the separate book signing table and finally the caterer's cookie table, I saw Mac wander through the arbor.

"Hi. Welcome to your library." I took his hand and kissed his cheek.

"Amazing. Stunning. Impressive. And the place doesn't look bad, either."

I rolled my eyes, but only on the inside.

He grinned. "What can I do to help?"

"That's so nice of you, but I think everything is done. Unless you want to help me check the sound system one more time?"

"Sure."

After checking that everything that should be plugged was plugged, I stepped up to the podium and flipped the switch. A deep thump pushed through all the speakers in unison, and birds, perched on top of the tents, flapped away into the trees.

"Test. This is a test. The last test before the real test." My voice slipped out of the speakers, clear and strong. Mac gave me two thumbs-up from the middle section of seats so I knew he could hear.

"I need to step inside for a second," I told him. "Want to save us a couple of seats?"

"Sure. But do you want me to come with you? Can I — I don't know — carry something?"

"Thanks, but I'm good. I'll be right back." I didn't want to go into any discussions about my nervous bladder, and there was nothing else inside the library that needed to come outside to the lot.

At the door, I turned around to see how things looked from that angle. It was pretty. All of my good friend Eleanor's demands had been a pain to comply with, but they made the lot look great. I did another panoramic glance and saw Old Man Greenwood on the bottom of his porch steps. He raised his arm and did a sort of salute. I waved and ran inside. He wasn't doing anything actively scary, but he would never not be creepy.

Back outside in record time, I saw Mac's

discarded brown jacket slung over the backs of two chairs near the middle and to one side. People filed in, families and couples and people I recognized from the library and people I'd never seen before. I looked around for Mac. He was fiddling with the cords on one of the speakers, arms over his head and legs against the tripod that was bracing the speaker.

"It stopped again," he called.

"Must have been you, because I didn't turn anything this time. Thanks." Julie's voice slid from behind the other speaker. I could see her feet standing on a chair. Apparently she was prepared for some cord-jiggling, too.

She stepped off her chair and half-dragged, half-carried it back to its place in line. She'd changed from jeans and a sweatshirt into a nice green dress. The look of satisfaction on her face made all my extra hours of preparation worth it. Nearly half the seats were filled, with more people wandering in.

I heard a sound like a foghorn had mated with chattering teeth. The hairs on the back of my neck stood straight. "What is that?"

Julie seemed to deflate over the back of the folding chair. "I think we're getting microphone feedback. We should have spent the extra money to hire a sound technician." Dragging the chair back to the speaker, she muttered unconventional-librarian words not very quietly.

I didn't know how to be helpful, so I did what I could. I made a list. "Maybe something's eating the cord. Maybe a squirrel dropped something on the plug. Maybe something kinked. Maybe a bird bit through a wire."

"Greta. Stop." She held her ears, but I couldn't tell if she was trying to block me out or the vibrating noise.

Since she and Mac had the "let's turn these plugs in their sockets" job handled, I walked back up to the podium. The sound throbbed through the speakers, throbbed and stopped, throbbed and stopped. From here, it sounded less foghorn-y and more like someone drumming on an organ while every key was pushed.

I glanced around to see if anything was obviously wrong with the microphone setup, but honestly, unless it was covered with slugs, I wouldn't have been able to tell if it was out of order. No slugs, by the way.

The noise stopped again, and I put my head under the podium. Maybe the cord was being pinched? Maybe the lectern thing was squishing it? On my knees in the shade of the little stand, I tossed up a prayer to the gods of literary gatherings.

When the noise started again, I knew what it had to be. In my hurry to get up off the grass, I bashed my head on the shelf and the impolite word I said boomed at me through the speakers. Nice. I was so fired.

But I shook it off, unfolded myself, and stood at the podium where Julie's mobile phone was vibrating against the wood. Repeatedly. Directly under the microphone. I grabbed it off the wooden stand and the noise stopped. Seven missed calls. Seven messages. All from Kevin's phone.

I turned away from the microphone. "Hi, Kevin. This is Greta. Everything okay?"

"No, it is not okay. If everything were okay, don't you think I'd be standing there at the library? Don't you think I'd be introducing you to your guest of honor? What is happening with you people? Can no one answer a phone?" His voice, tinny and shrill, verged on hysteria. I waved to Julie and pointed to her phone attached to my ear.

"I'm handing you over to the boss. Here you go." I wasn't within twenty yards of the boss, but I didn't want to deal with this version of Kevin. This was not your typical chill, relaxed Kevin, always ready to explain how things worked in the world. He was scary today.

I speed-walked toward Julie while she speed-walked toward me. Handing over the phone, I stood there, watching her face fall.

Even without knowing, I knew.

"Yes. Okay. Okay. No. I see. All right. Of course not. Thank you, Kevin." With each word, her voice got smaller and her chin moved closer to her chest. Her whole body rounded in on itself. She clicked off.

After a few long seconds of silence, she took a breath. Trying to grin at me, she bared her teeth. "We appear to be without a guest of honor for our party."

Chapter 24

"She didn't come." It wasn't a question in any way, but I needed an answer.

Julie's breath didn't seem to reinflate her. "She didn't. Kevin knew that, according to the publicist's demands, she should have been the first one off the plane. When the crowd from that flight surrounded the bag claim, he called the number the publicist had sent. Eleanor Richtenberg never even got on the plane. She changed her mind. Poor Kevin." She almost whispered the last part. It was so like her to worry about how Kevin felt. How he must have taken on himself the responsibility. How he had to be the messenger. Sweet Julie.

I was the opposite. As her voice got quieter, mine got louder. And more shrill. And less appropriate. "Changed her mind? Changed her mind? Is she insane? She is. She totally is. From demanding only green food to the seventy-degree car to the not even arriving? She's off her nut. Completely."

I stopped when Julie's hand touched my arm, and I looked at her face. Tears slipped down her cheeks and trembled on her jawline.

"Sorry," I said. "Not helpful. Sorry." I wanted to give her a hug, but I knew better than to hug a woman with tears on her face. It could only make things worse. I wished I had gummy bears. No dice. The only thing I had to offer was perspective. "The seats are filling. Someone is going to have to say something."

Okay, so that may not have been the most helpful perspective I could have offered. Her face sagged more, which I wouldn't have thought possible.

There was no way Julie could stand up in front of her patrons and tell them that their money was wasted, that the promised visit was not happening, that the hero they were waiting to meet had stood them all up.

"I'll do it." Wait. Where did those words come from? "I'll talk to them." I wanted to stop speaking, but the words kept rolling out of my mouth. "I'll explain."

She almost laughed, but it sounded more like a cough. Wet. And unintentional. "How can you explain this?" She shook her head, or maybe looked around really fast to take it all in.

"I'll give it a shot. And I'll be generous. And fair. And I won't mention the crazy." She looked at me as if she doubted my ability to not mention the crazy. "No, really. Not to anyone but you."

I stepped up to the microphone and waited for the crowd to settle. People craned their necks to catch a glimpse of Eleanor Richtenberg as the remaining loiterers found their seats.

"Ladies and gentlemen, friends of the library, neighbors, we are so glad you would join us today. We appreciate your generosity in being here, in buying tickets, and in all the ways you support us so that we can continue to be a crucial part of this community that we all call home." I read that part right off the introduction page. Now was the piece I had to make up.

"Um. As you know, we planned to have the remarkable Eleanor Richtenberg with us." Remarkable. Yes, I could make a few *remarks*. But I didn't. "Ms. Richtenberg, we have just gotten word, could not make it." I let the groans and the mutters carry for what felt like hours but was probably less than half a minute. A few hands waved from people wanting to ask questions. I was so not up for questions.

"Instead of hearing from Ms. Richtenberg, then, we will take a few minutes to let anyone else arrive and then we will share from our favorite Grimsby books. Kind of like a reading." *Kind of exactly like a reading,* I thought. I cleared my throat right into the microphone. "So, in a few more minutes, then."

I looked an apology over my shoulder and almost ran to the stack of Grimsby books we had for sale. Grabbing my two favorites, I hustled back outside. A huge crowd of people stood in a mass around the ticket table.

Bonita clutched the cash box, eyes bulging, fear written all over her.

I caught Julie's eye. "What do you want me to do?" I mouthed, pointing to Bonita and the Instant Refund Mob.

She shook her head and shrugged, which I interpreted to mean that I should carry on making things up. I went back to the microphone.

"Thank you for your patience," I said to the least patient group of people ever to assemble in this town or any other. "If you could please find your seats, we will begin."

I watched a few people drag companions back to folding chairs. Plenty of others stood their ground at the ticket table. I couldn't see Bonita from here, but I hoped she was protected from the wrath of the disappointed.

"We are all so sorry that Ms. Richtenberg can't be here with us, and I wish I could give some explanation." *Because, let me tell you, I could give you a few choice words. Oh, yes I could.* "All I can tell you is that we will miss her here."

People shouted over each others' demands.

"You're going to refund our tickets, right?"

"When will you reschedule?"

I held up my hand as though that might silence anyone, and it did. Bizarre. "I am certain that a large part of your donation was made with your expectation of seeing Ms. Richtenberg. And again, we are sorry that couldn't happen. But we are also confident that you still want to help the library."

I looked back and caught Julie's eye. She nodded, so I figured I could do whatever I wanted. What I wanted, however, was to get away before the pitchforks came out.

I took another breath and said, "We want you to be happy. If you need a refund, please send an email to the library help desk, and we will gladly get that processed.

If you'd like to stay and enjoy the evening, we are grateful for your generous contributions to our library."

I saw Marigold, typing notes into her laptop. Good thing my disaster was great material for her paper. At least some good could come of this awful night.

I held up one of the two books in my hands and put on a smile. "This is my favorite Richtenberg book. I've had two copies of my own because when I was small, apparently I ate my first copy. Not all at once, of course. A little at a time." I heard my mom laugh, and I looked up. She was sitting near the front and when I caught her eye, she did a smile-and-nod. Mac leaned back with his arm stretched over the empty chair beside him. I saw Will and his mom, sitting tall in their folding chairs and smiling too-bright smiles. Their faces reminded me that this was, in fact, not a total disaster. Will nodded at me and coughed into his elbow. I smiled back at them and opened the book.

When the talking was over and the mingling started, I found myself hovering near the edges of where Julie stood. She was putting on a brave face, but she did not look particularly okay. Mac and Will both seemed to sense it was a good idea to keep their distance from me. I was grateful because at a moment like this, too much kindness could lead to a major breakdown. I could keep this up as long as I needed to — just as long as nobody cracked through my professional exterior.

I directed some of the crowd away from Julie. I pointed people toward the table where Bonita was now selling copies of Grimsby books. Important community figures milled around, talking to each other.

I shook hands with the mayor and her husband. I had decided not to apologize any more for the weird turn of events. "Thank you so much for coming to celebrate with us," I said.

She was all graciousness. Leaning close to me, either to be heard over the buzz of the crowd or to keep her words for my ears only, she said, "You put together something special, and you handled the bumps in the road beautifully." Her voice was rich and deep. "This library has been an important place to me all my life."

She was still holding my hand in hers.

"I didn't know you grew up here." Suddenly, my mind flooded with questions. "Mrs. Cutler, can I ask you a personal question?"

She looked surprised. "You may certainly

ask," she said, implying that maybe she would choose not to answer.

"When did you graduate from high school?"

She laughed, showing all her teeth, and looked relieved. I guess she had dodged a lot of far more personal questions than that. "Nineteen eighty-two."

"Did you ever have any interaction with a Dr. Joshua Silver?"

Her face lit up. "You know about Dr. Silver?"

I wasn't sure she really needed more than a "yes" from me, but I leaned in and said, "I have a giant historical crush on him. It's the hat. And the all-around awesomeness."

She laughed. "That's a story we don't tell often enough in this town. My parents went to East, but my mother's youngest brother was one of the students that Dr. Silver drove on the bus to Central." She looked around, but seemed not to find who she was looking for. "His story is one of the great American tragedies."

I felt my face fall. "What happened? I can't find anything about him after he was replaced as principal that year — the year of the busing."

She looked around again, as if checking to see who could hear her. I was the only one listening, aside from her husband, who never left her side. "It's such a shame. They fired him. Sometimes when you shake up the system too hard, people get upset. The school board and the superintendent decided that he'd offended too many voters, so they let him go. He was young, so it was pretty public information that he hadn't retired. He taught some community outreach classes, but mostly he stayed home." She gestured toward the old Greenwood place. "Sometimes people find safety in seclusion."

I wasn't interested in adding Old Man Greenwood to the conversation, so I refocused. "So he did this amazing thing, this radical, generous thing — all for other people's kids — and then he lost everything?"

She looked over at her husband. "I wouldn't say he lost everything. But he lost his career, and for some of us that means identity. He couldn't get hired again in this town, but, you know, he has a legacy. People have privilege and opportunity now that they never had before, and that is tied directly to Dr. Silver's choices.

"For each person who disapproved of his actions in desegregating Franklin, there were ten who felt they owed him a great debt. And those ten have grown to be parents and grandparents. People who watched their children gain access that would have been unimaginable a few decades before. I'm not saying that things are fixed or fair, but doors are open to many of us that wouldn't have been opened without Dr. Silver." She laughed and leaned in again. "And you can quote the first African-American woman mayor of Franklin on that."

Mic drop. Wow. She was fantastic. And she was in demand. Apparently I'd been monopolizing her time for too long. Someone came up and took her by the elbow and led her to another point in the crowd. I looked around and saw that hundreds of people were still visiting on the lawn or sitting in chairs under the tents.

That little bit of Dr. Silver nostalgia helped me forget for a few minutes that my big plans were crumbling around me.

CHAPTER 25

"I tried not to believe it." Julie shook her head, jiggling the beaded earrings. "So many people contacted me when we made this event public. They said it would be a nightmare. They said she was impossible to work with."

In the past two hours, I'd heard Julie say variations of that theme a dozen different times. Mostly to herself, but I'd stayed near her for support.

I tapped her shoulder. "The mayor and her husband are leaving," I told Julie. "Want to at least wave?"

She nodded, hitched a smile onto her face, and walked over to say good-bye.

Will came to stand beside me. "You are an absolute professional. You were perfect tonight." He looked at his hands like he wasn't sure what to do with them.

I shook my head. "I'm sad."

"I know. Me too." His arm hovered an

inch above my shoulder, but he looked around and lowered it back to his side.

I could feel my shoulders, tight and tense, under my dress. My body felt like I hadn't taken a normal breath in hours. And it didn't have anything to do with worry over my patched zipper situation. "Thanks for being here. And thanks for helping set up."

He put his fingers on the back of my dress. "You know it. I want to stay, but I'm having trouble with gravity. The earth and sky keep trading places."

I shook my head. "No, of course." I reached up and patted his face. It was burning hot. "Oh, Will. You're so sick. Go home. Medicate. Rest. And really, really thank you." I turned him toward the parking lot and pushed him a little.

A few seconds later, I found Mac sitting under a tree. He shoved a frosted pastry into his mouth and stood up.

"Enjoy your fifteen-dollar cookie?"

He brushed crumbs from his face. "You handled that great, Greta."

I tried to smile, but my facial muscles rebelled in exhaustion. He could tell because his arm went around my back like he wanted to lift me out of this night, out of this lot, out of my life for a while.

He stood with me for several minutes, letting me breathe. He'd opened the buttons of his jacket, and I could see his pickup T-shirt flashing its message to the straggling crowd. I let my head rest on his shoulder for a minute, breathing in the bitter coffee smell of his horrible shirt. ("If I told you that you have a beautiful body, would you hold it against me?")

When I was ready to face reality, I squeezed around his waist and smiled up at him. "Thanks for being here tonight."

"I wouldn't have missed it."

My breath came out half a laugh, half a huff. "Eleanor Richtenberg would — did. She totally missed it."

He pulled me close again. "True. She missed. She lost. But you didn't. You were here. And look — all these people were here for your thing, your place." He gestured in a vague manner at the napkins littering the lawn, the folding chairs that no longer had any resemblance to the ordered rows of a few hours before, the crumby trays that had once held really good cookies.

"I never want anyone to tell me how much money we had to give back to these people. If you ever find out a dollar amount of refunds, promise me you'll never tell."

He crossed his heart. "I'll write it down on a piece of paper. Then I'll scribble the numbers out. Then I'll burn the paper. Then I'll scrape up the ashes and eat them."

"Gross."

"Maybe, but I'm willing to do anything for you."

"Really? Like what?"

He took a breath. "I'd take you to see that movie. The one all the girls in the coffee shop talk about. With the guy? And the dog? And the thing by the lake?"

"Wow. That is . . . sacrificial. What else?"

When he rubbed his hand along the side of his face, I could hear the stubble scritching under his fingers. "I would write you love poetry."

My heart stopped. For a long, long time. I couldn't breathe. He said *love.* Out loud. I heard it. Love. I forced my eyebrows up and asked for a sample. Then I went back to totally freaking out while he chewed on the edge of his thumb and pondered poetry.

"Now?" I said.

"When I get home."

I smiled up into his perfect face and said, "Then you better hurry home."

He tucked a piece of my hair behind my ear. "What if you don't like it?"

"Do you think I'd laugh?" I thought about the weird things he'd said before and about how I'd decided to forget things were weird.

"I wouldn't laugh. If I didn't like it, I'd hold in all my criticism. Because criticism breaks the spirit, you know."

He leaned close to my ear. I felt his voice more than heard it. "Please don't break my spirit."

He leaned in to kiss me, but I dodged and hid my face in his chest. I was so not up for making out at the scene of my latest failure. I hugged him and took a deep breath and tried not to think about anything.

"Good night," I said, and watched him walk away.

I moved through the motions of folding up the chairs and stacking them on racks. I hardly felt the times I banged my shins and scratched my arms. When my phone chimed, I saw this:

I sat in a folding chair on the lawn at the library this evening, watching you save the library, and wishing I could follow you everywhere, watch you, listen to you, soak in your thoughts and your beauty.

When I got home, I got on the computer before I even attempted to unstitch myself from my dress. I opened the window that held my virtual shopping cart, doubled my order, and clicked BUY NOW.

CHAPTER 26

Un-sewing myself from the black dress was inelegant and permanent. The dress would still look good on a hanger — as long as nobody turned it around.

Mac texted.

Did you make it home?

Thanks. Yes. Ready to tell me something?

Like what?

My soul is dry. Water it with poetry.

He didn't reply right away. I didn't want him to feel pressured.

I'll wait.

While he composed, I stared at myself in the mirror. Things weren't looking so great in the reflection. My face seemed to have aged during the course of the evening. I'd thought the black circles under my eyes came from mascara, but when I'd washed it off, the dark smudges remained. That'd be awesome, I thought, if the bruised-looking marks stayed there forever. I pressed my fingers into my face, hoping to squeeze away the pressure.

No luck.

I checked my phone. Nothing yet. The muse must have had the night off. It certainly wasn't working for me during the Richtenberg Fiasco, when I was inventing a monologue on the spot. Stupid muse. I could really have used it earlier.

I poked at a scratch on my shin, watching it turn from red to white and back to red. A surrounding bruise, red and blue now, would be dark purple by tomorrow. That was a relief. I needed something visible, obvious, to mark the stupid day. Nothing was worse than when you got hurt and nobody could see it to feel sorry for you.

I checked the phone again. Nothing.

Picking up the black dress, I pinched the broken threads from around the zipper, dropping each tiny, wrinkled string into a pile. The zipper went from the lower back to the middle of my shoulders. The string pile grew to golf-ball size. Still nothing from Mac.

At this rate I would have to go clean the bathroom or something.

I needed someone to tell me something good.

Will? Are you up?

No answer.

I put on my shoes and went outside. The streets were dark, but I was only going a few blocks. I'd take my chances. Besides, the odds of anything menacing happening were low. This was Franklin, Ohio. I pulled the sleeves of my hoodie over my knuckles and turned the corner. Franklin was sleeping.

When I got to his apartment, I could see his bedroom light was off, but I didn't care. I needed my Will.

I threw a pebble against his window. It made a thump that seemed to me like a sonic boom, but nothing happened inside. I walked closer, picked up another pebble, and threw it. This time I heard a crash inside, like Will had knocked over a table full of dishes or something.

I walked over so I could see in the window better.

He clicked on his lamp and opened the window. His hair stood up in seventeen directions, none of them intentional. He shoved his glasses on and squinted into the dark.

"Greta?"

"Who else would it be?"

He coughed for a whole minute.

"Are you still sick?"

He tried to laugh, but the cough overtook it.

When he caught his breath, he said, "What makes you ask me that?"

"I'm sorry. I wasn't thinking. Sorry. Go back to bed. Good night."

"No, I'm up now. What's up? What do you need?"

I shook my head. "It's nothing. I had a crappy night, as you know, and I wanted to talk to you."

"You wanted to talk to *me*?" He sounded surprised. And maybe a little doubtful.

"Well, yeah." I left it at that. Because that part was true. The fact that he wasn't my first choice could be left unstated, obviously.

He turned around and picked up something off the floor. "You texted me." He waved his phone at the window.

"Yeah, but I guess you were pretty tired."

He whispered a mild curse and looked at

me with surprise, which he tried to hide.

"What was that for?" I asked.

"I really, really hate missing texts."

"It's one text. No big deal."

"Right."

He coughed again and bent down so I couldn't see him. The cough kept him doubled over for a minute, but it took longer for him to resurface. When he did, he said, "I'm sure you don't want to talk about it, but I wanted to say that you handled today like a complete champion."

I shook my head. "I was a mess."

"Nobody's saying you weren't disappointed in how things happened — didn't happen — whatever." He stopped talking to cough again. "But nobody could have handled it better. You were graceful and eloquent and funny and generous and bouncy. You did a really good job."

"Bouncy?"

He shook his head. "Not like cheerleader-bouncy. Like you bounced back. Give me a break — I was asleep two minutes ago. I'm trying to tell you you're good."

I breathed those words in like they were clean air. "Thank you for telling me I'm good. I need to hear it. Regularly."

My phone buzzed. Mac. "Speaking of things I love to hear," I said, shaking my phone at him. "Thanks for keeping me company."

He smiled. "I hope he says all the right things. Good night, Greta."

Turning, I waved over my shoulder. "Night."

I didn't wait to get back to the sidewalk. I looked at Mac's message with my back to Will's window.

Today's poem is a haiku. In case you don't remember, it's Japanese. But in English: You never need to / Worry where I'll be. I'm here / For you every day.

I smiled at the phone. I might have laughed, and I might have sighed.

I thought maybe you fell asleep.

After I sent it, I started walking back toward my place.

No.

Long pause.
I almost sent back a follow up, but after walking another minute or two, I got this:

The only thing I love more than falling

asleep thinking of you is staying awake talking with you.

I stood still on the sidewalk in the middle of a block. Partly because I didn't care who saw me. Partly because I couldn't text and walk at the same time. I texted Will.

Ack. I'm melting. Mac is GOOD.

Yeah? How good?

Did I mention melting?

Mac again.

Sorry it took me so long to get back with you. I was thinking of the way you laugh and trying to make it turn into music. The music is never melodic enough.

Melodic? Mac had never said a word like that out loud; I'd bet on it.

How come you text so differently than you speak?

I knew he'd take some time to answer that one, so I shot another text to Will.

You know how some people can be different when you can't see them? Mac is like that.

Will answered first.

Like what?

Like, boring people can be funny online. Lazy people sound busy on the phone. Mac is more articulate in texts than in person.

Does it bug you?

I stopped again to key in my answer.

Not at all. I think it's fabulous that he tries harder when it's just for me.

He does try. That's obvious.

You always understand what's going on. That's why you're my favorite.

I decided to go as far as the next block before I stopped to type again. Will beat me to it.

Let's not overstate things here, Greta. Everyone knows I'm not your favorite.

That took the wind out of me.

Hey, now. Not fair.

Sorry. You're right. Tired. Sick. Sorry. Good night.

Mac came back.

I don't know why it's easier to say what I need to say to you when you're not looking at me. Maybe I can speak straight from my heart to yours when all the physical disappears.

Are you that easily distracted?

A minute later:

By you? Maybe. But maybe it's more. Maybe I want to know that what we have is more than how we look.

That's fair. I can see how you might be concerned that girls go for you because of how you look. You look really good. Really, really good. But. Don't freak out. Here's something I've wanted to tell you for a long time. Obviously it was your face and your hair and your eyelashes and your smile and your arms and your Everything To Look At that I noticed first. But the talking and the poetry and the messages — that's when I really fell for you.

Really? Talking?

Mostly this. Texting. When you really started saying things.

And talking out loud?

Sure. But you know — you text differently.

Better?

Obviously. How did I answer that?

More thoughtfully.

Smarter?

Yes. Definitely. About a thousand times.

Not necessarily.

I'm not dumb.

What?

Where did that come from?

I'm not dumb.

Of course you're not. You're deep and thoughtful and artistic and amazing. Maybe you need time to process what you're going to say. I don't mind. I love to hear it however it comes.

The answer came fast.

I'm not dumb.

Again.
I stopped on the sidewalk again to key in all the words.

Did you not get my reply? I know you're not. Nobody dumb could write the things you write. You're brilliant. You're spectacular. You're the whole package.

I walked an entire block before his reply came in.

I'm tired.

Okay. Have a good sleep. Talk to you tomorrow?

Come by on your way to work. Try not to be disappointed when I talk to you.

What was I supposed to do with that?

Never disappointed.

I put my phone in my pocket and it vibrated again almost immediately.

Did you make it home yet?

Will.

Not yet. I'm at Grants Pass Road.

You're not in a hurry.

I can't text and walk at the same time. I'd fall on my face.

Turn around and walk back this way. I'll meet you. I won't cough on you. I'll bring a blanket.

I walked back toward Will's place. In a block and a half, we met. He wrapped me up in a fleece that smelled like microwave popcorn. He shoved his hands into his hoodie pouch.

I walked up right beside him and put my head on his shoulder. "I'm sorry I say the wrong thing sometimes." I hated to even bring it up, but I hated more thinking he was hurt.

He took a deep breath before answering.

"You didn't. You're perfect. I just don't like to share. I believe we have discussed this before." His little boy smile looked like it always had. He nodded to a tree, and we sat down on the grass beneath it.

I positioned myself right up next to him. "Is that what we're doing? Sharing?"

He wrinkled up his nose. "Sounds creepy when you say it that way, doesn't it?" His laugh turned into a cough. "So, how's Mac?"

I was going to say fine. I was going to say perfect. I was going to say great. "Weird."

"What kind of weird?" he asked. "Wait. Do I want to know?"

I shifted on the damp grass. "I don't know. Eloquent one minute, and the next, just weird."

"Weird like quoting movies you've never heard of?"

"Weird like shifting from poet to caveman."

Will sat with his back against the chainlink fence. His heel tapped against the grass. "Maybe he has a multiple personality disorder."

I didn't say anything.

"Maybe you make him nervous."

I shook my head.

"Maybe he's sustained a traumatic head

injury." He didn't even sound sorry at the possibility.

I was finished brooding now. "Good thing whatever hit him didn't ruin his face." We both laughed.

"Right. Or his hair."

"I know, right? That would be a real tragedy. I mean, it's a shame that his personality shifts in the middle of a conversation. But if his hair was hurt? That would be bad."

"So what kind of personality shift are we talking about?"

"Minor." I stretched my legs out in front of me. "One minute it's all poetry and the next it's really defensive."

"Defensive beats offensive, I believe."

I nodded. "You're totally right. And because you thought I was being shallow, I've been paying attention to the things I like about him." He started to interrupt, but I didn't want to hear an excuse or an apology. I shook my head and kept talking. "He's a good guy. He's nice. And he's generous. And he's complimentary. And so what if I might sometimes wonder if he's looking up compliments on the internet before he gives them? He still says them beautifully. Tonight was weird. I told him I was falling for the text version of him, and he seemed like he wanted me to promise he was still hot. He is, by the way. Totally still hot."

Will leaned his head down. I couldn't see his face.

"Sorry. That was probably gross on every level." I pulled myself off the wet grass. "I should go to sleep. You should go to sleep. Your doctor would not love me if she knew I had you out here in the wee smalls sitting on wet grass."

Grunting, he hauled himself to his feet. Holding on to the trunk of the tree, he said, "Greta? Is it really the text version you love?"

"Did I say love?"

"You know what I mean."

I did know what he meant. Exactly. "I don't know." He deserved a better answer than that, but I didn't know how to put it.

He started to turn away, and I held on to his hand. "Wait."

He turned back and put his other hand on top of mine, sandwiching my hand between his.

I looked up at him. "I think it's all the versions. Except maybe the defensive part. He's the real deal, Willie-boy."

Will leaned over, my hand still between his. He kissed my forehead and whispered in my ear, "I'm happy for you. You deserve

305

the best, you know."

"Thanks. Good night."

"Night."

CHAPTER 27

I knew the next day would be an awful one at the library. I also knew that Eleanor Richtenberg's no-show was not my fault. One of those facts outweighed the other. Not so much in my favor. I spent the day organizing and preparing all the rented furniture for loading. Once it was carted away, I cleared out several more boxes from the basement and scanned documents and pictures for hours. It was two before I realized I hadn't eaten anything all day.

At four o'clock, Will walked in to the library with a huge tray in his hands. He headed for the circulation desk. Kevin sat at the computer in the corner answering emails with a polite form message: "We appreciate hearing from you. As soon as we can work out all the formalities, we will refund your ticket purchases, minus a small processing fee." Instead of doing a copy-and-paste, he was typing each message word by word, almost singing the words as he went. It was aggressively cheerful and, frankly, getting scary after a few times.

Julie was in her office, maybe hiding, maybe not. Will came over to the desk and stood in front of me. He pointed with his eyes at the giant plate of brownies balancing in front of him. Because of course he thought to bring the library staff a huge plate of brownies the day after the failed fundraiser. This was Will, after all. I reached over and lifted the brownies off what I thought was a tray. It wasn't. It was a huge wooden picture frame.

"Is Ms. Julie here?" Will asked in his most polite, cultivated library voice.

"She is busy in her office. Can I help you?" I smiled back at him.

"Actually, she might want to see this."

I waved toward her window to get her attention, but she didn't look up. I went over and knocked on her door. "A patron has something for you," I said.

"Is it a box of rotten fruit?" I was pretty sure she was joking, but I shook my head no, just in case she meant it. I could tell by her posture as she walked to the desk that maybe she meant it.

"I have something I'd like to give you," Will said, handing the frame across the counter. When Julie saw it, she made an O shape with her mouth, but no sound came out. She held the frame and stared for a long minute. Then she held it up for me to see.

Half of the large frame was filled with the photo of Joshua Silver and Dr. King standing outside the library. The other half held a copy of the old newspaper article about Dr. King's visit to Franklin.

Julie wasn't saying anything, so I said, "Wow. That looks great."

Will smiled his thanks. "I thought it might look really nice hanging on the wall."

Julie still didn't say anything. I moved to take the frame out of her hands, but she pulled it toward her. "This is beautiful. Thank you for thinking of us." She put out her right hand, and Will shook it. I could tell she was trying not to get emotional.

"I'm really glad you like it. But I brought brownies in case you didn't."

She looked where he pointed. "Those are beautiful, too." She set the frame on the desk and stepped over to the wall. She pulled a painting off a nail and up went Dr. Silver and Dr. King.

"They look perfect there," Julie said to Will. "This is lovely of you." Then she turned to me. "You," she said quietly, "are a lucky girl. Hold on to this one."

My mouth might have flopped open trying to deny that I was holding on to Will. She sounded like she thought he was my boyfriend. And that was not even close to the case. But obviously I should keep him around. Ack. What? I had no idea what I was supposed to say. Or think.

I picked up the plate and held it out to Julie. "Brownie?"

When I walked up my porch steps that night, I almost ran into a box at the door. Not just a box. *The* box. I lifted the corner with my shoe so I could get my hands under it. It weighed a ton. Lurching and staggering, I managed to get the box into my arms and stand almost upright. Who would have thought that forty skinny metal signs and stakes and eighty magnet sheets could weigh so much? I guess everyone who thinks about mass and volume.

I am nobody who thinks about mass and volume.

Once I was standing nearly vertical, I balanced the box against the door and turned the knob.

Locked. Of course. Because I'm not an idiot. I lock my door when I leave my apartment.

I slid the box down the door and held it against my bent knee with one hand. The other hand fished around inside my bag for keys. I pulled out two packs of gum, a broken pencil, a pen with yellow ink that was practically invisible, and a bracelet I hadn't seen in months. The box tipped dangerously to the left, and I dropped everything else to steady it. I reclaimed the bag from the ground, shook it, and totally heard the keys. They were in there somewhere; all I had to do was keep digging. Or dump.

I poured the contents of the bag onto the box that was cutting off my circulation. Aha! Keys.

All the other bag fodder slid onto the porch as I unlocked the door and pushed it open. The box nearly dropped to the floor, but I didn't let it, because my toes were down there.

Upon inspection, I found what I expected to find.

They were magnetic signs, the kind people slap on the sides of their cars to advertise their business. Innocuous, simple: "Don't Forget to Vote on November 6" in red, white, and blue. With stars. I'd ordered them in bulk from a sign vendor. I didn't use library money. This was personal.

I stuck the magnetic signs on top of the other signs, lining up edges perfectly and hiding the message underneath. They looked seamless. Then I hauled a few at a time through the neighborhood, on the public access ways, and on busy corners surrounding the library.

I shoved the metal legs of the signs into the grass. I knew if I waited another week the lawns could freeze, and it might be too hard to slide the bars in. I didn't need this project to have any elements that were too hard, so I took another breath and another "Don't Forget to Vote" sign and planted it for everyone to see.

CHAPTER 28

A text rang in on my phone.

Today has been a beautiful day. Make it more beautiful by showing me your face.

Hi, Mac.

What are you doing?

I looked around my apartment. I had straightened up enough that a casual visitor wouldn't know how much I hated cleaning. There was a thriller I'd checked out from the library sitting open, upside down on the arm of a chair, waiting for me to come back and read it. My "Daisy Buchanan thinks you're a beautiful little fool" mug sat on a coaster holding the cold dregs of last night's cinnamon tea.

I thumbed in a message to Mac.

I am doing literally nothing.

Even without making plans, you manage to shape the movement of the world with your brilliance and your vibrancy.

Wow. That was awesome. What would you have said if I told you I was replacing all the ductwork in my building?

Every step you take brings this world closer to the perfect vision you have of it.

Not bad. Not bad at all.

Want to come over?

Yeah.

If you're hungry, please bring food. My fridge is bare.

So many things to do besides eat.

Exactly. I'm going to put you to work.

Not work.

Did he mean he didn't want to work? Or what he was planning wasn't work? Either way.

You're perfect for this job.

You going to pay me?

Depends.

I spent the next ten minutes brushing my teeth and organizing my hair. I actually did have work for Mac and me to do, but it didn't hurt to help things along. When he rang the bell, I opened the door to see him smiling, holding a bright yellow sunflower.

"Hi," I said, smiling. "You didn't have to bring me anything."

He cleared his throat and, with a look of intense concentration, said, "Like a sunflower moves through the day following the sun's light, I watch for you from sunrise to sunset." Then he nodded to himself, stepped inside, and pulled me close to him. His kiss was sweet and tender, growing more intense as he moved us toward the couch.

"So I wasn't kidding about making you work today," I said as I leaned away from him.

He shifted closer and put his hands around my waist. "Play first," he said, kissing me again. He broke away and whispered in my ear, "Work later."

I laughed and kissed him back, but pulled

back after a minute. "Okay, so here's what I need."

He made a gesture that seemed to tell me not to worry. "Pretty sure I know what you need." He reached for me again.

"Mac, I'm serious," I said, still smiling at him but moving up onto the side of the couch. I held my arms out straight in front of me like I would somehow try to push him away. Yeah, right. "Help me write some tweets for the library."

He looked at me like I'd sprouted an alien head.

"For real?"

I nodded and picked up my phone. "Totally. Help me come up with some good tweets to remind the public that they love the library."

He pointed from his face to my face and said, "Are you actually stopping this" — and then he pointed to my phone — "for that?"

"You're a natural. Come on. Write a few tweets for me, and then we can watch a movie or something."

"I vote for the Or Something." He was awfully attractive when he was trying to convince me to kiss him.

"Focus, please." I think I was talking to both of us.

He shoved over as far from where I was

sitting as he could while still remaining on the couch. "Fine. Focused. What do you want?"

I explained that I needed to keep interest in our library going, and that most of my librarian account followers were people who worked in libraries in other communities. "So I just need a few tweets that I can send out over the next couple of weeks. Keep Franklin in people's minds."

"Why do you want my help? You're a good writer."

I slid over next to him. "But you're the best. Please?" I grinned and batted my eyes. He leaned in and kissed me. I moved away again. "No. Wait. Words first."

He let out an aggrieved sigh. "Okay. 'Support your library.' Now get over here."

I laughed. "Try again, please."

"I am trying. So, so much." He was fake-whining.

I knew exactly what he was trying for. "Try to write me some good tweets."

"Right. That. Um, 'Books are good? Go read something?' "

I stared at him.

"No? How about 'We need our library.' Is that better?"

My head shook without my permission.

"Okay." He nodded. "I know. Put your

317

face on it. Tweet a picture of you and the words 'Check me out at the library.' People will pour into the place."

My heart thudded in a decidedly non-romantic way. My jaw clenched and I moved away. "That is sweet of you," I said as I stood up from the couch. "But not at all helpful. Can't you come up with a few great one-liners? About the library? Please?" I wasn't sure I could have explained why I was getting so upset. I told myself that it wasn't his job to organize my social media presence. *He's here,* I told myself. He was flirting like crazy. He was interested in me. *And look at him,* I kept telling myself.

He shrugged his shoulders and held out his hand to me. "Maybe I need some inspiration."

We got all kinds of inspired over the next few minutes, but when I asked again for some ideas, he kept coming back with nothing. And I mean, really nothing. After a little while of total non-productivity, I told him I was going to my mom's house for dinner.

I was not going to my mom's house for dinner.

"Do you want me to drive you over?" he asked.

"That's sweet, but I need to get a few things done first."

He picked up his jacket and headed for the door. "Have fun with your mom," he said, as if that were even a faint possibility.

"Thanks." I managed a smile, even though what I was thinking was less smiley. As I kissed him again and closed the door, I let myself rage just a bit. Why wouldn't he give me something for the library? Why wouldn't he use his great one-liners to help me? Was it really asking so much for him to redirect his cleverness from wooing to saving?

I needed Will.

I called his cell. "Are you busy?"

"I am grading essays written by really nice kids who can't remember to capitalize the first word of a sentence."

"Don't their computers do that for them?" I asked.

"See? It's attitudes like that that cause all our society's problems."

"All of them?" I said, flopping down on the couch.

He laughed. "I stand by my emotional overstatement — *all.*" I heard him click shut his laptop. "What are you doing?"

"Coming up with clever tweets about the library." Which obviously I'd been failing to do. I inspected my fingernails.

"Oh, like that Einstein quote? 'The only thing you absolutely have to know is the location of the library.' How's that?'"

"Did he really say that?"

Will made a *psht* noise. "If not, it's the kind of thing you can research at the library."

I pulled a pen and a notebook off the side table. "More please."

"Hang on." I heard him open his laptop again and start typing. "Okay. How about this? Doris Lessing. 'A public library is the most democratic thing in the world. . . . If you read, you can learn to think for yourself.' There's more in there, and it's really good, but you'd go over your characters."

"That's awesome. What else have you got?"

"Ray Bradbury said, 'Libraries raised me.' Ooh, listen. He also said, 'You don't have to burn books to destroy a culture. Just get people to stop reading them.' This guy's quotes are on fire." He did his over-the-top pun laugh. Because he was being so useful, I laughed too.

I heard him clicking some more on his keyboard. "Jorge Luis Borges said, 'Paradise will be a kind of library.' I don't know who that is, but I like him."

I sat up. "I do. He was from Argentina. He wrote magical realism and short stories.

That's a good one. Hang on." I put his call on hold and opened my librarian Twitter account. "Borges: 'Paradise will be a kind of library.' Don't wait for heaven! Go to the library. #SaveFranklinLibrary"

I patched back to the call. "Thank you for helping me with this. You're a peach."

"Mmm," Will said. "Peaches. Of course I'll help you. This is important to you, so it's important to me."

That stopped me. I couldn't answer him. I couldn't make the right words come out, and I was afraid of the wrong ones. It was important to me. Obviously. And so it was important to Will. Because Will loved me. So why wasn't it important to Mac?

I listened and took notes as Will continued to research what cool people said about libraries.

"Did you tweet that Argentine guy?" Will asked.

"Yeah."

"Save this one for tomorrow: 'A library is not a luxury, but one of the necessities of life.' Henry Ward Beecher. That's timely."

I scribbled it down.

Will shouted into the phone. "This! Ready? This is the one. Eleanor Crumble-hulme. Hang on." He spelled out her name to me and then typed some more on his keyboard. I loved hearing that sound come through the phone. "Okay, she's a Canadian librarian. Ready? 'Cutting libraries during a recession is like cutting hospitals during a plague.' We have to get that on a shirt for you. And you need to follow this woman on Twitter. Her name alone should make you love her forever."

I felt myself getting weepy. My throat went thick. "Totally. Will, thank you for doing this. This means a lot to me."

"No big deal."

I actually could not speak for a couple of seconds. My voice shook with emotion. "No. Really, really big deal. Thank you for caring about my thing."

He paused before he said, "I care about all your things. You know that."

"I do. I know that." I needed to hang up, because I was getting teary. "Bye."

"Bye."

CHAPTER 29

I found Julie hunched over with her nose an inch from a computer monitor. I didn't ask, but I walked really close to her chair so she'd notice me.

She did. But I didn't hear any "glad you're here" words. She was in grunting mode.

After I clocked in and stashed my bag, she pointed to the monitor so I could see what she was reading. It was an online version of the weekly paper. We had one of those? The site had a section where a reader could access all the letters to the editor by subject. Julie slid her cursor up and down pages and pages of text.

Apparently people had opinions about the library bond. After a few more minutes of reading and scrolling, Julie slid her chair out from the desk and rubbed her eyes.

I pointed to the screen. "Can I?"

She held the chair out for me and nodded. She didn't leave, though. She leaned over my shoulder and read the letters again.

The citizens of this community work hard for their money. They support multiple programs, endeavors, and policies. But the funding for pet projects is not the job of the government. Basic needs are being met by the tax dollars we willingly pay. No one should ask us for more to support something that should be privatized. Bring your little library into the twenty-first century and get your own funding. Let our neighbors keep the money they work so hard to earn. Vote no on Bond Proposition 4.

Jerry Mandalay
Concerned Citizen

Dear Editor,
  Mr. Mandalay clearly misunderstands the long and storied tradition of public libraries as a government institution.

There was a long paragraph that I skipped, even though the writer amused me with her "storied" pun, but I didn't care at the moment for her take on the historical value of American library system and Benjamin Franklin. She ended with this:

We are happy to keep the library we have, but we don't need to spend more money. What we have is enough. I'll also vote No.

Stephanie Wilkins
Bonner's Glade

The library has the same books that have been there since I was a child. We should be reading the classics. Everything new is smut and filth anyway. Let's make do with what there is and be grateful that we have any books at all. Vote No. Keep it clean.

Julie's eye roll was practically audible. I didn't say anything.

As a member of the city council, I plan to listen carefully to all sides of the library bond issue. I have had opportunities to hear from citizens and library patrons and developers, and I refuse to come to a snap judgment. I hope all the voters in this town will do the same. Become educated. Inform yourself. Talk to people. Take into consideration what is best for this community that we love.

Ms. Marnie Blum, attorney
City Council Member

Julie shook her head. "You know when people try to be so fair that they say a lot while saying absolutely nothing? If I ever need a lawyer, remind me not to call Ms. Marnie Blum, attorney."

Everyone needs a library! The soul of Franklin resides in that rickety old Victorian house. Walk inside. Breathe in the glow. Allow it to penetrate your barriers and move you to greatness.
Mary Elise Gold
University Student

I resisted saying a word. Any word. In fact, I held my breath well into the next letter. Because an ill-timed snort about souls and barrier penetration could ruin this day. But I bet Marigold would have loved that one.

I love that beautiful old building. If the library has to close, I hope the city will turn it into a gallery for the community artists to exhibit their work.
Mr. Henry Tran

Julie blew out a breath and popped two green gummy bears into her mouth. "Has Mr. Henry Tran ever come inside this beautiful old building? Did he manage not to see any of the local art we display every single day? Dear Mr. Tran, let's add a new pair of glasses to the bond for you." She swept a stack of waste paper into the recycle bin. "Why do we even write letters to newspapers anymore? Does anyone even read the paper? And who needs a newspaper when we can Google anything in the universe? And while we're at it, who needs paper at all? Honestly, can you think of anything" — her sarcasm tuned to fake innocence — "anything at all that is better with paper than without it?" With a pointed look at the restroom and a shrug, she went back into her office, muttering.

There was one more letter.

Who Needs the Library:
An Honest Look Inside

In the upcoming election, voters will see an article on the ballot for a tax increase. This tax will serve to give our town's public library an even larger percentage of tax revenue. If voters look honestly at the situation, they will come to see that the library is an outmoded and unnecessary piece of Americana that we can allow to bow gracefully out of our community.

The library is a place to find and borrow books. Books are available for free online or from multiple retailers. Most of us have digital reading devices in our mobile phones, in our computers, and on our other handheld devices.

Once, libraries were a research facility. Now, every man, woman and child can access a wealth of information on every subject imaginable from the comfort of home. The thousands of dollars spent on reference materials, outdated almost before they reach the shelves, are dollars better spent on useful civic projects.

Libraries do not support authors. Thirty, fifty, or a hundred families may read the same borrowed copy of a book, but the author sees royalty for only one sale.

Libraries have become free day-care centers where parents drop off their children and come back for them hours later. This is not an activity that should be paid for through our taxes.

In this digital age, the library of yesteryear is but a glowing memory. We do not need a library, and the one we have certainly does not deserve a greater portion of our money.

Vote No next week and let the memory of the Franklin library rest in peace.

I clicked the browser window closed. Well.

At least we knew how people felt.
And I felt sick.

CHAPTER 30

Saturday.

I slid my bag under the desk. Julie was on the phone, so I mouthed, "Morning."

She flicked her wrist in a small hello wave. Then she pointed to a padded envelope on the counter. It had my name on it. I hadn't ordered anything, but here something was. A surprise package. A present.

No return address.

Stamped in town, though.

How mysterious.

I ripped open the envelope, unwilling to drag out the mystery. Inside was a folded piece of fabric. I pulled it out and shook it.

A black T-shirt with white letters across the front: "Check Me Out." There was a graphic of book spines under it.

I carried the shirt to the workroom in the back. It almost covered the little table when I stretched it out. I shot a photo of it with my phone and sent the image to Will.

What is this?

He responded within a minute.

Looks like something Mac would wear. If he worked with books.

Did he send it to me?

?

He didn't say anything to you?

Not about T-shirts. Or books. Or checking him out. Or checking you out.

That narrows it down considerably. Thanks for that.

There was a pause.

Maybe he's showing you he cares about what matters to you.

Well, that would be a pleasant change.

That makes this whole thing far more ador-able than freaky.

Perspective — it's what I offer.

331

That's why I keep you around. Time for working.

Go deliver culture and entertainment to the masses.

Right. While I still can.

Have a good day.

You too.

I picked up the T-shirt and held it out in front of me. I stared at it for a few minutes. I wondered what Julie would say if I put it on. I could imagine a few different responses she might have to using me as visual propaganda. The thought amused me for a minute. I realized I should probably do something more work-related than stare at a T-shirt, so I grabbed a handful of thumbtacks and hung the shirt on the bulletin board.

Grabbing the recycling box from the corner of the workroom, I went to the front desk and added the papers and cans from that bin. Julie was still on the phone, so I pointed to the box in front of me and nodded toward the Dumpster outside.

The only benefit of having Mr. Greenwood for a neighbor was that we could tuck our ugly green commercial mini-Dumpster up against his side of the lot and people wouldn't connect it to the library at all. It almost disappeared among the piles of trash spilling across his yard.

A once-blue metal barrel leaned next to the green trash box, slightly holey from decades of rust. Tetanus waiting to happen, that's what it looked like. I peeked inside the barrel. I knew it was weird even as I was in mid-lean, but I wanted to see what was in there. An old rubber tire, or what was left of it, kept the barrel from crumbling to the ground.

A stack of moldering phone books, probably from the decade before I was born, lay piled beside the barrel. I almost picked them up and put them in the recycling bin, but the thought of touching them with my bare hands? No thanks. I shook the recycling from inside box to outside bin and turned back to the library. From this angle, I could see the stained glass windows. The maple tree shading the backyard was starting to drop its red leaves.

I stood staring at the windows, my breath leaving little clouds in the air.

Today was Saturday. The election was Tuesday. How long would it take them to shut us down if the vote went badly? A week? A month? These were questions I couldn't ask Julie. And even if the people voted for a new building, what would happen to this place I had worked in for so many years? What would happen to me? I'd built an identity around this place. I loved this building like it was capable of returning the feeling.

The vote couldn't go badly.

But I knew it really could.

My stomach hurt. And my arms couldn't seem to decide if they were having a shiver or if they'd been punched. Like there was a stretch in there that I couldn't get out.

I turned around and kicked the barrel. It rang out with a sickly clang. I kicked it again. Pieces of the rusty metal flaked off from around the holes. I kicked it again and wondered how long I'd have to work to make a real dent. One more kick. It didn't make a dent in the barrel, but may have broken my toes. Ow. I wasn't really done punishing the stupid barrel, but if I kicked it again, I'd cry, and there was no way I was touching that thing with my hands. Stupid.

They'll vote for the tax increase, I told myself. *People are basically decent,* I told myself. *My signs will work,* I told myself.

And the signs *under* the other signs would

work. My signs had to work.

We'll see, I told myself.

CHAPTER 31

Thirty-nine. I had to rearrange thirty-nine more signs. The first one was in front of my apartment building, and the next was only a couple of blocks away, at the corner by the convenience store. I waited until the sun went down, so I'd be a little more subtle. I knew traffic wouldn't be a huge issue on a Sunday evening in Franklin, but I expected at least a few cars to slow down and notice me. Nothing. I leaned over the sign, pulled the outer magnet off, and revealed the sign beneath it. I allowed myself a smile as I re-attached the "Don't Forget to Vote" part underneath, to the metal legs. Both sides. Now the real message stood out above the generic one, out there for everyone to read.

Could it be that easy? I wondered.

After seventeen signs (times two magnets each), my fingers were screaming in pain. It was cold. Really, really cold. And a tiny bit creepy alone in the dark. I started to wish

I'd asked someone to help me. Mac would have been my first option, but Mac might have requested that we take a break after unmasking each sign to kiss. Not exactly an efficiency boost.

I could have asked Will to help me. He would have. But he wasn't exactly . . . subtle. When a car came around, I could slink into a shadow. Will did not slink. I amused myself for the next several signs imagining Will slinking, skulking, and scurrying in various situations. Before I knew it, I'd removed and replaced all the magnets. They now sat on the legs below the signs I'd intended for everyone in town to see, eventually.

Eventually was now.

I shifted the biggest sign from the grass patch in the library's front yard to the corner of the lot and jammed the metal legs into the ground. Pulling the magnetic "Vote" signs off this larger sign felt more real, more of a statement.

A statement that was about to get a little — or a lot — more clear.

I dragged Mr. Greenwood's rusty, holey barrel from the back of the lot up to the sign. It screeched across the gravel, completely unsubtle. Pulling on rubber work gloves, I went back for a pile of phone books. Then another. And one more. I leaned over the barrel and took a breath. It was time.

It only took a few seconds. The crinkly, crusty paper lit so fast that I practically ran off the lot and around the corner. Fine. My plan was to circle the block anyway. I slowed my steps as soon as I cleared the Greenwood house. I took deliberate steps past each house and building on the block. I checked my phone: 8:45. When I got half a block from the library, I turned around and started to circle the block again in the opposite direction.

I sent out a tweet from my librarian account. "Shut down the Franklin Library in November. Book burning party in December. #SaveFranklinLibrary #CheckOutTheLibrary"

I took as long as I could to walk without looking like I was loitering or waiting for something. By the time I got close to the library again, I could hear people muttering. Then I was there.

I smelled it before I saw it. The ugly, oily reek of rubber on fire. It rose through the air and hung there, close to my face. Inescapable. Rounding the corner at the Greenwood house, I saw the barrel. I tried to see it as a person seeing it for the first time: a

338

huge metal barrel like they have in construction sites on the side of the freeway standing in the lot beside the library's front door, belching black smoke. Ashy paper floated up and spun in the hot air.

Then I saw the sign. The one that I'd placed there. The largest. The last of the forty signs, looking sinister and horrible, all backlit with fire like that.

> Franklin may not have extra money,
> but the library's got books to burn.

I knew what it said. Of course I knew. I'd created the images and made the order, and I'd had the box of signs in my bedroom for weeks. I'd stuck every metal post into the ground, the "books to burn" message hidden beneath the innocent voting reminders. But seeing the total effect of what I'd done nailed me to the ground. I couldn't move. My feet felt glued to the sidewalk. Legs stiff, I lurched but still couldn't make my feet move.

Come on, feet, I told myself. *You have to keep walking.*

This was not how I'd planned it. This was, in fact, the opposite of a nonchalant stroll.

Becoming aware of the buzzing is the next thing I remember. The humming, muttering noise of a lot of people trying not to say the same thing very loudly. I turned my head away from the burning barrel and saw a decent crowd. It had only been about fifteen minutes, but the neighbors gathered. And probably made some calls. They stared at the sign. They pointed past me, or maybe at me. They shook disapproving heads.

They were horrified. Disgusted. Sickened. Angry.

No. This was not how it was supposed to happen. This was not the plan. They were supposed to be shocked by the message. They were supposed to be enraged on behalf of the library. They were supposed to be a tiny bit impressed. Not offended. Not revolted.

The crowd grew like crowds do, and I stayed stuck to the sidewalk.

I heard Julie. I shouldn't have been able to hear her, not over the crackling and popping of the fire, not over the grumbling crowd, but I did. I heard a gasp. A croaking, gagging sound. And I knew it was Julie. Her house was on the back of the next block, so it wouldn't have taken her long to get there. I slid farther into the shadow.

Turning toward her from my place on the outside of the crowd, I looked at a horror movie version of my boss. She stood at the edge of the parking lot, her face lit orange and shadowy from the fire. Eye sockets haunted and mouth drawn down, she looked ragged and frightening. Her head seemed to shake back and forth on its own; she didn't seem to have any will left. More ashen pages lifted on the air currents as she stared.

I knew what was burning. And even to my eyes, the fact that these were several years' worth of ancient telephone books didn't lessen the ghastliness of the whole thing.

All my clever ideas came down to this. What I'd done as a symbol — as a metaphor — became an ugly reality.

I knew I should go to her. She tipped dangerously to the side as she watched the black smoke rise out of the burning barrel. She could pass out. She could fall over in front of all these people, none of whom seemed to know what to do any more than I did.

But what if she asked me how this happened? Could I lie? Could I tell her I didn't know?

The firelight flickered orange through the oily black smoke. Other lights bounced off the smoke and the buildings. I looked around. Four police cars. Two fire trucks. A TV van with a dish on the roof. The red-

and-white ambulance. Ambulance? Someone was overreacting.

A couple of police officers pushed their way through what was by now a deep line of watchers. They took Julie inside the library, maybe to take her statement.

What kind of statement, I wondered. What could she say? She didn't know anything.

I stayed beside the oak tree. I couldn't go in there. I couldn't let them ask me anything. I couldn't say I didn't know. Because I knew more than anyone else knew. And all of a sudden, I really wanted to forget.

My phone buzzed in my pocket. It was Marigold.

"Where are you?" It didn't even sound like a question. It was a demand.

"I'm walking." Not true. I stood rooted to the sidewalk, but she didn't need to know that.

"You have to come down to the library."

I couldn't make any more words come out.

"Greta?"

"I heard. Are you there?"

"You heard what?" She sounded both excited and sick. I recognized the feelings.

"I heard you tell me to come." She was here somewhere. I looked around without moving too much, but I couldn't see her.

"Some activist is calling the people who won't vote for the tax increase Nazis."

"Mm." It was all I could manage.

"This is perfect for my paper."

I couldn't even grunt this time.

Her voice kept coming through my phone, way too pleased. "It's amazing. Fantastic. What a show." She laughed. "Wish I'd thought of it."

My ears started buzzing, and heat rushed up the back of my neck.

"I'm sick. Have to go." I clicked off my phone and turned away from the firelight. I leaned against Mr. Greenwood's monstrous oak tree, tipped my head up, and closed my eyes.

Breathe, I told myself. *Breathe in and out, and don't cry. And don't vomit.*

Those were a lot of directions for my brain to take in at once, so I repeated it all in my mind until I felt myself relaxing. Preparing myself to open my eyes, I took another smoky breath and felt a hand clench my shoulder.

I couldn't help it. I screamed. Then I opened my eyes and screamed again. If Mr. Greenwood was scary in the daytime, it was nothing to what he looked like in the spooky glow of a trash fire. His sunken cheeks looked twice as deep. Orange sparks reflected in his hooded eyes.

"Quiet, please." He didn't let go of my shoulder, but he pivoted me farther behind the tree. Blocked from the glow of the fire, he stopped looking like an ancient demon and resumed looking like an ancient grouchy man.

He stared at my face, and I tried not to think serial killer victim thoughts. His hand that was not clutching my shoulder was moving up and down between us, and I realized he was directing my breathing, guiding me to inhale and exhale. Staring at that moving hand was far easier and much less terrifying than looking at his face, so I watched his hand and felt myself calming. After a couple of minutes that could have been several lifetimes, he dropped both his arms to his sides. He reached into a pocket and handed me something. I was afraid to look, but I did it anyway. A perfectly folded square of fabric with a flower sewn into the corner. A handkerchief.

He pointed to my face. "Clean yourself up. Maybe you should breathe through it. This mess you've made is bound to make you sick." He gave me a pointed look and turned away. Somehow he knew it was me. Maybe he saw me. Walking slowly to his porch, he looked back and shook his head. The firelight did strange things to his face. It almost looked like he was smiling at me. Beckoning?

Weird. And scary.

I followed him anyway.

You will not, I told myself, *enter the house. You will not, for any reason, go beyond the porch.* My memory of the piles of rusty metal on the porch removed most of the comfort from that thought. All kinds of horrible things could happen to a person even on the porch.

When I got to the steps, I squinted to find Mr. Greenwood. He sat on the edge of a rusty metal chair, pointing to the swing at the side of the dark porch. I picked my way across without speaking, almost without breathing. What was I doing here?

When he spoke, his voice was quiet. "What's your plan?"

I wasn't sure how to answer that. Which plan could he be asking about? Was this conversation really even happening? He waited.

When I opened my mouth to speak, nothing came out. I cleared my throat and tried again. "I love the library. Lots of people do. I just thought I'd give people who hadn't quite decided how to vote a little nudge."

"That's your justification, not your plan."

"What?"

He cleared his throat. His voice sounded rusty, disused. "You seem like an intelligent person, and I would assume you know the difference between a justification for a previous action and a plan for a future one."

Who was this guy?

"Right. Yes. I do."

He waited.

"So. My plan. Wait for the vote?"

He said nothing.

"Okay, I guess I don't have a plan." I sneaked another look at him. My eyes had adjusted to the dark porch, and I saw him shake his head. But he was still smiling. So if he was planning to murder me with a broken yard decoration, at least he was happy about it.

"Mr. Greenwood, what am I doing here?"

He either coughed or laughed, but I swear, it sounded like he barked. When he started shaking his head, I decided he'd laughed. He got up from his chair and stepped close to me.

This is it, I thought. *The part where the camera pulls back and reveals the gullible young woman who has knowingly put herself into the clutches of Evil.*

When he was about a foot away from me,

he stopped and held out his hand. I put my hand in my pocket to give him back his handkerchief, but apparently he had something else in mind.

"It appears we have not been properly introduced. The last Mr. Greenwood to live in this house was my mother's father. My name is Joshua Silver."

CHAPTER 32

My gasp may have sucked in all the remaining air from the neighborhood. Several seconds passed before I noticed that the old man was waiting for me to shake his hand, introduce myself, or close my mouth. I couldn't manage to do any of those things.

"Joshua Silver? Dr. Joshua Silver? That's you?"

He nodded. "Joshua Greenwood Silver. And you're Greta, as I recall."

That bumped me out of the zone, and I took his offered hand. "Greta Roxanne Elliott."

"A pleasure to meet you officially, Miss Elliott."

He took a step back, but I didn't let go of his hand, and my mouth ran off without my brain. "You're my hero. You're the notorious civil-rights activist hero of Franklin. You're the man who integrated the Midwest. I have a historical crush on you." I slapped my other hand over my mouth to stop myself. A little too late.

"And you seem to have a tendency toward overstatement." He removed his hand from my clutch and turned to look at the lot and the gathering crowd. "You also have something of the activist in you."

Was he angry? He hadn't seemed angry before, but now his back was to me and I couldn't tell.

"Joshua Greenwood Silver?" This was probably not the most important part of the conversation we were having, but it was the part my brain stuck on. "Was your mom a Greenwood?"

He looked surprised. "Yes. Her name was Evelyn. She lived in this house."

I may have done another gasp. "I know. She sparked in the back garden with a man named Walt."

He either laughed or cleared his throat. Maybe both. "Walter Silver is my father's name."

If I clapped my hands together, I did so quietly. "I have a package of their love letters at the library," I said. "You have to come and see them."

Mr. Greenwood-turned-Dr. Silver possibly decided that I'd dodged the important subject long enough.

"What's in the barrel, Miss Elliott?"

I pointed to the side of the house where I'd cleared out the junk around the lot. "A few dozen phone books from the pile. I only used the most damaged ones." I couldn't believe how calm I felt telling this man I'd stolen his garbage and lit it on fire in his driveway. When I took a deep breath, I smelled the reek of hot rubber and felt compelled to continue my confession. "And a tire, but it was in the barrel already. A few squirts of hand sanitizer to make it start burning fast. I learned that in high school chemistry."

He looked over his shoulder at me, one eyebrow raised. "You're staging a protest on my property."

I started to fidget. "Actually, there's a property easement in the gravel there." I pointed to the lot. It occurred to me that if I had planned to deny my involvement, I'd waited too long. "Dr. Silver, I love this library. I just wanted to stir people up so they'd remember they love it, too."

He turned to face me again. "I understand the urge."

A laugh escaped my mouth. My shoulders relaxed, and I looked back to the burning barrel.

"And," he continued, as if a chatty conversation about radicalism late at night on his porch in November wasn't at all strange, "I understand the connection one can feel to a beautiful old building."

My thoughts were uncharitable at best. *Right. You love this house so much that you cover it in garbage.* I glanced at him to see if he heard my thoughts.

Possibly.

"Look inside, if you please." He reached over and opened the front door. Dim lamplight revealed an immaculate living room decorated with what looked to me like gorgeous antique furniture. The paintings on the walls were tasteful and elegant. He looked at me to make sure I'd seen, then closed the door.

"It's a historical monument, this old house. It's on the register. There's a marker." He waved behind his back, somewhere toward the street, in a dismissive gesture. "The building is important to the historical society." He looked at me again. "The building. Not who lives in it now, or who may have lived in it before. So according to the powers that be" — the lift of his eyebrow left me in no doubt of his feelings — "I must not throw anything away that belongs to the home."

He stopped talking, and I waited. Nothing

else seemed to be coming, and so I followed his gaze to the piles of trash and junk littering his porch and lot.

When understanding hit me, it hit hard. An unfeminine "Ha!" escaped my mouth. Followed by, "You're protesting?" The words came out faster, louder, and far higher in pitch than I'd intended. "The garbage, the mess — it's in protest?"

He could have been offended. He probably should have been. But when he looked at me, I saw his eyes crinkled up. The half-smile on his face made him look at least a decade younger. He didn't answer, exactly — he just gave a single nod. We had achieved an understanding.

"How many years have you been staging this particular protest?"

He didn't answer the question directly. "When my employment situation changed suddenly several decades ago," he said, "I found refuge in this old house. My parents had both passed, leaving me in comfort, at least financially." He looked toward the window, but curtains made it impossible to see inside. "Sometimes a place we love can shelter us. Buildings were meant to protect people. But a building is more than bricks and mortar. What happens inside tends to shape the spirit of the place."

Marigold would adore this guy.

"Mr. Silver," I said, still grasping for belief that I was talking to the one and only Joshua Silver, "I had no idea that my, um, demonstration might make trouble for you. What can I do to fix this?"

He shifted on the junk-filled porch to stand with his back against the door. "Don't do a thing. Don't say anything to anyone. Keep silent. Let's see how it pans out."

I felt dismissed, like I should walk away, but I had to make sure. "Does that mean you're not going to report me?"

The left side of his face lifted again in that half grin, and I could see the suit-and-hat-wearing man from the photographs, still there under years of aging and sadness.

"I am certainly not going to report you. But I will expect a little something from you."

Shoot. I was so stunned to find out that Old Man Greenwood was actually Dr. Joshua Silver that I had forgotten to protect myself from the possible crazy murderer. I took three quick steps backward, nearly upending what looked like a paint can full of nails.

"I know that to your mind, I'm some old man who happens to live next door to your work." Was that all he thought? Well, then, that was a win for everyone. "But I do have some experience that can be useful to you. I expect you to make use of your resources. Ask me questions. Compare your experiences to mine." He reached for the doorknob. "And the next time you're looking for a job, I want you to come to me first." He bowed in my direction before letting himself inside.

I ran off the porch and pushed through the gathering crowd toward home, every few steps looking at my hands. I'd met Dr. Silver. I'd shaken his hand.

I let myself inside and locked up.

I got on my librarian Twitter account and tweeted, "A vote to close the Franklin library is like a vote to burn books. #SaveFranklinLibrary"

Then I pulled up the shared file I was making on my Dr. Silver research. Reading over both my notes and Will's notes about Dr. Silver's protests, I couldn't help but see some similarities in our stories. He had pushed boundaries to help people get the educational opportunities they deserved. Some people hated it. I pushed some boundaries of my own. And sure, not everyone was thrilled. But maybe I could help bring about the change of heart needed to keep the library open.

When I slid into the bed, I smelled the reek of oily smoke in my hair. I fell asleep smiling.

When I slid into the bed, I smelled the reek of only smoke in my hair. I fell asleep smiling.

CHAPTER 33

I sat on the couch, clutching my laptop and looking up every news story that mentioned what happened at the library. It was all over the internet, but it was the same basic story on every site: "Local library unconnected with act of protest and vandalism, blah, blah." I couldn't decide how to feel about it.

An hour of morning TV news later, I heard a knock on the door. I glanced through the peephole. Will.

"Hi," I said as I opened the door.

He didn't say anything, just held out a bag from Ruby's.

I took it. It smelled like onions. "Did you buy me an omelet?"

"You probably want to eat it while it's hot. And I have to get to work." He smiled. "I hope you have a great day."

"Will," I said as he headed down the stairs to the parking lot, "thank you for this. You always know what I need."

He smiled up at me over his shoulder. "I try."

And then he was in his car. Not a word about the fire, or the protest, or the way he was going to use it in his civics and debate classes that day. Because of course he was going to use it. It was high-school-teaching gold. So why didn't he mention it?

He knew. Of course he knew. He'd wait until I was ready to talk about it, and then he'd listen to me and tell me the truth. Whatever the truth was.

The thought made me sad.

I had rarely been more grateful for a Monday off. My mom called and wanted me to meet her for lunch, but I knew how that would go. A forty-five minute conversation bouncing between the library protest and my relationship with Mac? I felt good about telling her I had other plans.

My plans consisted of eating half the omelet for breakfast, standing under the shower until the water went cold, going back to bed for several hours, eating the rest of the omelet for lunch, and obsessing over TV news, internet news, and Twitter.

I didn't hear from Mac all day.

I was thankful for the early sunset. I went to bed at six-thirty.

■ ■ ■ ■

Election day dawned cold and gray and icy. I tried not to see that as an omen. When I slipped into the polling station before work, I kept my sunglasses on. I knew it was silly to think anyone would recognize me, or if they did, would connect me to the fire, but I found myself hunching over the ballot and glancing over my shoulder.

The longest day only lasts twenty-four hours, but this one seemed so much longer. I went to work just before ten and spent the next eight hours checking my phone for messages from Mac or Will (there were none) and looking at the county election results website (which was apparently not working). I busied myself in the basement (braving the creepies since Kevin was at school) moving boxes around. When I had to come upstairs, I ignored everyone who looked like they had a question. But I listened. And I noticed who said the words *library* or *fire*.

Getting out of the library for lunch was nonnegotiable. I wanted to ask if anyone wanted me to pick up anything, but I found that I could not, in fact, speak. Icy drizzle leaked from the sky. I pulled my hood over my head and hid in my coat all the way to Happy's.

I patted Mr. Greenwood's — *Dr. Silver's* — oak tree as I walked past.

Julie was on the phone when I came back, so I waved, swiped my time card, and ran up the stairs to clean up kid book messes. There were plenty of misplaced books to keep me busy for a half hour. I was glad to be up there. I dreaded speaking to Julie. More specifically, having to answer questions. Or make eye contact.

I walked down the stairs with my arms full of downstairs books. A woman with helmet-y hair stood at the circulation desk.

"Greta," Julie said, "this is Marnie Blum."

I recognized her name; she was the woman of all opinions from the newspaper. I nodded.

Ms. Blum held her hand out to me. "I'm representing the city council." She turned back to Julie and leaned her elbows on the counter.

Julie took a tiny step back from the other side of the desk.

"I wonder," she continued, "if you'd like to make a comment about the disturbance Sunday night." She was facing Julie, but I couldn't make myself walk away.

"Thank you for asking. I think I'd rather

not." Julie sat with her head perfectly straight, looking directly at Ms. Marnie Blum, attorney. I knew that meant she was ready to end her visit as quickly as possible.

"I wonder if you've heard any response from the community."

I couldn't breathe. And I still couldn't walk away.

Julie shook her head.

Ms. Marnie Blum, attorney, leaned farther over the counter. "Because between you and me, I can't imagine this little stunt will hurt you at the polls today."

The shiver that overtook me was so violent, I almost dropped the stack of books I carried. Was she accusing Julie? Did she suspect me? Gathering up the sliding books, I skittered past the desk without looking at anyone. After I put a few books away, I peeked around the corner to see how Julie was holding up.

It didn't look so great.

Ms. Marnie Blum, attorney, was gone, but Julie still stood in the same place.

Bonita walked past and touched Julie's shoulder. I stacked a few more books. Looked again. More touching. Sometimes a squeeze, sometimes a pat, sometimes a little circle rubbed on her back.

I knew how Bonita felt. Julie looked damaged, and we wanted to fix her. Bonita tried to fix her in her own way, and I tried in mine. I went to the north corner and dusted the stained glass windows. I turned all the computer monitors to face the same direction, checking every ten minutes to see if the election result website was back up. It wasn't. I put chairs in front of tables so they lined up like perfect geometric formations. After every little job, I'd sneak back to where I could see her.

I had to hear what she heard.

If someone told her anything, I wanted to know it.

My better side shouted at me through the smoke and haze of my guilt, "If anyone tells her anything it should be me." But I couldn't tell her. Not now.

Not as long as she kept turning around and seeing me there and saying, "Greta, I'm glad you're here."

Minutes lasted ages, but hours moved fast. I wasn't the only one not talking. The library was as quiet as any stereotypical old-lady librarian could have wanted. And it felt so wrong. I wanted the life-filled library, not the waiting-for-the-death-sentence one.

Kevin came in at four. He perched in his spot at the counter and repaired paperbacks. I couldn't help thinking these were books we'd have to give away, sell, or recycle if the bond didn't pass. He refreshed the election website every ten minutes, and every ten minutes, he told us it still wasn't working. He gave long, theoretical possibilities as to why. We all ignored him.

At six, I was supposed to go home. I didn't. Neither did Bonita. We found little jobs to keep us busy, shivering in the wind every time the door opened. The door didn't open all that many times. Will sent a message asking if I was home, but I answered that I was staying late. He asked if I wanted him to come in. I said no. I couldn't think how to talk to him. Or anyone. At eight o'clock, Julie turned off the lights and shooed us all out the door.

"We'll find out tomorrow," she said, as if we'd been having a conversation.

Bonita nodded and patted Julie's shoulder. "Tomorrow. It will be good news."

On the way home, I passed the senior citizens' center that was being used as a polling station. One of my signs stuck out of the grass at a strange angle. Someone had moved it. Maybe someone took it away because it was offensive, and someone else put it back because of free speech. Maybe it was too close to the door so it blocked entry. Maybe I was overthinking. But the sign was there. No money to burn. Plenty of books.

Someone had taped a paper sign on top of my magnetic sign. It said, "#Save-FranklinLibrary." I felt a glimmer of gladness. I hadn't put it there. Someone else cared.

I knew Mac was closing Beans that night, so I stopped in for a quick minute and a cup of cinnamon hot chocolate. I felt exhausted from the day — like there was a physical weight on my shoulders. And things had been uncomfortable and weird between us, and I was through with things feeling uncomfortable and weird. I wanted to make things light and happy in at least one corner of my world.

The bell announced me, but Mac didn't look up. He was absorbed in the customer in front of him. She was looking absorbed too. They were in a definite lean. I walked to the end of the line and stood (hid) behind the large man standing behind the girl. Mac looked down at the counter and then up at the girl through his eyelashes. Apparently he knew how well that look worked. It had certainly always worked on me. He shook those perfect curls, and I felt a sick swoop in my stomach. My neck felt like it was on fire.

He reached across the narrow counter and

put his hand on hers. She leaned and gig-gled.

The big man in front of me cleared his throat, as though he had something better to do than stand in line watching Mac hold some girl's hand.

Mac looked up at him, gave his perfect smile, and said, "I'll be right with you." Then he leaned closer to the girl again.

I heard him say, "Grab a seat at that table over there. The red chair. Then I can see you from any angle behind the counter."

Wait. No. He didn't. But yes. He did.

I wanted to throw up, then die, then punch him in his perfect nose, then die again. That chair was mine. That spot. Those were words he said to me.

When she turned away, I saw her shirt. It was a feminine version of his black T-shirt with "I Love Your Pickup Lines" printed across the perfectly fitted front.

Had he sent her that shirt in the mail? Had it arrived at her work in an un-signed package?

I hated her. I envied her.

I hated her. I hated me.

Cocoa was a definite no at this point. I turned around and started to sneak out the way I'd come in, but from somewhere below the humiliation and self-loathing came a tiny spark of self-respect. I tapped the guy in front of me and said, "Sorry, excuse me, I need to ask a question."

Mac jumped when he heard my voice. "Hey, Greta," he said, his syrupy voice all low and insincere. His shirt flashed today's pickup line at me. I ignored it. He did a tiny toss of his perfect hair, though it looked a whole lot more staged and less spontaneous tonight.

The girl stopped on her way to the red chair. I could feel her watching Mac talk to me. "This will only take a second," I said, but I wasn't sure who I was trying to reassure.

I knew before I said it that my words would sound stupid, scripted, trite. But I didn't know what else I could say. "Know what today is?"

Mac sucked in a gasp. "Is it your birthday?" He stood up straighter and said, "You get a free cookie." His smile was perfect. Gorgeous. Insincere.

I felt my eyebrows come together in confusion. "Seriously?"

"Excuse me," the guy who was now behind me said. "I would like to order some coffee."

I turned around. "Pardon me. Just one minute." I looked at Mac again. "Not my birthday. Election day."

Mac looked relieved. "Oh, yeah. Right. Your little library thing."

The words went into my ears and registered in my brain and settled there.

My little library thing.

My little obsession.

My little job. My little career.

It seemed so obvious now. None of it mattered to him. And if it didn't matter to him, *I* didn't matter to him. Not when it meant so much to me.

"I'm done here," I said.

He looked confused. "You didn't order anything."

Seriously? "I mean, I'm done with us."

"No. Wait," he said in a soft voice.

But then —

I watched him glance over at the girl in the red chair. Nail in the coffin. I shook my head and turned away. "Bye."

I didn't flounce out of the room. I didn't storm. I didn't stomp. I just turned around and walked out the door like I'd done a thousand times before. But this time it felt like the right thing to do. And final.

My hands tingled. I found myself blinking. A lot. Was I going to cry? Blink, blink. I waited for the crosswalk light. Blink, blink. I told my eyes to stop it. *Stay open,* I told

366

them. They disobeyed. I held my lids up with my fingers, but only for a minute, because I felt — and possibly looked — like a lunatic. But no tears came. I walked a few blocks before I looked at my phone. Nothing. Mac hadn't apologized. He didn't explain. I texted Will.

Mac is a sucker. He sucks. There is so much suck there.

He replied right away.

Are you okay?

Meh.

What happened?

Nothing.

Liar.

Okay. Fine. He's a jerk-face goon.

Did he hurt you?

Those words felt so protective, so concerned. I wondered again if I'd cry.

No. Nothing like that. It's dumb. He's not

367

interested in the things that matter to me.

Where are you?

At the intersection of Humiliated and
Should Have Known.

Where are you physically?

Oh.

Madison and Elm. Heading home.

I'll meet you.

Nah. I'm going home to fall into bed.

Sure?

On all counts.

Seen the polls?

I rubbed my face with the hand not holding the phone.

The site was down. All day.

Up now. Good news. Looks like your bond
is passing.

I stopped in the middle of the sidewalk. A family walked out of the guitar store and almost crashed into me. I didn't care.

Really?

No guarantees. But it looks good.

Thank you. I love you. I needed that.

I shoved the phone into my pocket and started jogging home.

CHAPTER 34

I turned on a news radio station as soon as I woke up on Wednesday morning. I listened for stories about the library while I scrolled through my phone reading the local news. Oh. Stories. So many stories. Yes. Stories that carried photos of my signs. Stories that pointed to my signs as the reason the news was good, the reason the bond passed. Franklin was getting a new library. A big, expensive, modern, book-filled library.

We won.

I tweeted "Way to go, Franklin voters! Thanks for the new library. #SaveFranklin-Library #Saved"

We won.

So why did I want to throw up?

Will knocked on the door with a take-out hot chocolate and a chocolate cake donut in his hand. He congratulated me on the bond passing, and then sat at the kitchen table with me, speed-talking about absolutely nothing while I pinched up tiny bites of the donut. I kept nodding. He kept talking. He never mentioned Mac. I never spoke at all.

After about fifteen minutes, he put his hand on my hand. I looked at his face. He wrapped his fingers around mine and squeezed. "Want me to stay? I can get a sub."

"No, it's okay. I can do it."

"Which part?"

I breathed in and out a few times. "Every part. I'm going to tell her."

He pulled my hand to his mouth and kissed my knuckles. "I'm proud of you. You can handle today."

I nodded. He was right. I could.

Entering the library, I looked for the marks on the lot from the burning barrel. It had only been two and a half days, but there was no remaining sign of the "protest."

It was still a few minutes before ten. Julie hadn't unlocked the front door yet. Inside, I stood on the patrons' side of the circulation desk. I hadn't stood there to ask a question in years. The whole desk arrangement looked small and shabby from this side.

"I need to talk to you." There was no way Julie could have heard me. No sound even came out. But I did make the shapes of the words. "Julie?" I tried again. "Can I talk to you?"

"Sure, Greta. What do you need?" She almost raised her head from the computer monitor in front of her.

"In your office, please?" I didn't wait for her to say yes. Trudging behind the tables, I walked into her office and held the door open for her.

She didn't say anything. She came in and sat on her desk, facing the chair I should have sat in. I stood, back against the closed door.

"I know what happened. I mean, everyone knows what happened, but I know how it happened. I know why. And it's my fault." *Breathe,* I reminded myself.

Still she didn't speak. So I kept going. "The signs were my idea. I had them made. I put them up around town. I thought it would be . . ." Helpful? Funny? Effective? Useful? There was no good way to finish that sentence. I shifted my legs, which were tingling. I cleared my throat. "Anyway, the barrel thing, the burning thing? That was me, too. I didn't mean for it to be like that. Well, I think maybe I did mean it, but I didn't recognize how scary it would be. Maybe I could have stopped it, but I didn't. It was legal, though. I got a permit to protest, just in case. And they weren't really books."

Her posture looked like she had turned to stone. I saw no emotion in her face at all.

"And I'm sorry. Really, really sorry."

She looked at her fingers for a long time. Then she said, "I need you to go home now."

"What?" I felt like all the air had been shoved out of me.

She looked at me again. "Thank you for telling me. You need to go now."

I nodded. "Okay. I'll see you tomorrow."

"No." Her voice was professional and emotionless. "No. Don't come back until we contact you."

CHAPTER 35

It was a long day at home. A long, lonely day. Late in the afternoon, my phone buzzed. Will.

Are you there? Are you home? Are you available?
Can I come over? I need to talk to you.

Course. Come.

He clicked off, and a few minutes later, I saw his car pull into my parking lot. I watched from the window as he walked slowly to the door. He looked awful — pale and slumpy.

"What happened?" I asked, opening the door and pulling his arm. He walked to the couch and sat.

"I went to the library after school to talk to you."

"Yeah. They sent me home."

"So you told her?" His voice was quiet, like he wasn't sure he was allowed to have figured it out.

I nodded. "I said I would tell her. So I did."

"I know. I wasn't sure you could . . . you know." I knew. He looked at the floor and then back at me. This time his voice was barely more than a whisper. "Are you fired?"

I shrugged.

We sat there, not talking, not looking at each other, for at least two minutes. I picked my feet up and wrapped my arms around my knees.

He took a big breath. "I can't do it anymore."

I waited a couple of seconds for clarification. He didn't offer any.

"What are you talking about?"

"I can't help Mac."

I hadn't given Will any more information about walking out on Mac. I figured Mac would tell all the details of my not coming back or calling or anything if he wanted Will to know. I rubbed my hands along my arms to keep them warm. "Help with what?"

"I'm not helping him get you back. I'm done telling him what to say." He folded onto himself, his chin hitting his chest. He looked pathetic. I felt pathetic. What a pair.

I waited for him to elaborate, explain, something. He didn't. "I don't get it."

He picked up a pillow from the couch and squeezed it. "I know I started this, but I don't want to do it anymore. I'm not doing it anymore. I won't do it anymore."

Frustration built. "Did I walk in on the middle of a conversation? Why do I not understand you?"

"You understand me. It's Mac who can't understand."

Now I was annoyed. "No, actually, I really don't know what you're saying. I've had an unpleasant day. In fact, I may have been fired. And now you're speaking a foreign language. Don't be bugged that I don't understand your code words."

He sat up. "I'm not helping him look and sound smart anymore."

I shook my head. Not making sense yet.

"He needs me to keep this up if you're going to make it work, and I'm done making it happen." He gestured between me and the empty space on the couch, as if Mac were sitting there.

I still didn't understand. "Keep what up?"

"Making you like him. Earning your respect for his brilliant mind. You clearly already respect his face and his hair and his —" He paused, like he wasn't sure what to

376

say. "His shape." He waved his hand in front of him like he was indicating Mac's body.

"Gross."

Will laughed like it was the least funny thing he'd ever heard. When he spoke again, it was a little louder, a little more firm. "There will be no more depth coming from Mac. Because I'm done telling him what to say."

"There's no more anything. It's over." I wanted to say it loud and clear, but it came out muttered and muted.

He kept going, like he hadn't heard. "He's not going to send you any more poetry."

"I know."

"You know?" He looked hopeful, almost happy.

"I kind of told you." I tried not to sound whiny.

"What did you tell me?"

I put my head on the back of the couch and stared at the ceiling. "He doesn't care, remember? It wasn't very long ago."

"Of course I remember that. But you didn't say it was *over*. Over-over?"

"There's this other girl." I managed to say it without any tone. It only sounded like heartbreak on the inside.

Will moved forward to the edge of the couch in what would have been a leap to his feet if Will was built to leap to his feet. "What? Who? For how long?"

I put my head on my knees. "I don't want to talk about it."

He made me sit up. "Seriously. How long?"

"Officially yesterday. Unofficially? Who knows?"

At that point, Will said a few things about his cousin that even I hadn't had time to think.

"Don't," I said.

He almost laughed. "The guy's a complete —" He stopped. "What's the last thing he said to you? The last text he sent?"

"Please, Will," I said, tears stinging my eyes. "I can't do this right now." That seemed to convince him I was not okay.

He cleared his throat. "Has Mac ever said anything that would make you think he deserved you? That he was good enough for you?"

"I don't know what that means."

I thought he'd stop. He didn't. "I want you to tell me if he talked to you."

The sigh wouldn't stay inside. "Of course. He always said charming, sweet, clever, romantic things. Every day."

"Anything longer than a sentence or two?"

"What are you saying?" I was getting tired.

Of everything. Including this dumb conversation.

"Answer the question."

"Yes. Totally. His texts were almost always long and amazing and thoughtful and romantic and perfect." I was starting to rethink my decision to end things. What's a little flirting with a pretty girl when you put all the rest of Mac in the balance? So he didn't care about the things that mattered to me. So what?

Will handed me his phone.

I took it and held it in my hand. "What do you want me to do with this?"

He reached over, pushed the icon for texts, and clicked on Mac's name.

I read the last one.

Don't worry. I'll handle it.

He scrolled up. I wasn't sure what I was reading. It sure appeared that Will had sent some extremely adorable texts to Mac as well as a few bossy ones, telling him to do this, go there, try this, say that. But then it started to look familiar.

I can't stop thinking about the way that one piece of your hair slips across your forehead when you're leaning over a book.

I'd never need to read again if I could fill my eyes and my memory with the sight of you. You are all the story I ever need.

I looked at Will, but he stared at the floor.

When you laugh, all the happiest sounds in the world come together at once: the music on the ice cream truck, the drip of melting snow in the spring, the elementary school recess bell, the sound my phone makes when you send a text. Your laugh brings everything perfect together.

The sound I made right then might have been a laugh, but it certainly did not sound happy. Not at all.

I sat in a folding chair on the lawn this evening, watching you save the library, and wishing I could follow you everywhere, watch you, listen to you, soak in your thoughts and your beauty.
I look at my fingers and they seem barren without your hand to hold. I am only complete when you're with me.

I scrolled through dozens of familiar texts. So many words I'd read before. So much I'd sighed over, swooning like a stupid little girl.

I wanted to stop, but I couldn't. I kept reading all the words. Message after message that Will had written and then sent to Mac, who'd then sent them to me. And I'd had no idea.

No idea at all.

Openmouthed, I stared from the phone in my hand to the guy who was supposed to be my best friend. I couldn't help but feel deceived.

"You wrote these." It wasn't a question.

He nodded anyway.

"All the sweet, romantic, poetic things that Mac sent to me, you wrote."

He nodded again, but wouldn't look at me.

"And the smart things he'd say out loud? Did you send him those, too?"

I heard him sigh, but now I couldn't look at him. "Let's assume so."

"So what you're telling me is, he never thought any of those things about me."

He shook his head. "He thinks you're beautiful. Obviously," Will said to the floor.

That was the least of my concerns. "Shut up."

He did.

I could feel heat coming off the back of my neck in waves. Breathing became more difficult than usual, as if my lungs had shrunk. "Did you tell him what to say to me from the beginning?"

He had the grace to look ashamed. But he didn't deny it.

"Rilke?"

He almost laughed. "Do you really think Mac reads Rilke?"

My heart felt bruised. "In management?"

He shrugged. "You have to admit, you *are* kind of a snob. You'd never have moved forward so fast if he'd told you he worked in a café."

I would have liked to deny the accusation. I couldn't.

My brain pounded against my skull. Hands shaking, I whispered, "Idiot."

"I know. I'm sorry." Will reached for his phone. "It was a stupid idea."

I didn't give it to him. I wasn't ready to release the proof of how I'd been fooled. "Not *you* idiot. *Me* idiot. This is what happens when I ask for what I want?"

His voice came out quiet and even. "Not always. Sometimes you get polka-dot socks."

Not amused. "Stop it. Stop. Do not make fun of me right now. Even though I am the biggest idiot in the world, I need you to not mock me. Nobody else would have been fooled by this stupid game, but I couldn't see what was staring me in the face. Or talking in my ear. Or on my phone."

His hands held his head, elbows on knees. It looked like he was assuming crash position. "No, Greta. You couldn't have known."

"If I wasn't such an idiot, I could have guessed." I finally pushed up off the couch and started pacing the room.

"You're not an idiot." Will sounded so tired.

I stomped across my tiny living room. "So, what was this, then? You were looking for a pity project?"

Still on the couch, he shook his head. "I have never pitied you. You can't pity what you admire."

"Stop it. This was a project. Admit it. You wanted to know if you could make some dumb girl swoon? You were trying it out on me? Like I was your stupid canvas for some experimental art project? 'I wonder if Greta would believe these words if someone else was saying them.' That's awesome. Thanks so much for making me look like a fool." I knew I should stop. Somehow I couldn't stop.

I threw his phone onto the couch. It bounced. He ignored it.

He rubbed his hands through his hair. "You never looked foolish. You never looked anything but happy. I just wanted you to know what it felt like to have everything you wanted."

I had never hated Will before, but I was starting to now. "This was you being clever for my benefit? It's all about me? Yeah, right."

His inhale took forever. "I did it because I wanted to, and because you wanted it, too. I didn't expect it to turn out this way." He sounded both pathetic and strong. It was uncomfortable.

"You lied to me."

"I didn't."

I snapped out a harsh laugh. It hurt coming out. "Every day. You lied to me every single day. You made him say things you'd never say yourself. You said things you didn't mean."

"Never."

It came out so quiet I almost didn't hear it.

I plowed over him. "He lied to me, too. You both did. I believed those words, Will. I believed every single one. And he didn't mean them. He didn't even write them." Tears burned my eyes. Angry tears. Humiliated tears. Frustrated tears.

I couldn't stop. "When was this going to end? What if I'd never walked away from him? Would you have kept telling him what to say to me until you made him propose? Until you named our kids? How could you have possibly thought this was a good idea?"

He shook his head and opened his mouth to answer me.

"No." I didn't shout, but he had no doubt I meant what I said. "No talking. You can't possibly give me a good reason for what you did. It's impossible. No good reason exists. You lied to me. You tricked me. You made Mac lie to me, too. You made me fall in love with someone who doesn't exist. You jerk. You big, fat jerk."

And there it was. I'd said the words I couldn't take back. I'd brought fat into it, and now, no matter what else we said or didn't say, that was what this was about.

Yet I couldn't apologize because I wasn't sorry. "Go home."

"Greta." His voice shook, like he was trying not to laugh, maybe. Or not.

"I need you to leave. Now. I want to be alone. I need to burn every one of those stupid lies out of my memory." Breathing was becoming a challenge. I leaned over. It was easier if I wasn't upright.

His hand touched my back. "I meant every single word."

I straightened up and pushed him away. "No," I yelled. "No." Pointing him to the door, I shoved him hard.

He walked away.

As I drove the dead bolt closed, the tears fell hard.

CHAPTER 36

I put my phone in airplane mode so I could listen to angry music and ignore all calls and texts. That lasted for twenty-four wrathful hours. When the music ended and the anger burned off, I flipped the cell connection back on. I ignored all the texts that came in. For a while. Then I had to know.

Nothing from Mac. Nothing from Will. Nothing from Julie.

Congratulations from my mother and a couple of other people.

When a new text arrived, I ignored it for at least ten minutes. I was afraid that this time it would be Will. Or even Mac. When I couldn't ignore it any longer, I checked my phone.

We both won! You get a pretty new library, and I'm getting an A!

Marigold.

Thanks. Meet for a muffin?

Sure. Where?

She knew enough to ask, which meant she knew, or at least guessed, I didn't want to see Mac.

Yeasties. 38th street. 20 minutes.

I beat her there, so I ordered three muffins. Two of them were gone by the time she walked in.

She came over and put her cheek next to mine, almost like she was going to kiss me. My eyes started to tear up. She held her face against mine and put her hand on the other side of my head. I wanted to sit there for the whole day, smelling baked deliciousness and being comforted by a friend.

When she pulled away, I wiped my eyes and smiled at her. "The banana walnut is really good. So is the apple spice."

"That looks like blueberry," she said, pointing to the muffin on the plate.

"It is. I don't know if it's any good. I haven't gotten to it yet."

She raised her eyebrows at me but refrained from verbal judgment.

"Okay. So you didn't try anything with

chocolate in it?"

"Well, I haven't left yet."

She smiled. "Be right back." She dropped a newspaper on the table. I ignored it and stared at the brick wall, thinking of the brick walls in Beans. Thinking of the muffins in Beans. Thinking of Mac in Beans, and all the days and dollars I'd spent there. Lots of days and dollars. Then I thought of Mac outside Beans, and all the kisses and all the texts.

All the texts he didn't even write.

Why would Will do that to me? What was wrong with him?

Marigold waved from the counter, probably making sure I was still upright. I pinched a bite of the blueberry muffin, but I was suddenly not hungry. I crumbled the bite onto the napkin in front of me.

What was wrong with Will that he would fake messages like that? What was wrong with Mac that he couldn't say those things to me himself? What was wrong with me that I never even noticed? Everything was a total mess.

Marigold pulled out a chair and slid a plate with three muffins on it across the table. "Chocolate chip. Salted caramel chocolate. Chocolate mocha — that one's for me. Now. What's going on?"

I pushed the plate back to her. "Let's see. I got fired, I think. Also Mac and I broke up, and he's already got someone else, and he's a jerk. And it's possible that Will is secretly in love with me."

She laughed.

I did not. "Which of those things seems funny to you?"

She forced a look of serious concern that might have convinced me once. "None of them."

I shook my head.

Her smile came back. "Sorry. Of course Will is crazy about you. It's not much of a secret. You're the only one who didn't appear to know about it."

"Pretty sure Mac didn't know," I muttered.

"Mac knew. How else could Will write all those . . ." Marigold broke off, suddenly intent on her muffin.

"All those what?"

No reply.

I pulled the plate away from her. "Write what?"

She looked uncomfortable. Good. "You know — a few texts. A few poems. Some scripts."

"Scripts." The word felt as weird in my mouth as it sounded coming from hers.

"You know about the texts?"

She shrugged. "A few weeks ago, I went to Beans for a coffee, and Mac said he wanted to practice a few lines."

Dumbfounded. Gobsmacked. Stunned. "He practiced lines on you?"

"No. Not like that. Just, you know, rehearsed. 'Does this sound right?' Stuff like that." She took a bite of muffin. It turned her teeth momentarily black.

"So Mac is going around reading scripts" — the word still felt wrong in my mouth — "to girls who come in and order coffee."

"It's cute, though, right?" She ran her tongue over her teeth and offered me a bite of her muffin. I declined. She pulled the plate closer to her. "I mean, Mac couldn't have come up with any of those conversations on his own. He can make a decent beverage, but there's not a whole lot going on behind that pretty face."

I stared at the pile of crumbs in front of me. "Don't be mean."

"I didn't mean it to sound mean. I thought you needed a good post-breakup wallow."

I ate a blueberry. "I'll wallow the nice way."

"Which way's the nice way?"

"Where I say all the pleasant things in public and keep the insults for my private moments," I said.

"Like when you write them on the walls of public spaces with permanent marker?" She was squinting at me and trying not to smile.

"Maybe."

Marigold pushed the hair out of my face. "I'm not sure you're very good at this wallowing thing. We could go to the gym and put on boxing gloves. What do you say?"

"Pass the muffins." I reached for the plate.

She pretended not to watch me eat the top off the salted caramel one. "Want to talk about the job?"

"No." I wiped my hands on my jeans. "Yes." I set down the muffin. "I love that job. I love that library. I have loved that library all my life. And I've loved that job for ten years. Ten years. That's a huge percentage of my life, you know?" I took a big breath. "I don't know if I'm really fired, but what if I am? What do I do? It's not like there's a huge population of libraries in this town."

"There's one at the university," she said.

I nodded. "And what's the likelihood that anyone's going to hire someone so recently fired for such a public reason? Do you see what this means? I have a totally useless master's degree. I'm unemployable."

She shook her head, just a little, and I could see she was trying not to argue with me while I was ranting. I was present enough to recognize that as thoughtful.

"So, what, then? I move home with my mother?" I dropped my head to my arms and breathed out a shaky laugh. No way. "Or I leave town? Leave Will?"

Marigold looked at me. I could actually see questions flickering across her face, but she didn't ask any of them.

She watched me unwrap the bottom of the muffin. She nodded in sympathy. "You tried something. And it worked — mostly."

"I did. I tried. I tried everything I could think of to save my library. I did all the smart things. Then I did the dumb thing." My throat was getting scratchy. Like anaphylaxis. I wondered if I'd developed a muffin allergy. Then I realized I was crying.

Marigold sighed. "Nobody got hurt."

I put my head on my arms. My nose almost touched the table. "Nobody got burned by actual fire, but plenty of people got hurt. I'm such an idiot."

"You're not."

I sighed. "How could I not be an idiot? Even you knew that Mac wasn't sending me the messages I thought were from him."

"This might be one of those things you

need to look at from a distance." She pulled the chocolate chip muffin toward her and pulled the top off. "Think about the first time you met Mac. What do you remember?"

"I really don't want to talk about this."

"Too bad. Hot guy walks into the library looking for poetry, am I right?" she asked.

"Basically."

She nodded. "Right. What's not to like?"

I chose not to answer that.

"But the thing is, that wasn't enough. You asked for more."

I shook my head. "I don't know what you're talking about." I brushed crumbs off the table.

"You asked for him. Birthday wish number twenty-four, if I recall."

I raised my head. "How do you know that?"

"Will told me," she said, as if it should be perfectly clear that she and Will discussed my birthday wishes all the time. I made a mental note not to introduce any more of my acquaintances to each other. She went on. "You told Will that what you wanted for your twenty-fourth birthday was nothing less than perfection, remember? A perfect man for you. Perfect face, perfect body, perfect mind? Sound familiar?"

My mouth fell open.

"You asked for the soul of a poet. He delivered." She shrugged, as if that explained everything. The problem was, it didn't explain anything. Will always gave me what I asked for, but he'd never deceived me before in the process.

"So you're saying that the guy I want doesn't exist. I can have half of what I want but not all of it."

She knocked her knuckles against the table. "Pretty much. And you should be impressed that I understood any of your muttering into your arms."

I muttered some more.

"Sorry. I missed that. But you maybe missed my point. Maybe right this minute, you can only have half of what you want at a time. The good-looking guy exists. The poet exists. Maybe you can't have it all, not all at once."

I moaned into my arms.

Marigold petted my head.

I slapped her hand away without looking up. She did it again.

"Are you petting me?" I asked.

"Purr," she commanded.

I shook my head. "You're weird."

"Do it. You'll feel better."

"I'm not ready to feel better."

"Come on."

I growled.

"Close. Try again."

I was glad my head was down. I didn't want her to see that she'd almost made me smile. I breathed out a long, heavy sigh.

"That was even closer." She scratched the back of my head between my ears, and suddenly that whole stupid idea about being a cat seemed pretty brilliant.

I purred.

Marigold laughed. "Good girl."

I raised my head and looked at her. "If I really was a cat, I could sit on the couch in the sun all day long and you could feed me tuna and pet my head and I'd never have to get another job or talk to a human male ever again." I may have gasped in wonder. "This is sounding like a better idea all the time."

Marigold laughed again and kept petting my head until I was ready to go home. It took a long time. As I got up to leave, she put the newspaper she'd brought with her into my hand. "When you're ready. Page two. Top of the fold."

"It's not like you to be vague and mysterious," I said.

She shrugged. "It's not like you to have a nervous episode and then pretend to be a domesticated animal."

I opened the paper and found her essay. The one by Mary Elise Gold. Mary Gold. *Marigold.*

Was there any end to the ways in which I was capable of misunderstanding people?

Old and New by Mary Elise Gold

Citizens of Franklin voted this week to build a new library. The approved bond will cover the cost of building and running a state-of-the-art facility, complete with performance spaces, a café, study rooms, light-filled open spaces, collaboration rooms, an arboretum, a science research center, computer stations, art studios, and space for three times as many books as the current library.

To some citizens, this is a vast improvement. The casing for the library will be modern, efficient, clean, and beautiful.

To others, the new building represents a tragic separation from tradition. The Franklin library has been housed on Pearl Street for generations. The building matches the historical feeling of the neighborhood. The weathered brick, stained glass, narrow staircases, anachronistic light fixtures, wobbly bookshelves, and distinctive aroma are, for many people, the very definition of what a library should be. Many who have spent their lives in this community feel a deep connection to the building.

Will a new exterior change the soul of the library?

This question leads this reporter to ponder questions that reach far beyond the confines of brick-and-mortar buildings.

What is the delineation between a *house* (traditionally a building to live in) and a *home* (the place you feel loved and accepted)?

How does a community determine the necessity of traditional institutions in a modern society?

When you read a printed book, do you connect with the story differently than when you read digitally?

How important are traditions, and what makes them matter? What traditions should be phased out to make room for modern improvements? And who is to determine what is considered "improvement"?

Does a person's physical presence determine how others respond to him or her as much as a building's does?

What is the responsibility of the local government for making public places fully accessible?

Does upgrading, renewing, and updating

always mean improving?

If a reader becomes uncomfortable answering any of these questions, remember that discomfort often offers a place to begin a dialogue. Whether you voted for or against the library bond, you, as a tax-paying citizen, will have a responsibility and a consequential reward for the community's choice. The time for choosing has passed, but the conversation — the way Franklin looks at the future of its traditional gathering spaces — will continue for generations into the future.

CHAPTER 37

After four days without hearing from Julie, I decided I had to tell my mother what had happened. I called her and asked if we could meet for lunch.

She offered to cook for me. As much as I hated the implication that I couldn't afford to eat out, I had to face the possibility that my discretionary income was — at least for the foreseeable future — gone.

When I walked up to her house, she was sitting on the porch. I knew I could either finesse this conversation or I could rip the bandage off. I ripped.

"Mom? I might be fired."

I had a long list of responses to expect. None of which was, "Oh, is that what the lawyer is calling about?"

"Pardon me?"

"You got a few calls from a lawyer woman. But never mind that. Do you need to come home?"

I chose to accept the generosity of the offer without actually accepting the offer. "Thanks for your concern, Mom. I'm fine." Of course, I had no idea if I really was fine, but she didn't need to know that.

She ushered me into the kitchen and pointed to a chair. As she served me a chicken salad croissant, she performed her latest litany of Eligible Single Men. Aunt Josi's coworker at the bank was handsome and well groomed. The next-door neighbor was having her windows replaced, and by all accounts, the handsome window replacement man, who occasionally worked shirtless (gasp), was single. Grayson Shelton was back from grad school — had I heard? — and looking to settle down.

I wore my polite and pleasant face through it all, knowing that if I voiced any of my reasons to veto her list, it would only end in a fight. I didn't have any fight left in me. Finally, after I'd eaten the sandwich and the carefully sliced carrot sticks, she passed on the message. Ms. Marnie Blum, attorney, had asked her politely if she'd let me know she was looking for me. She'd like me to return the call at my earliest convenience. She left an office number and a cell.

My mom handed me the kitchen phone. I didn't argue.

When I called her, she knew who I was right away. "Greta Elliott from the library. You're a difficult young woman to get in touch with," she said.

"Sorry. My phone's been unreliable." That almost made me laugh. Yeah. Unreliable in how it occasionally led me to misunderstand the origins of certain text messages.

"I'd like you to meet me. I have something I'd like to talk to you about."

I suggested Yeasties. We met there the next day.

Her hair was still the same helmet, but she was more forward than I expected her to be. More than "your agenda is my agenda," anyway.

She got right to the point. "I love your moxie."

"I don't know what that means." Of course I knew what that meant, but I didn't know what else to say. She knew. Somehow, she knew what I'd done.

She cleared her throat. "Guts. Panache. Courage."

Maybe she was waiting for me to say something else, or maybe she lost her groove, because a few seconds later, she reset and said it again. "I love your moxie, even if I don't approve of your methods. You've got great ideas. With some coaching, you'd probably execute the right ones. I'd like to offer you a job."

I picked up my hot chocolate and took a long sip. When I put down the mug, I made a throat-clearing sound. "I'm sorry. Could you please say that again?" Stalling wasn't my best thing.

She laughed. "You've got your finger on the pulse of the rising generation. I could use someone like you in my corner."

I thought she could use someone like me to write her some cliché-free lines.

"Which corner is that, exactly?"

"Looking ahead. I'm running for state senate next year. Come to work in my law office, do some phone work, some filing. When it comes up, I'll have campaign work for you to do. You can help me see things from the perspective of the youth."

I watched her stab a bite of coffee cake, set it down, and smash it with the back of her fork. Was she nervous? Maybe putting everything out on the metaphorical table was the right move.

"I'm in kind of a lot of trouble. Maybe."

She shrugged. "You staged an anonymous protest."

I sank back into my chair. Desperately wishing for more hot chocolate, I said, "Apparently you know my trouble."

"I'm not finished. The protest was on government property, and your pyrotechnics endangered a historical building."

I cleared my throat and put my hand up. "Technically not on government property. I was careful about that." She quirked her eyebrow in disbelief. "Obviously, I'm the kind of person you want working for you," I muttered into the table.

"I came to you. I think that makes it clear that I do, in fact, want you working for me."

She was smart, but I had to make it clear. I pushed the words out on a heavy breath. "My employment record is not stellar."

She tried not to laugh. "You've had a single job for over a decade, including your time in college and grad school. Employment records don't get much shinier than that."

I found my spine and sat up straight. "Right up until the end."

"You've made all kinds of impressions with the community, but it seems like most of them were good ones." She lifted up her coffee cup and smelled it, but didn't drink. "You've made a good impression with me, too. Despite today's effort to show me you're not interested, I'd like to leave the offer open. I think that when you take some time to think about it, you'll recognize a perfect opportunity." She pushed back her chair and stood, wiping coffee cake crumbs from her pants.

It occurred to me, much later than it should have, that I should not screw this up. "Thank you," I said, screeching my chair against the floor. "I will think about it. I'll be in touch."

She reached across the table to shake my hand. Smiling, she said, "You think you're a librarian, but what you are is a public servant. It covers a lot of ground, what you and I do." She slid her card across the table. "Congratulations on saving the library."

When I got home that afternoon, I sat down at my computer and started the letter I knew I needed to write.

Dear Julie

Dear Ms. Tucker,

Dear Julie,

For ten years, you have given me a purpose. For longer than that — for as long as I can remember, practically — you have given me a place.

I appreciate the purpose.

I cherish the place.

The things I learned while working for you and beside you at the library are things that will stay with me all my life. Specifically, I learned that all the important work that gets done happens because people care about each other. That relationships matter most. That habit and tradition are crucial, but not static.

You have given me opportunities far beyond what I deserved, and I am grateful. I have loved learning from you. Thank you for being an excellent employer and a dear friend.

<del>Love,</del>
<del>Sincerely,</del>
<del>Yours truly,</del>
Love, Greta

CHAPTER 38

I sat with my back against my apartment door, my face raised to the weak fall afternoon sun. I didn't need an almanac to tell me we were going into a long winter. Closing my eyes, I let the breeze that was shaking the leaves breathe through my hair. Mac would have had something romantic and perfect to say about the combination of sunlight and wind and hair.

But no, *not* Mac.

Will.

For the first time in years, I wished I still lived at home. And that Will still lived at home so I could look from my kitchen and see if he was in his bedroom. I pulled out my cell.

Are you home?

Hi.

Come over?

Three minutes. Maybe two and a half.

I was still sitting against the apartment door when he pulled up. He heaved himself up the staircase and stopped in front of me. "Hi."

"Hi." I patted the ground next to me. "Want to sit?"

"Hi," he said, lowering himself onto the concrete stair.

"You already said that," I said.

"Right."

We sat there, the cold of the concrete seeping into our legs.

I'd asked him to come.

I should be able to make conversation.

But what was a best friend for if not to sit in uncomfortable silence on uncomfortable concrete?

After a long inhale, the words came out all at once, like one word. "Why did you do it?"

I felt Will's body turn toward me, but I kept looking ahead.

"Are you sure you want to talk about this?" His voice was quiet, but close.

I laughed. "No. Turns out I'm not sure about very many things."

He rubbed his eyes. "I wanted you to have what you wanted. I wanted you to have the perfect guy."

Snort. "He's not exactly perfect."

"No, but he looks perfect."

"Will," I started.

"Don't lie. He does."

"You're totally right. He does."

He shrugged. "It makes sense. His looks. My brains and personality. A lethal combination. No girl could have withstood the united perfection." His smile was sad.

"So he's what you'd choose to look like if you could pick?" I was sure he could hear the subject change from a mile away, but I wanted to lighten the mood a little. A lot.

He shook his head. "No. But I knew he'd be what you'd choose."

"Well, you chose right, I guess." I let my head fall back against the bricks behind me. "Who would you choose, though? Who would you look like?"

He answered right away, as if he'd actually had occasion to give it some thought. "George Clooney, circa 1994. I have the hair for it."

"You totally do. And the eyes. Clooney's eyes are almost as good as yours." I nudged his arm with my elbow.

"Who would you choose? If you could

look like anyone?" he asked.

I rubbed my nose. "Coincidentally I'd also choose Clooney '94. I'd stare into the mirror constantly."

"Be serious." But he was smiling so I knew he didn't mind.

"I am completely serious. I'd be the most confident person in Ohio."

"You're weird."

I shrugged. He had a point. "Okay," I said. "Doris Day."

"Really? You're not even blonde."

"Maybe she wasn't either."

"Movie magic?"

"Something like that. She's perfect, though. Cute and dimpled and sexy all at once. She's the package. Also, she could sing."

"No fair. Looks only. No bringing talent or personality into it."

"Look who's so hard-core about the rules. You're like the Mussolini of Fantasy Faces."

He sat up straighter. "Rules are important to me. Rules like 'don't lie.' And I didn't. Ever."

"Will," I tried to interrupt. The abrupt change of tone made me uncomfortable.

"Just wait." Now he was the one who looked straight ahead. "Let me say this, and then you never have to hear it again." He

410

waited for a second, maybe to see if I'd argue. I didn't.

"I meant everything I said. I meant everything he said, as long as he was on script. I never lied to you. I wrote every word for you. Every poem, every message, every thought was straight from my heart to you. All the time."

He tugged on the laces of his shoes. "With the benefit of hindsight, I can appreciate that it was not a perfect execution. But I wanted you to hear the words. I wanted you to feel what I felt — what I feel." He shifted on the step, having a hard time sitting still. "Can you understand? Do you get why I did it?"

I wasn't ready with a yes or a no. "I'm not sure I buy it. Your motives were nothing but altruistic? All you wanted was for me to have a perfect boyfriend?"

He breathed out a loud sigh. "No."

"Because?" I prompted.

"I wanted to be the one to make him perfect. He couldn't do it without me. I wanted to wear a Mac-face mask and play the part of the perfect-looking guy. Because you'll never care how clever I am, how poetically I can speak, how much of a gentleman I am when I look like this."

My words came out shuddery. "I've always cared."

He shook his head. "Not like I want you to."

"So where does that leave us? You and me?" I swiped at a tear that was trying to fall.

"We're the same. Come on, Greta. We're adults. You're my best friend. That's not going to change just because you happen to know I love you, right?"

I wasn't sure. Did it change? Did it have to?

I stared at my hands, remembering the times Mac had held them, touched my fingers and made my pulse fly. And then remembering how sometimes Will's touch could feel strangely electric. And how often had I admitted — even to myself — that no one had ever kissed me like Will Marshall had.

But Mac's face. His eyes. His hair.

Was I really that shallow? Did I really love a guy because he looked like that?

Because if he hadn't, would I have? If Mac hadn't been in between, would Will's words have made me feel the same way about Will? Was there any conceivable way I could have felt that way about Will? Under any imaginable circumstances?

I realized that wasn't the question he asked me. He asked why anything might have to change. Not even that, really. He asked me to agree that nothing would change. But would it?

Will wasn't asking me to love him. But did I? If anyone had asked me that — just those words, *Greta, do you love Will?* I don't know what I would have answered. How do you answer that?

Did I like his company? Of course.

Did I want to be with him? Well, obviously. Look at my scheduling record. All my non-work, non-Mac, discretionary free time was his.

Did I feel happy when we were together? Always.

Did I like his affection? When I thought about Will holding my hand, Will hugging me, Will kissing me, I got squirmy inside. Not because I didn't like it. More like I didn't know how to feel about how much I sometimes liked it.

And what about the words? The words I claimed made me fall for Mac? Would those words be that different coming out of Will's mouth?

I couldn't decide, and the fact that I couldn't made me sick.

I realized that the last thing Will had said

to me included the words, "I love you." And that I'd failed to reply. In any way.

I had to say something.

"You're my best friend." I shifted on the frozen concrete. "I like a million things about you," I said, and then I stopped.

He looked like he wanted to say something else, but he waited. That was so Will.

I stood up, but my legs tingled so hard that I felt wobbly. "I like a million things about you," I repeated, because that was the important part right now.

"But?"

I shifted on my sparking legs. "I don't know how to move forward yet. Can you give me some time? I'm kind of on a bounce right now," I reminded him.

He had the decency not to mention that I was only halfway on the bounce from Mac — the rest was all him. When I broke up with Mac, I kind of broke up with Will, too. This was too weird.

CHAPTER 39

No Mac. No Will. No work. I cleaned my apartment like it had probably never been cleaned before. I avoided several of my mom's telephone calls. I trashed useless files from my laptop. I stared at the walls.

There was an email in my inbox from Julie. "Please come to the Franklin Public Library to pick up some personal effects." That was it.

I'd started my job when I was fourteen. Add to that all the years that the library had been my childhood home away from home. And now, I was being summoned to gather my personal effects. I wanted to throw up. A tiny thought about a letter of recommendation flickered past my brain, but even I couldn't talk myself into expecting anything like that now.

I stood outside the library for several long moments. I looked at the angles, the lines, the windows, the cracked bricks, the layers of paint. I loved this building, but I loved even more what it stood for. I loved the guts of it — the books, the people who came in looking for understanding and entertainment and connection. I watched a family pull up in a minivan, the mom hauling kids and bags through the sliding door. I remembered the years I'd spent inside the library: the hours after school that I sat upstairs reading, waiting for my mom to get off work, my first day of work, my last day.

My last day.

I breathed. I walked inside.

Kevin sat at the circulation desk, face curtained by his hair. When he heard me clear my throat, he looked up from his pile of books and grinned. "Hey, Greta. Good to see you."

"Hi, Kevin." I was going to cry.

Bonita came around the corner, pushing an empty book cart. "Hi, honey," she said, her voice soft and low. "We got in a new art history book. Want to see?"

I understood what she was doing. I nodded and followed her to the nonfiction section. She perched on the arm of a chair and looked at me. I waited, but she didn't say anything. "Did you really get a new art history book?"

"We did." She nodded.

"Did you want to show it to me?" I asked.

"No." She slid from the arm of the chair into the seat. Her hands held her knees.

This was my chance. My opportunity. "Bonita, I'm sorry about how things ended up."

Her eyebrows arched. She didn't believe me.

"Well, no. Not totally. I'm glad the bond passed — really glad — but I'm sorry that I handled it in a way that hurt you."

She didn't take her eyes off my face. "Honey, I'm fine. But that was a dangerous thing to do."

I nodded. "I know. Don't play with fire."

She made a *psht* sound. "The fire wasn't the dangerous part. You spoke for people without asking. You accused our patrons of terrible things. You used fear and hate to control a political decision."

I could only nod.

She was quiet for a minute.

I stared at the quilting books on the shelf in front of me. "Does everyone hate me?"

The noise that came out of her mouth almost sounded like a laugh. I looked at her. She shook her head. Not everyone, then.

I pointed through the wall where Julie's office was. "Does she, though?"

Bonita appeared to change the subject.

"There was a council meeting last night."

I nodded. I knew. I'd stayed far away.

"Julie asked to be on the agenda. She stood and explained." Bonita stopped talking and rubbed her left knuckles with her right hand.

My voice came out quieter than I planned. "That's good. Nobody around here should get in trouble. Everyone knows it was only me."

Bonita shook her head. "No. I mean, she explained that you did what you did because you love this place. That you used those tactics to reach an audience that had stopped listening to reasonable arguments."

I wasn't sure I understood. "She defended me?"

Bonita waited until I was looking at her. "More than that. She showed that you'd gone through all the legal channels. She found out that you'd requested a permit to protest. She mentioned your careful placement. And she asked the board to consider that your unconventional methods might be what this town needs to bring a fading institution back into the spotlight." Bonita looked right into my eyes. "She recommended you as head librarian at the new building."

Silence. I couldn't speak. I could barely

breathe. I leaned against the shelf behind me. Bonita pushed herself out of the chair. She stepped toward me and kissed me on the cheek. "I've got to get back to work. We're short-staffed right now, and we're experiencing something of a renaissance around here." She tapped my collarbone with her bent finger. "Greta Elliott. Making libraries cool again." She turned, winked over her shoulder, and walked away. I stayed there for a minute, leaning and thinking.

When I pulled myself together, I went back to the circulation desk. Kevin was still there, still hiding behind his hair.

"Is Julie around?" I tried to see into her office, but that was hard to do from this side of the counter.

He didn't exactly answer, but he handed me two envelopes. "She asked me to give you these." Then he pulled a couple of Cards out from under his computer monitor. "And I wanted to give you these."

Blinking back the hovering tears, I said, "Oh. Right. Got it. Thanks." I took the envelopes and the cards, waved my fingers, and left.

I waited until I was standing behind the huge oak tree. Dr. Silver's tree. The cards were on top of the little pile. "What's going to happen to this building?" was typed on the card, followed by seven penciled tally marks. "Was that book-burning thing as cool/dangerous/big as they tell me?" followed by a penciled-in comment, "variations on a theme," and thirteen tally marks. The third one said, "How can they legally call it a seedless watermelon if it has some seeds in it?"

I tucked the Cards into my pocket and stared at the first envelope for a few minutes. Maybe several hours. Hard to say. Eventually, I opened it. What had I been expecting? A thank-you card? A huge check? It was a letter. But not to me.

To whom it may concern,

I have been Greta Elliott's employer for ten years. In that time, she has been the most excellent worker. She is dedicated, careful, and consistent. She continually puts her whole heart into even the simplest projects. She gives her best effort to a work she considers important.

A recommendation. I almost couldn't believe it. It went on for several paragraphs, but I stopped reading because I thought I might cry. Instead, I opened the second envelope. This one was handwritten.

Dear Greta,

I have spent days processing what you did. I think I understand it, but I can't condone it, not specifically. Your actions brought about a wonderful and greatly desired conclusion, but you took several missteps getting there.

I cannot continue to employ you. Not here. Not in the library you misused. You leveraged this building to cast aspersions on members of our community — decent people who want to be financially and socially responsible. You accused them of unspeakable things, which is wrong in every way. You hurt me, and I need to keep my distance for a time. Perhaps until I retire. Were I to speak out against you, you would be unemployable in this town.

I will not speak against you.

I have recommended you for the head librarian position in Franklin's new building. This is not certain. You would need to apply and be accepted by the board. And you'll need to find an interim job for a year. I recommend the university library. There is still much for you to learn. Some of it is about running a library.

None of this is a perfect solution.

Maybe there is no perfect solution. We can't always have all the things we want and love and expect at the same time.

If the librarianship of the new branch is not what you want, please consider using my letter of recommendation. I meant every word. You have been a model employee, right up until the end.

Sincerely,
Julie Tucker

I held the paper against my chest, trying to gather my thoughts. So many ideas and feelings had flown through my mind in the past few minutes. Did I want to apply for the new head librarian job, even when there was a strong possibility the board would reject me outright?

Wouldn't it be easier to take the offer from Marnie Blum?

Easier — for sure.

But not better.

I didn't want to be a politician. I didn't want to be a glorified secretary. I didn't want to put my finger on the pulse of anybody's generation.

I wanted books. I wanted people.

I wanted to do what I'd trained to do. What I'd learned to do. What I'd been born to do. What I'd always known I was meant to do.

I turned and walked up the steps of the old Greenwood home and knocked.

When Dr. Silver shuffled his way to the door, I took a bracing breath. I knew I had to say what I wanted to say before I let myself feel what I was trying not to feel.

He undid the bolt and pulled the door open just enough to put his head and shoulders out. I didn't look past him to try to see the interior of his house. I understood that was private, that he kept the outside for the public and the inside for himself. I understood something about that now.

"Hello, Miss Elliott."

"Dr. Silver." I held out the first letter from Julie. "Sir, I would like to talk with you about a possible opportunity. I have a letter of recommendation from my previous employer," my voice snagged on those words.

"Previous." He wasn't asking, and I wasn't about to explain. I didn't need to. He knew. It was only fair. And familiar. We had both taken a risk and broken some rules for the benefit of a place we'd loved. And we'd both lost something for our efforts. He understood.

I looked up at the corner of the doorway for a second. "In the short time we've known each other, I think you've seen that I am continuing to develop a wide range of skills, from research to yard work to minor acts of radicalism."

He didn't laugh, exactly, but he breathed out a short breath that, if you listened just right, could have signaled amusement. I chose to feel encouraged.

"I am going to apply to run the new Franklin library when it's built in eighteen months, and I'd like you to join me."

He squinted into the sun that was sinking in the trees behind me. "That's kind of you, Greta, but I don't need a job. I haven't needed a job for many years."

I stood up straighter. "No one can argue that you don't need an income, sir, but everyone needs a job."

He did that left-side grin. We were communicating now.

I cleared my throat. "With all the respect in the world, Dr. Silver, this isn't actually about what you need. This is about what the town needs. And we need someone to connect us to our history. Someone who's been involved. Someone who understands."

I let that sink in for about three seconds before I went on. "I want you to take on the local history section, and I want it to be a force. I want it to be something people will be interested in. Proud of. Connected to. I want paper, photos, newspapers, journals, and I want digital access to all of it. I want audio and visual recordings of important events. I want it to be accessible in every possible format — including interviews with someone who was present for some of the most essential moments."

"That's quite a list." I couldn't tell if he was impressed by my passion or concerned for my sanity. I didn't worry too much about it.

"I'm just getting started. Dr. Silver, I want you to be the face of the history of Franklin."

"Like you're the face of the future?" he said with a grin.

I felt my cheeks flush. "Oh, no. I'm not the face of anything."

He nodded once. "Don't be so certain."

"So?" I asked. "Will you?"

He leaned against the doorframe and folded his thin arms across his chest. I realized it was rude of me to keep him out here in the chill. He looked from the library building to me. "Will my answer determine whether or not you'll go ahead with your plan?"

I thought about it for a couple of seconds before I shook my head. "No. I mean, no, sir. I plan to begin applying for the position this afternoon. Letters and introductions and whatnot. I'd like to know I have someone on my team."

He rubbed his chin with his hand. "I understand. I think it's fair to say you have someone on your team. If you receive the appointment, I'd be honored to join you."

I put my hand out to shake his. "Thank you."

He wrapped my hand in both of his. "And I thank you." His eyes gleamed with an excitement and energy I recognized from his photographs. "Good luck."

"I'm not really the kind of person who leaves things to luck," I said as I stepped off the porch and down the stairs.

A church bell rang four o'clock. Flocks of birds lifted from trees with the sound. I pulled out my phone and texted Will.

Are you still at school?

On my way to the car.

Meet me?

He answered fast.

Of course. Anywhere.

Not exactly anywhere.

Ruby's? Happy's?

I was sure he'd keep making offers until I agreed to one.

Not hungry. Burton Park? Our bench.

I'll be there in ten minutes.

I took my time walking to the park. The ground was coated in dry leaves, and the air was noisy with birds. When I got to the bench, he was already there, holding two take-out hot chocolates from Beans.

He stood up as I held my hands out for a cup. "I've missed this," I said, saluting him with the drink.

"Is it bad?"

I took a sip. "No. It's great. Tastes perfect."

He shook his head. "Not what I meant."

"The thought of seeing Mac? Not at all. As far as I know. I haven't tried it." I laughed a little and wrapped my fingers around the cup for warmth.

"Sorry. Again."

I took a deep breath and blew it out. A

frost cloud hung in front of my face for a second. "I'm sorry, too. And I miss you. And I'm all done pouting. So can we move on?" I said it so fast I wondered if he'd even understand me.

He sat. I did too.

"You mean go back to being best-friends-since-elementary-school Greta and Will?" He sounded hopeful.

I shook my head. "Not exactly."

He shifted on the bench to put more space between us.

"I miss more than my best friend." Could I do this? I could. I had to. More than that, I *wanted* to. I'd been thinking about it for days. Weeks. And the more I thought, the more I understood that somewhere in my heart I'd been thinking about it much, much longer. "I want something else, too. I miss your words." I pulled my hand away from my drink and held it out to him.

He stared at it like he'd never seen it before. He didn't make any move to take it.

"Will?"

"What?" He kept looking at my hand, hanging there, waiting.

"Are you saying no?"

He shook his head, like he was clearing it. His eyes snapped from my hand to my face.

"I'm not sure I understand what you're asking."

Hand still held out, I said, "I want you to say your words to me."

His voice was steady and low, like he was trying not to startle me. "Do you mean it? Say what I mean and what I think and what I feel, right to you, without a pretty face between us to make the words look good?"

I reached up and touched his cheek with my fingers warm from the hot chocolate. "I like this face. This is a good face." I kept my hand against his face. "I have loved you for so long it became as natural as breathing. You and me. Me and you. But now, I want us. Together. I want you and me for real."

He reached out and took my cup out of my hand. He set both cups down on the grass. Then he leaned closer, hugging me. I put both my arms around his neck.

"Are you sure?" he whispered, and I could hear a dozen different emotions in that question.

For weeks I'd been wondering the same thing. But now, I could honestly say, "I'm sure I want to try."

He hugged me closer. Then he pushed himself off the bench. Pulling me to him, he put his forehead to mine and whispered.

"Standing here, wind gusts around us,

"And all that's warm and comfortable is in my arms.

"Darkness surrounds us, but sunshine streams from your eyes to mine."

Little shivers of pleasure mixed with shivers of cold. "Wow. Looks like I made the right call." We stood, arms around each other, and smiled into each other's faces. "But I think we should put the poetry on pause for a minute."

"Pause?" He glanced at the bench, the very place he'd once told me that we were never actually finished kissing. I knew exactly what he was thinking.

Was he blushing? He might have been blushing.

I grinned and pulled his mouth to mine and un-paused. The kiss was warm and comfortable and delicious and familiar and not even a little bit weird.

He pulled away and brushed my hair across my forehead with his fingertips. "I have been waiting a very long time for this," he said. And then, again, "Are you sure?"

"Yes, I'm sure." I smiled at him and slid my hands to the collar of his jacket. "Besides, you really did just toss out an awesome poem," I said.

"There's more where that came from if this is my reward," he said, and leaned in again. I closed my eyes and let myself feel how right this could be.

How right it all could be.

ACKNOWLEDGMENTS

I have had the great privilege of having wonderful public libraries in all the communities I've lived in, and I want to thank Julie Hersberger for giving me my first job, when I was only fourteen, in the Batesville Public Library. I learned important things at that job, and a few of them relate to books.

My writing community is large, strong, and generous. A giant thank you to all who encourage and inspire, with a special shout-out to Josi Kilpack, who reminds me when I forget exactly why we do this. Brittany Larsen and Jenny Proctor are always willing to read manuscripts over and over; thank you both for honesty and gentleness and dear friendship.

A giant thank you to my editor, Lisa Mangum, who took a chance on me, pulled me from the slush pile, and made me shine. Thank you to the entire Shadow Mountain team: Chris Schoebinger, Heidi Taylor, Julia McCracken, Sarah Cobabe, Malina Grigg, Heather Ward, and Richard Erickson.

Our Novel Writing class at Wasatch High School only lasts one semester, but the memories we build there will stay with me forever. Thank you to my students who are all thoughtful and brave — and especially to Dylan Parker, for pulling the title for this book out of thin air.

Biggest love and thanks to my family for supporting me and believing that my words can matter. And for seeking out the things you love. You make my world beautiful.

ABOUT THE AUTHOR

Becca Wilhite, author of *Bright Blue Miracle* and *My Ridiculous Romantic Obsessions,* is a happy wife and a mom to four above-average kids. High school English teacher by day, writer by night (or very early morning), she loves hiking, Broadway shows, food, books, and movies. You can find her online at beccawilhite.com.